Ben M. Baglio's

ANIMAL
Where animals come first ®
ARK

Kitten
Collection

SCHOLASTIC INC.

New York Toronto London Auckland Sydney
Mexico City New Delhi Hong Kong Buenos Aires

Where animals come first

Kittens in the Kitchen, ISBN-13: 978-0-590-18749-7, ISBN-10: 0-590-18749-X. Text
copyright © 1994 by Ben M. Baglio. Illustrations copyright © 1994 by Scholastic Inc.

Kitten in the Candy Corn, ISBN-13: 978-0-439-68758-4, ISBN-10: 0-439-68758-6.
Text copyright © 2004 by Working Partners Limited. Created by Working
Partners Limited, London W6 0QT, United Kingdom.
Illustrations copyright © 2004 by Scholastic Inc.

Kitten in the Cold, ISBN-13: 978-0-439-09698-0, ISBN-10: 0-439-09698-7. Text
copyright © 1996 by Working Partners Limited. Original series created by
Ben M. Baglio. Illustrations copyright © 1996 by Scholastic Inc.

12 11 10 9 8 7 6 5 4 3 2 1   7 8 9 10 11/0

Printed in the U.S.A.   40

ISBN-13: 978-0-545-02819-6
ISBN-10: 0-545-02819-1

First compilation printing, June 2007

Contents

ANIMAL ARK®

Kittens in
the Kitchen

Ben M. Baglio

Illustrations by Shelagh McNicholas

To Jenny Oldfield, who loves animals,
and to Peter and Benjamin,
the kittens in my kitchen

Special thanks to Jerry Oldfield, and to C. J.
Hall, B.Vet.Med., M.R.C.V.S., for reviewing the
veterinary information contained in this book.

One

"Mandy, you're very eager to get to school all of a sudden," Dr. Adam Hope said. He watched his daughter stuff old newspapers into her backpack. She flung on her school jacket, flicked a brush through her dark blonde hair, and snatched a mouthful of toast. "It's only ten to eight. Are you sure you're okay?"

"Very funny!" Mandy said. "Of course I'm okay. It's just a special day, that's all." She'd fed her rabbits and done her morning chores at Animal Ark. Simon, the nurse, had come in to look after the animals and take temperatures and give medicines. Now she was free to go.

"School trip?" Dr. Adam took a guess as Mandy unlocked her bicycle padlock and put on her bike helmet. He got no reply. "New boyfriend?"

"Ha, ha!" Mandy said. "No time now, Dad. I'll tell you later." She set off up the driveway, her long legs pedaling like mad. She waved at her mother.

"What's the rush?" Dr. Emily Hope rolled down her car window.

But Mandy had already sped by, under the wooden sign, "Animal Ark, Veterinary Clinic." She took one look back at the old stone cottage with its modern vets' extension to the rear, then she pedaled hard again.

"She's up to something," Mandy heard her mother say. "She's got that determined look on her face."

Mandy knew they wouldn't have a clue what she wanted with the old newspapers. But she ignored them and charged up the lane toward Welford village. She'd keep her mystery until evening, after her mother came back from her round of visits to the sick cats, dogs, goats, and hamsters that made up the busy practice of Animal Ark. She gave her mom and dad one last wave before she turned out onto the road. "See you later!" she yelled.

"This is it! This is the big day!" Mandy greeted her friend James Hunter. As usual, his straight brown hair flopped onto his forehead, and his glasses sat halfway down his nose.

"Hi," he said. "Do you realize I've dragged myself out of bed half an hour early to meet you outside this rotten store?" He was breathless from pedaling. "My dad nearly dropped dead with shock!"

"Come on!" Mandy said, ignoring his protests. "Let's go and see!"

Mandy and James rode their bicycles out of Welford on the two-mile stretch into Walton. Past all the sleepy cottages and wide-awake farms with their collie dogs at the gate, she never once stopped chattering.

"It's going to be today, I know it!" She had a feeling about these things. James nodded and panted to keep up. "I'm so excited I can hardly wait!" The ground sped by under their wheels. "She's been looking for a warm, dry place, and that's always a sign! Anyway, she refused her food yesterday." James nodded again in agreement. "I did see her on the custodian's porch yesterday after school, behind the stack of logs. She's a very smart cat!"

They pedaled down the final hill. Mandy's short hair blew back in the wind. The new one-story houses of Walton greeted them, spick-and-span. Walton Moor School lay behind the housing development, another new building that backed onto open countryside. Mandy and James rode through the gate into the deserted playground.

Mr. Williams, the custodian, strode through the yard, setting out parking cones for the garbage truck. It was Thursday, trash collection day. "Morning!" Mandy called, with James running to catch up. But Mr. Williams was a man of few words. He ignored her greeting.

"Shh, now!" Mandy warned James. They'd left their bikes locked up in the shed and came up behind the custodian's house. "We don't want to disturb her." Carefully they peered over the beech hedge, neatly trimmed by Mr. Williams. They scanned his pink rose bushes and the porch at the back of his house.

"Mandy," James dared to whisper, "does Mr. Williams know about this?" He was cleaning his glasses on his school sweater. "I mean, what will he say if he finds us snooping around on his porch?"

"He won't mind," Mandy whispered back. How could anyone mind about animals? "Mrs. Williams sometimes puts out food. I bet that's why Walton has chosen their porch to have her babies on!" Mandy's face shone with excitement.

"Walton?" James didn't realize the cat had a name. It was small, black and white, and rather ordinary. As far as he knew, it was a stray. But then,

Mandy had kept details about the cat pretty much to herself up till now.

"I named her after the school," Mandy said. "According to Mrs. Williams, she just turned up on the main doorstep one night, dumped inside a plastic bag with tiny airholes to breathe through. Can you believe it? People can be so cruel!"

Mandy could feel the prick of tears in her eyes even now. "She was only a young cat, and someone just dumped her!" She sniffed and tried to pull herself together. "She would've died if I hadn't come along early next morning and gone to the teachers' room for some milk for her. She was really neglected. I had to build her up." She squared her shoulders. "Anyway, that was six weeks ago. She's the school cat now, only a sort of half stray. So it's up to us to look after her!"

With that, Mandy eased open the back gate into the Williamses' garden. "Walton! Walton!" she coaxed, bending low and looking under the raised porch into the dark space there. James peered up onto the porch itself, behind the stack of logs. No cat.

"Walton!" Mandy called, a bit more loudly.

A black-and-white shape trotted across the long shadows of the lawn and over the flower bed; a round, heavy shape, nearly as wide as she was long, with a low belly. James spotted her first. "Mandy, look!" he said.

Mandy breathed a sigh. They'd gotten here in time. "Hello, Walton," she said. "Here's a nice, comfy place for you to give birth to your lovely kittens, see?" She climbed the porch steps. The cat followed. Mandy delved into her bag and pulled out the old newspapers. She showed them to Walton and let her sniff them. "See, nice and warm and dry!"

Then she and James banked up some of the logs to make a sort of den for Walton. They lined it with the newspapers, carefully overlapping them in thick layers. "See!" Mandy said again.

Walton brushed against Mandy's bare legs. She tilted her head up toward the special bed of logs and newspaper. Her delicate nose and whiskers seemed to approve, for she climbed, slow and heavy, up onto the ledge.

"It's in the sun, nice and warm," James said. "Good idea!" He grinned at Mandy, then blushed. In the distance, the morning bell sounded. "Was that the bell?" he asked clumsily. Then he shot off for homeroom before Mandy could reply.

"You hear that, Walton?" Mandy said. "That's the bell. I have to go." But she felt the strong pull that the cat had over her. Perhaps it was because she,

Mandy Hope, age thirteen, of Animal Ark, Welford, Yorkshire, England, was very like Walton, the school cat. They were both adopted. Her own parents had died in a car crash, too early for her to remember them, and Adam and Emily Hope had taken her in. Now she would do the same for Walton.

Softly she stroked the cat, then she caught hold of herself. "I'll stop fussing now and leave you to cope." She knew animals liked privacy at this time. "No one will bother you, and I'll be back later to see how you're getting along." Quietly she backed down from the porch, then quickly she cut across the garden, through the gate, and over the asphalt of the playground. The second bell had rung.

Mr. Williams, in his padded green vest, his old corduroy trousers, and his big laced boots, crossed paths with Mandy as she ran into school through the main door. As usual, he only grunted, head down and grumpy. Mandy thought it was best not to say anything to him about Walton and her arrangements for the birth. Leave it till later. Even Mr. Williams's heart would melt once he saw Walton's kittens nestling on his back porch!

Mandy rushed into class. She tried, and failed, to concentrate all the way through math, geography, and English.

* * *

At half past three James was waiting for Mandy at the lockers. "Ready?" he asked. Animals were the most important thing in James's life, too.

Dodging the crowds, they sprinted together up the slope to the custodian's house. Mandy could hardly breathe, she was so excited. This was Walton's big day!

"Walton!" Mandy called, opening the gate and crossing the lawn. They turned the corner up onto the porch. Mandy half closed her eyes. There Walton would be, tucked up in her newspaper bed, shielding her new kittens! She couldn't wait!

She opened her eyes. The bed was empty! Clean and dry and quite empty. Mandy looked at James. They felt the bottom of the world fall out.

"Where is she?" James gasped.

Mandy shook her head. "It's today. I'm sure it's today." She couldn't understand it. She'd seen enough cats giving birth to kittens at Animal Ark to know just how they looked when the great day came. Mandy and James stood on the porch, confused and alarmed.

"Listen!" Mandy said. The Williamses' back door stood open in the afternoon sunshine, and Mandy was sure she'd picked up a sound from inside. A tiny, high-pitched squeaking sound!

James stared at her. "What is it?"

Mandy stepped across the kitchen threshold. "Mr. Williams?" she whispered. "Mrs. Williams?"

The kitchen was neat and clean, scrubbed to perfection. Its lace curtains shone pure white. Its black-and-white tiles looked like an advertisement for floor cleaner. But it was empty. The squeaking noise was slightly louder. "In here!" Mandy said.

They tiptoed into the empty room.

"It's still very muffled," James said. He looked inside cupboards, trying to find the noise.

They looked under shelves, behind the vegetable bin, but still the noise escaped them.

"Walton!" Mandy called gently.

But Walton, wherever she was, didn't want company. Only the muffled, faint squeaking continued. Mandy followed it until she finally tracked it down.

There was a laundry basket in the corner of the kitchen, by the washing machine. It was an old-fashioned straw one with a lid. Mandy put her ear to it. The squeaking came from inside!

Gingerly she lifted the lid. It was dark and warm in there. The high-pitched noise rose to a wailing chorus. Mandy adjusted her eyes to the darkness and peered inside. She saw the black-and-white patches of Walton's fur; she saw the cat's eyes glint as she looked up. Obligingly, Walton lifted a paw and shifted sideways. "Look," she seemed to be saying, "four perfect kittens!"

Mandy could just make them out — four tiny curled-up things, gray and blind. Skinny, helpless creatures. She thought they were the most beautiful things she'd ever seen!

"Aren't they wonderful!" Mandy breathed, as James came to look over her shoulder.

He saw their blunt little faces and blind eyes. "Ye-es," he said. He clearly needed more time to get used to them.

"Oh, but they are!" Mandy cooed. She touched Walton gently under the chin. "Good girl!" she said. The kittens squeaked louder in protest at the light and the cooler air. Mandy gave in and replaced the laundry basket lid.

And then their luck ran out. Someone crossed the porch and filled the kitchen doorway. He was tall, bulky, and his feet made a noise across the wooden floor of the porch. "Amy?" he called. He paused, wiped his feet, then stepped into the kitchen.

"Mr. Williams! Um, hello!" Mandy said feebly. James stood alongside her, straightening his school tie, trying to look braver than he felt.

"What the heck!" Williams bellowed with shock.

"Amy! Where are you? What the heck!" he said again.

His wife came tottering through from the front room. She was slightly deaf, slightly nearsighted. "Don't shout, Eric," she sighed. "I can hear perfectly well without you having to shout!"

"Oh, can you?" her husband fumed. "I'll bet you heard these two prowling around in here perfectly well, too!"

Mrs. Williams sighed again. "Sit down, all of you," she said. "Everybody sit down while I make us a cup of tea!" It was clearly her cure for everything.

Mandy and James sat down as they were told, as far away from Mr. Williams as possible, while his wife made the tea. "Well!" he said over and over. "Can't a man even call his house his own anymore?"

"Oh, shush, Eric!" his wife said, giving him his favorite mug and a butter cookie. "Just give them a chance to explain!" She was little and skinny, half his size, but Mandy and James could see who was boss. "Well, then," Mrs. Williams smiled sweetly at Mandy. "I'm sure there's a perfectly good explanation!"

"There is," Mandy agreed. She looked wildly at James for help.

"The cat had kittens!" James blurted out.

"In your laundry basket," Mandy finished off.

"What!" Mr. Williams shot to his feet. He backed off into a corner.

"Wait!" Mrs. Williams went to investigate. She lifted the basket lid and peered inside. "It has," she confirmed calmly. "It had kittens, all right."

"On my best shirts!" Mr. Williams stammered. "It had kittens on my best shirts!"

"Calm down, Eric!" Mrs. Williams shook her head. "It's only a stray cat!"

"Only!" The custodian rolled his eyes in helpless anger.

"She won't do any harm," Mandy broke in.

"They've very clean animals. She won't leave any mess!" She tried to reason with him. "If you just leave her and the kittens there in peace for a few days, they'll soon be on their feet. Then you can make them a better place — a cardboard box, for instance. Just line it with newspaper and put it out on the porch. That should be fine!"

"A few days!" Mr. Williams repeated. His face seemed to be stuck. His mouth had dropped open; his eyes were bulging.

Mrs. Williams took Mandy and James aside. She shook her head. "It's no use. He can't stand them."

Mandy was slow to catch on. "Can't stand what?" Only now was she beginning to sense that there was a problem.

"Cats. He can't stand them. They set his nerves on edge."

Mandy breathed in deeply. How could people hate cats?

"He says they dig up his garden. He can't abide them." Mrs. Williams sounded sorry, but she sounded as if they'd just have to understand. Her husband was stubborn as a mule over cats. She turned and started clearing away the tea things.

"Just a few days!" Mandy said, dashing from one to the other. "We can't move them for a few days, in case the mother decides to abandon the kittens.

She might, if they get moved. Please let her stay where she is!" She felt breathless with fright, but she tried not to show it.

"Stay? In my laundry basket?" Mr. Williams snorted. "On my best shirts?" He tossed his head. "A load of smelly cats!"

"They're not —" Mandy interrupted, but James stopped her. He had a better idea of when to answer back than Mandy.

"Not likely!" Mr. Williams headed straight at Mandy and James to shoo them out of his kitchen. "Go on, you two. Get moving! I won't warn you again!"

Mandy and James backed off toward the door. Mr. Williams towered over them. "Please!" Mandy pleaded. She felt sick at heart.

"No!" Mr. Williams thundered. "They've got to go!" He glanced at his wife. "And there's no use you looking like that, Amy. I'm saying no, and I mean no!" He looked down at Mandy's terrified face. "I'm telling you once and for all, I'm not having them kittens in my kitchen!"

Two

Mr. Williams said his final word, then stormed out of the room. Tears sprang to Mandy's eyes. She looked in desperation at Mrs. Williams.

The old woman raised her eyebrows and rolled her eyes. She patted her neat gray hair. "Just give him a minute to cool down," she said. She lifted the laundry basket lid to take a peek for herself. "My, my," she murmured.

"He can't mean it," Mandy said to James, who was trying to drag her out of the kitchen onto the back porch. "He can't just sentence four perfectly harmless kittens to death, can he? It isn't fair!"

James shook his head and kept on pulling. "Come on, we'd better go!"

"Mrs. Williams!" Mandy pleaded.

The custodian's wife carefully washed the rose-patterned teacups. She put them away in a high, glass-fronted cupboard. "I'm saying nothing," she said steadily.

Mandy shook herself free of James. "But it isn't fair! I mean, what have those poor little kittens ever done to anybody? They deserve a chance to live, just like anyone else! You can't just chuck them away because they happen to have been born in an unusual place!"

"On top of my husband's best shirts," Mrs. Williams reminded her. "My Eric's very particular about his shirts." She turned to face Mandy, who was a head taller than she, but thin as a piece of string. "Anyhow, whoever said life was fair?"

"But if he moves them, they'll die! Walton will abandon them!" Again the tears pricked her eyelids.

Mrs. Williams stared up at her. "Walton?" She folded her arms and kept her gaze steady.

"The mother cat. I've called her Walton after the school. I wanted her to sound as if she belonged somewhere! As if she was looked after, and had a home, and somebody who cared!" Mandy rushed on.

The tears were rolling down her cheeks now. They ran with a salty taste into her mouth. She remembered the half-starved cat being dumped in the school doorway. She thought of herself. What would have happened to her if Emily and Adam Hope hadn't taken her in and cared for her when she was tiny?

"Mandy!" James whispered. "Don't cry. You see worse things than this at the Ark every day of the week, remember."

"No, let her alone," Mrs. Williams said thoughtfully. "She's right. They deserve a chance." She took Mandy by the hand and sat her down at the table. Late afternoon sun filtered in through the white net curtains. "But for goodness' sake, dry your eyes, young woman. I can hear my Eric coming back across the yard, and he can't abide waterworks!" She pulled a clean handkerchief out of her apron pocket and handed it to Mandy. "Quick, blow your nose!"

"Will you help us?" Mandy whispered. The custodian's big boots tramped up the steps and across the porch. "If you let the kittens stay, I'll come here every day, twice a day, to help look after them! I'll —"

"Shush!" Mrs. Williams warned. Her husband hung his cap on the door peg. She stood up and leaned forward evenly, with clenched fists down on the table.

"What the —!" Mr. Williams's face darkened as he caught sight of Mandy and James. "I thought I'd told you to clear out! What's the matter; are you deaf?"

"Now, Eric," Mrs. Williams began steadily.

"Don't you 'Now, Eric' me!"

"Now, Eric!" she insisted. "This young girl has been explaining to me again about these kittens being moved. It seems the mother won't have any more to do with them if we interfere. They have to be left alone."

A loud meow of agreement from inside the basket backed up the end of Mrs. Williams's firm speech. Thin squeaks followed after in a kind of chorus. Mr. Williams paced up and down the kitchen.

"Stand still, Eric, and listen!" Hands on hips, the tiny woman in the flowery apron confronted her heavyweight husband. "Where's the harm in it? You've got a drawer full of shirts up those stairs, most of them hardly worn. There's even one still in its package, pins and all — the one that your sister gave you last Christmas!" She eyed him sternly.

"You know I don't like shirts straight from the wrapping," he grumbled. "They're stiff and they itch!"

"I'll wash it." She didn't flinch. "Then you can wear it this Sunday to church, all right?"

Mandy held her breath. She had the good sense not to interfere in this argument, even though the little wailing sound from inside the basket was tugging at her heartstrings. James still stood sentry by the door, ready to escape.

Mr. Williams pointed an accusing finger at the basket. "My best blue shirt! My favorite!" he reminded her angrily. But it was the last trace of resistance. He knew when he was beaten.

"Now, Eric, it won't come to any harm. This young girl knows all about animals, don't you?"

Mandy nodded and gasped. "My mom and dad are both vets. In Welford, at Animal Ark!"

Mrs. Williams nodded, too. "See, she's a good girl. She promised to come in here twice a day to help look after those poor little things. They won't get under your feet. They'll just stay in there nice and cozy while Walton tends them."

"Walton?" Mr. Williams interrupted, looking curiously at Mandy.

"The mother cat," Mrs. Williams said, steady as ever.

"Crazy name for a cat," he grumbled, but he was definitely weakening.

"Well?" the fierce little woman demanded.

"Well . . ." He scratched his lined forehead with broad, work-worn fingers.

"All right, that's settled!" she said, like a suitcase snapping shut. "The girl will come in here each day until the kittens can begin to fend for themselves."

Mr. Williams grunted.

"That means yes," she reported to Mandy and James.

Mandy jumped up from the table, able to breathe at last. "Oh, thank you!" she said in a rush. "I'll go right away and get some food and extra vitamins and things for Walton. I'll be back as soon as I can. Walton will need lots of looking after, being such a small cat, and we may have to help her feed her kittens. I'll bring milk and a dropper just in case. She won't have that much milk herself, and four is a lot for her to feed, especially being so run down when she was a stray! We'll need to —"

"Whoa, hold your horses!" Mr. Williams backed off against the wall. "Not so fast." He turned to James. "Now listen, boy, maybe I can talk sense to you!"

James stood at attention, ready to listen.

"Man to man, I'm telling you straight. My wife, Amy, is too softhearted by far. Everyone knows that. And I've agreed to let those darn kittens stay put on top of my shirts because of her. I don't like it, but I want a quiet life. And when my wife makes up her mind about something, I generally give in."

Mrs. Williams smiled at Mandy, her hands clasped meekly in front of her.

"But," said Mr. Williams, "I just want to give your girlfriend here a word of warning."

Mandy saw James's face turn red at the word "girlfriend." But Mr. Williams thundered on.

"Now, I'm a mild-mannered guy, but before you both go running off for food and vitamins and whatever else, I want to make it clear that I won't put up with these smelly things camping out on my best shirts for a day longer than necessary, is that clear?"

James nodded. Mandy moved over to the door to stand beside him. They watched Mr. Williams's face take on the old angry look. "Quiet life or not, I'll give you just one week," he warned. "And that'll be that! After that, it's the end for the nasty little creatures!"

Mandy felt her heart go thump. She felt the blood drain from her face. "What do you mean?"

"I mean what I say. I'm giving you seven days. Find good homes for those kittens within the week, or else!" He stood with his feet planted wide apart, his face like a storm.

"Or else what?" Mandy gasped.

"Or else I'll deal with them myself!" He turned and stamped out of the kitchen, slamming the door after him.

James and Mandy flew back home on their bikes, up and down the hills to Welford. At the back of her mind hammered the horrible phrase "deal with them myself." Meaning what? Pictures of kittens drowning, hanging, being dumped in a sack by the side of a highway flashed through her head.

She yelled good-bye to James at the turn near the Fox and Goose tavern and hurried on up the road to Animal Ark. When she arrived, she threw down her bike in the backyard and rushed straight into the office.

"Mom!" she called. She dashed past Jean Knox in reception, who was busy signing out Miss Martin's Yorkshire terrier, Snap.

Jean looked up and smiled. "She's in the exam room," she said, but the door was already swinging shut.

"Mom!" Mandy slowed herself down and lowered her voice so as not to disturb the animals in their rows of cages and kennels.

"Hi, Mandy, over here!" Dr. Emily called. She had a blue-gray Persian cat up on the treatment table and was carefully feeling behind his left ear. She gave the cat a gentle stroke and popped him back in his carrier. "You're just about ready to go home," she promised. She turned to Mandy. "Now, what's all the drama?"

Her mom stood there in her white coat. She wore her long red hair tied back as usual, but it was always escaping. With her big green eyes and friendly face, Dr. Emily had the knack of calming Mandy down. "The school cat had four kittens," she reported.

"Ah!" Dr. Emily smiled. "That explains the newspapers. Good bedding for a birth. Did you get there in time?"

"Yes, but she didn't like the place on the porch that we'd fixed up for her." Mandy fiddled with the catch on the Persian's basket.

"No. They often don't." Dr. Emily hooked her thumbs in her coat pockets. "So?"

"So she gave birth in the custodian's kitchen instead."

"And?"

"And Mr. Williams, the custodian, hates cats!" Mandy looked at her mother with her wide blue eyes.

"Ah!" Dr. Emily settled back against the table. Dr. Adam came out of one of the treatment rooms to join them.

"Mo-om!" Mandy began to plead. "He's given us a week. We have to find homes for four kittens in a week. Otherwise he's threatening to take them off somewhere and put them down!"

Dr. Emily looked at her husband. "Hmm."

"It's not fair!" Mandy exploded. "He cares more about his stupid shirts than about the lives of four innocent animals! How can anyone be so mean?"

"Calm down, Mandy," Dr. Adam said. He was rubbing his beard thoughtfully. "What's this about shirts?"

Mandy explained. "Anyway, the kittens will be up and about in a few days, then it'll be okay to move them out of the stupid basket. Then he can have his rotten shirts back!"

"Mandy!" her mom warned. "Don't be rude. Some people just don't like cats, and you have to accept that." She lifted the cat basket and began to head for reception.

Mandy realized that her chance was slipping by. "Mom," she said, "can I take some milk and some vitamins back over there tonight?" She knew from watching her parents at work in Animal Ark what help Walton would need to feed the kittens.

"Of course," Dr. Emily nodded. She was already on her way out.

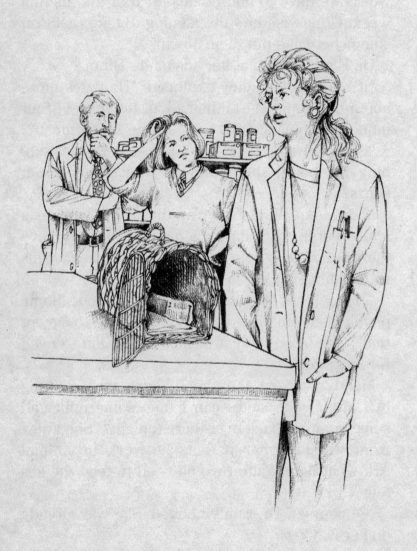

"And, Dad, can we take the kittens in here at the end of the week? Please!" Mandy sidled up to him.

"Ah!" Dr. Adam put an arm around her shoulder. He knew his wife was still listening. "Now, Mandy, you know our rules about that."

"I know, Dad, but this is different!" Mr. Williams was going to kill the poor little things if she couldn't find them homes!

"We don't take in strays, you know that. We're not a charity, remember. We're vets." Mandy guessed that it was a rule he might have bent a little. But his wife had a very firm business head. She came back toward them.

"The answer's got to be no, Mandy." Dr. Emily was kind but firm. She put the cat basket down and spoke gently. "Listen, the custodian has already done you a favor and given you a week, hasn't he?"

Mandy hung her head and nodded miserably. "It would only be for a while, Mom. We'd only have to have them for a while until Walton's finished feeding."

"Then what, hmm?" Dr. Emily glanced at her husband to check. "That's right, isn't it, Adam? We can't suddenly change our rule about strays. We'd be overrun with them in no time. You've got to understand that, Mandy."

Mandy nodded again. Her mom was always right,

but it hurt a lot to agree with her sometimes. She thought of the four helpless kittens being carefully licked clean by a proud Walton.

"Now, listen," Dr. Adam said in his cheerful voice. "Cheer up, this is a challenge!"

Mandy sniffed and looked up. "How do you mean?"

"You've got a whole week; look at it that way! One week to find four good homes for four furry bundles of fun. You can do it!"

She looked up at his lopsided, cheerful grin. "I can," she agreed. "Or rather, *we* can!"

"We?" her mom asked.

"Me and James."

"You and James!" her mom echoed, raising her eyebrows. "Well, then!"

Mandy ignored her. "Yes! Four homes for four kittens!" Mandy began packing sterilized droppers and vitamin drops in her pockets. "Easy. No problem!"

"Good girl," Dr. Emily said, satisfied.

Dr. Adam winked at his daughter. "That's my girl!"

Mandy was dashing about, back to normal. "I'll come up with a plan, just you wait!" She was out through reception, jumping on her bike, and pedaling up the driveway before her parents had time to draw a breath.

Back at school, Mrs. Williams opened the kitchen door to her and watched as Mandy carefully lifted the lid off the laundry basket.

"Hello, Walton," Mandy said gently. Inside the basket it was warm and dark. The cat purred up at her. "Come on, come and have some food!" She picked up the warm, soft cat and cradled her. The four kittens wailed miserably. "Sorry, but mother cats need looking after, too!" Mandy said as she closed the lid.

"There!" Mandy said as she set out milk and food on the kitchen floor for Walton. The cat arched her black-and-white back and rubbed against Mandy's legs. Then she settled quickly and daintily to her supper.

"Come and look!" Mandy whispered to Mrs. Williams. "Walton won't mind." Walton raised her head briefly as Mandy lifted the basket lid once more, then kept on lapping milk. They peered together into the dark nest. Clean and dry, the four kittens nestled on Mr. Williams's best blue shirt — blind and helpless, but quiet now — and snuggled against one another.

"Oh, my!" Mrs. Williams shook her head. "They look liked drowned rats!"

"No, they don't. They're beautiful!" Mandy whispered. "Look!"

"Well, at any rate they all look the same to me, all gray and furry and curled up like that."

"No, they don't. They're very different; can't you see?" And Mandy promptly decided to give them names. She picked them up, one at a time. "This one's Smoky, and this one's Patch." She looked carefully at the two remaining kittens, then grinned. "And this one's Amy. And this one's Eric!"

"Oh!" Mrs. Williams stood back, slightly shocked, then pleased in spite of herself. "Are you sure? I mean, I don't know what my husband will say!" She tut-tutted and smoothed her apron.

Mandy smiled and stood up as Walton finished her meal.

The cat leaped up into the basket, back on duty. She sprang down into the dark well, ready to let the kittens suckle. "I think we'll let her manage for now." She put the lid back on, testing it to make sure the cat could push it off easily by herself. "Maybe tomorrow we'll start giving the kittens extra milk."

"Hmm." Mrs. Williams nodded. "What time will you be back in the morning, then?"

"About eight o'clock. Before school starts."

The custodian's wife showed her out. "Make sure you don't forget!"

"No way!" Mandy waved, picked up her bike, and set off for home.

The sun was setting over the field as she rode past the new houses out onto the open road. The sky was pure red, the horizon dark brown. Mandy felt the wind. She was pleased with the day, happy that Walton had had such a good birth. She'd be a wonderful mother, even though she was so young herself.

Then Mandy's heart jolted. Smoky and Patch, Amy and Eric were all snuggled up for the night. There was a new world waiting outside for them, a big and dangerous place. Right now they were asleep. But Mandy tensed against the handlebars as she took the final curve down the hill into Welford. Her face frowned. She had a week to find four homes. Mr. Williams's threat lurched out of the lengthening shadows like a giant from a fairy tale. "Find good homes for them kittens within the week. Or else I'll deal with them myself!" he roared. Mandy knew he wouldn't relent. He meant what he said. A death sentence hung over the poor little kittens, and only she could save them!

Three

Dr. Adam glanced up from the television as Mandy wandered in. The living room was low, with wooden beams, a big stone fireplace, and cozy red-patterned rugs on the old stone floor. It was a cold evening, and a log fire crackled. "Got any home-work?" he asked.

"I've already done it." Mandy flicked through a magazine. She was frowning and restless.

Dr. Adam looked at her again. "Why not take that back to your grandmother's?" he suggested.

Mandy nodded. She was thinking, thinking; what to do to find homes for those kittens? But she picked up the little magazine and drifted off down the hallway.

"Where are you off to?" her mom asked as she came in through the front door. She'd just gotten back from her yoga class, relaxed and smiling as usual.

"I have to clean out the rabbit hutch, then I'm off to Grandma and Grandpa's," Mandy said absent-mindedly. She waved the magazine, still deep in thought.

"Say hello from me!" Dr. Emily shouted after Mandy, but she got no answer.

Mandy let Flopsy, Mopsy, and Cottontail out into the run in the backyard while she cleaned out their hutch and laid down fresh straw. Satisfied that their water was clean and that they were safely bedded down for the night, she set off up the lane to her grandparents' cottage.

In the cool evening light, the mass of white lilacs in her grandfather's garden gave off a strong, sweet scent. Even at this late hour he would be out in his greenhouse, puttering. "Hi, Grandpa!" she said with a wave. She stood to wait for him by the new camper sitting proudly in their side driveway.

"Hello, sweetie!" His face lit up, and he came out to greet her. He slid the greenhouse door closed.

n. Your grandma's inside writing

her in through the kitchen and into k room. The lamps cast a yellow glow and u owered curtains were closed. "Hello!" Mandy's grandmother gave her a wide smile. "Guess what I'm doing."

Mandy sat down opposite her at the table. "Writing a letter?" She loved visiting her grandparents. Even when she felt down, like now, somehow they cheered her up.

"Not just any old letter!" her grandmother announced. "This one is special. This one is to the prime minister!"

"Oh!" Mandy tried not to sound too surprised. She was used to her grandmother knitting impossible cardigan patterns and making gallons of rhubarb-and-ginger jam, not writing letters to prime ministers. "What is it about?" she asked.

"It's about our post office. There are nasty rumors in the village that they want to close it down. Mr. McFarlane told me about it when I went in to pick up some stamps earlier today."

"Why do they want to close it?" Mandy couldn't imagine life in Welford without their little post office.

Grandma raised her glasses onto her forehead. "They say it's too expensive to run. Too expensive, I ask you! Honestly, they don't know what they're talking about! We have to stop them!"

"So Dorothy's writing to the prime minister. Always go to the top is what I say," Mandy's grandfather said. "On her best notepaper, of course!" He winked and handed her a glass of homemade lemonade.

"On my official notepaper. I'm writing as chairperson of the Welford Women's Club!"

Mandy looked impressed. Even the prime minister would have to listen to her grandmother when she was on her high horse. "They won't close the post office," she said. "Not after they've read your letter!"

They all chuckled. "You've spoiled my concentration," her grandmother said. She put pen and paper aside. She looked at Mandy's fidgety hands. "Anyway, you have something on your mind, I can tell."

Mandy didn't need a second invitation. The story of Walton and her kittens poured out — how she was the school cat, but Mandy felt she must take charge. How Mr. Williams had no heart at all. How she, Mandy, had to find homes for the kittens. Her grandparents tut-tutted and nodded in all the right places. Mandy paused at the critical point and took a deep breath. "Grandma," she said, trying to sound very reasonable, "I've been thinking."

"Yes?" Her grandmother gave her a sideways look.

"Well, I've been thinking that a cat would be the perfect thing for you here in the cottage. I mean, it's lonely this far up the lane, and you hardly see any neighbors, and a cat is really good company for . . ." She faltered and blushed.

"For old people?" Her grandfather finished the sentence. He grinned. He was sixty-five — a gardener, a walker, a bicycle rider. He was fit as a fiddle.

"Yes," she admitted. "Anyway, they're sweet, clean animals, and you don't have to fuss over them. They look after themselves, and —"

"Whoa!" her grandfather said. "Hold on!" He looked helplessly at his wife.

"Look, honey," her grandmother spoke gently. "It's a good idea, and it's very good of you to be thinking of us like this, it really is. You're our beautiful, warmhearted girl, you know that!"

Mandy saw a great big "But" looming on the horizon. "Yes?" she said, feeling her heart sink.

Her grandfather took over. "But we've just bought our camper. You know, our retirement treat!" He jerked his head sideways. "There she stands in the driveway all shiny and new, waiting to take us to the Italian Alps, to Provence, to Portugal!"

"To Scarborough, the day after tomorrow!" her grandmother put in.

Mandy nodded. "So?"

"So we won't be at home to look after a pet as much as we were when your grandpa was working. We'll be out on the open road, the freeway, with the wind in our hair and the sun on our faces!"

Mandy was shocked. She wondered if she'd ever see her grandparents again!

"Not all the time," her grandfather corrected. "I still need to keep an eye on my tomatoes!"

"But too much of the time to be able to take in one of your kittens," her grandmother said finally.

And Mandy had to accept that. Smoky was the one she'd been planning for them to have, with his perky face and his way of pushing the other three kittens out of the way when they were feeding. Now Smoky wouldn't be sunning himself on her grandfather's patio after all. Mandy tried to swallow her disappointment.

"But . . ." her grandmother said, sweeping stray hair up into the bun at the back of her head, "we can still help!"

"How?" Mandy leaped at the promise. Her eyes lit up.

"We'll help you look for homes. How many kittens are there? Four?" Grandma got on her thinking cap. "There's Eileen Davy at the Old School House, but she's on the main road, and she's already lost two cats to the traffic, poor things. There's Myra Hugill, but she has to look after her sick sister in York right now. There's Dora Janeki from Syke Farm, but she's a loony old thing, and her new husband isn't known as an animal lover."

Mandy seized each name, then let it drop as her grandmother counted them off on her fingers. She was beginning to feel hopeless again.

"Wait!" her grandfather said. "I've just had a brilliant idea!"

Mandy swung around to face him. "What?"

"The post office!" he said, raising a finger.

Mandy looked puzzled. "Not right now, Grandpa. We're talking about Walton's kittens!"

"I know. That's why I mentioned the post office. That's my brilliant idea!"

"Oh, I see!" her grandmother said. "Yes, Tom, of course!"

"What? What?" Mandy didn't see at all.

"The bulletin board in the post office! That's what!" Her grandpa took a postcard out of the bureau and uncapped his old fountain pen. "Watch."

He wrote in beautiful old-fashioned letters:

WANTED!
FOUR GOOD HOMES
Cat lovers needed to provide
homes for kittens.
Please call Welford 703267.

"There!" he said, standing back and looking at his work of art. "You can take it down to the post office first thing in the morning."

Mandy took the sign. She nodded and smiled. "Brilliant, Grandpa!"

He screwed the top back on his pen. "It's nothing, my dear," he said modestly.

"Yes, it is, it's brilliant! We'll get millions of calls, you'll see!" Welford was full of animal lovers, and this was the perfect way to find them. Everyone went into the post office at some time during each day. Mandy hugged both her grandparents.

"Maybe not millions," her grandmother advised.

"All right, dozens!" Mandy said, laughing at her own habit of exaggerating. They all laughed together.

She left the house, smiling and happy. She closed

the gate with its Lilac Cottage sign, waved, and set off down the lane. Tomorrow was Friday. She'd be at the post office first thing in the morning. She'd spend the weekend answering all the phone calls. She ran home full of plans and preparations.

Mandy had arranged to meet James again to go to school early. She'd already been into the post office and pinned up her "Wanted" sign right in the center of the bulletin board. She greeted him cheerfully with, "You're seven minutes late, James Hunter!"

James pushed his glasses back onto the bridge of his nose. "Sorry," he said. He screeched to a halt on his bike. "I had to walk Blackie. Dad's away. And then I had to feed Benji."

"Oh, well, then," Mandy forgave him. Being late because of a dog and a cat was quite understandable. "Let's go!"

They made up some time on the journey. Traffic was still light, and they knew all the back ways. By five past eight they were knocking on the Williamses' kitchen door.

Mrs. Williams opened it with a worried face. "I thought you weren't coming! Come in, come in," she said.

"Is something wrong?" Mandy was unpacking cat food and a carton of milk on the kitchen table.

"I'm not sure. It's too quiet in there for my liking. Not like yesterday with all the racket. Even Eric noticed." Mrs. Williams watched anxiously.

Mandy lifted the basket lid. "Hello, Walton!" she said. But the cat lay on her side and only managed a feeble meow. "Leave me in peace," she seemed to say. She raised her head, but she didn't stretch and make her way out into the daylight to get some breakfast.

"Poor thing, she's exhausted!" Mandy said. "James, you'd better open that can of food. I'll lift her out." She reached in, tenderly lifting the tired cat. "She'll be all right in a minute," she told Mrs. Williams. She knew from helping out at home that there was nothing seriously wrong. "She just needs a little extra care." And she set the cat down to feed.

Walton wobbled, steadied herself, and eagerly got to work on the dish of meat.

"What about the kittens?" James said.

Mandy cast an expert eye over the four huddled shapes. "Fine!" she said. "But we'll have to feed them. We'll need the droppers. And we'll have to use the ordinary milk for now." She'd seen her mom and dad do it often enough. Now she hoped she could manage it all by herself.

James got the droppers from her bag. Mandy

gently heated the milk. Then she lifted one of the featherlight bundles. She sat with it on her lap and eased open its tiny mouth. "Come on, Patch, come on!" she coaxed.

She squeezed the rubber bulb of the dropper and took in milk from the warm pan. Then, while she held open the kitten's mouth with two fingers, she eased the glass tube between its lips with the other hand. She squeezed again and watched Patch's tiny tongue lick and then swallow the liquid. "See?" she said to James. "Now you try it."

He nodded and took another kitten, Smoky, out of the basket. Afraid but determined, he copied Mandy's actions with a second dropper. Smoky looked surprised, then gulped. James looked up in triumph.

"All right!" Mandy said.

It was fifteen minutes later and they were just finishing with the last two kittens when Mr. Williams tramped back in from unlocking the school. James and Mandy were busy stroking the kittens' throats to encourage them to swallow. Mr. Williams heard the tiny mewing from the basket. "What's up with the mother cat?" he barked.

"Tired out," Mrs. Williams said. "And you would be, too." She hovered by the sink like a worried relative.

"Hmm." He turned back out of his kitchen, grumbling.

"This place is being turned into a cat hospital! A man can't even call his home his own anymore!"

Mandy and James finished the feeding and cleaned up the room to perfection. Walton was sitting on the step, in the morning sun. She gave herself a thorough licking. Mandy bent to stroke her. "Good girl," she said. She was relieved when Walton decided it was time to return to her kittens. They watched her walk across the shiny tiles, jump up, and nimbly lift the basket lid with one paw. Then she disappeared from sight.

"Smart cat!" James said. He looked at his watch. "It's a quarter to nine," he reminded Mandy.

They said a hurried good-bye to Mrs. Williams and ran out through the garden and across the playground. A strong wind blew white blossom petals diagonally across the pavement. "What do you think?" James asked, pausing before they passed under the great stone arch of the main entrance.

"Oh, Walton will be all right," Mandy said. "She'll just have to take things easy." She hitched her backpack higher onto her shoulders and brushed cat hairs off her navy blue skirt. "But I'm not so sure about the kittens now."

Mandy didn't want to scare James, but she

thought the cat's milk might dry up. This sometimes happened when the mother wasn't strong. If
so, the tiny things would soon starve to death.
"We'll have to wait and see. Perhaps Walton will be
able to go on feeding them herself."

"What if she can't?" James wanted to know.

Mandy thought of the kittens with their gradually
opening eyes, their fluffier coats, their attempts to
struggle up onto all fours. They still tumbled and
collapsed like rag dolls. She could hold them easily
in the palm of her hand. "Well, we'll just have to
keep on feeding them ourselves," she said.

All morning long Mandy had kitten worries on
her mind. There was the old one of finding four
good homes in less than a week, and the new one
that she wouldn't confess even to James. But the
question kept crowding in on her. It wouldn't go
away. Walton was exhausted from the birth. The
kittens were clinging to life by a thread. And the
question still whirled in her head as Mandy sat and
ate her packed lunch in B Hall with Kate and
Melanie: Would they need to find homes for the
kittens after all? Would the poor little things even
survive?

Four

Mandy decided that the best answer to her question was a great big "yes!"

You have to think "yes" all the time, or life will get you down, she told herself. She and James would hand-rear the kittens if necessary. So she set about finding homes for them with even more energy than before.

She and James fed Walton and the little gang of kittens right after school, then they rode their bikes back to Animal Ark. "We're going to make more signs!" Mandy announced. She led James upstairs and rummaged under her bed, looking for some neon-pink poster board she'd stored there before

Christmas. "Then we'll be sure that every single person in Welford will read one!"

She liked to work in her room; it was an art gallery of animal posters. Horses and rabbits, dogs and cats stared down from her walls. Hardly an inch of wallpaper showed through, just how Mandy liked it. Mandy and James knelt on the floor to cut out small rectangles of pink cardboard. They chose broad black felt-tips and began designing their own signs. "Where will we stick these?" James wanted to know.

"Shh, I'm thinking!" Mandy said. She wanted eye-catching words to draw people's attention. Finally she wrote in big capital letters:

KITTENS IN THE KITCHEN
Bring love into your life.
Cats make cozy companions.
Adopt a kitten. Call Welford 703267.

It was catchier than her grandfather's sign. She was pleased as she knelt back to judge the effect, while James finished his much more practical notice:

HOMES NEEDED FOR FOUR KITTENS!
Remember, pets are for life!
If interested, call Welford 703267.

"I could put this one on your board in reception," he suggested.

Mandy nodded. "Good idea. Let's go down and ask Jean before she leaves for the day." She knew Jean liked to know exactly what went up on the bulletin board in reception.

They went downstairs and through the house into Animal Ark. Jean had closed the appointment book and was searching for her car keys. She had been their receptionist for five years and she was always losing her keys. Mandy knew all the places they were likely to be. She began helping Jean search.

"Here they are!" Mandy lifted the blue book and handed the keys to Jean.

"Oh, silly me!" Jean said, as she always did. She wore her glasses on a silver chain around her neck and still managed to forget where she'd put them.

James tried not to smile. "Can we put a 'Homes Wanted' sign on your board, please?" he said.

Jean took the sign, looked for her glasses, found them hanging down around her neck, and read the words. "That looks fine. Just find a space over there beside all the others," she said.

"Others?" James looked at Mandy. They scrambled across to the board. In the bottom corner there were at least six other "Homes Wanted" signs. James and Mandy's faces fell a little.

"Only three of them are for kittens," James said. Two others were for puppies, one for a pony.

Mandy counted up quickly. "Yes, but that's fourteen kittens needing homes altogether!" Fourteen kittens in a tiny place the size of Welford.

"Come on, chop-chop!" Jean said. She was busy locking cupboards, windows, drawers, and anything else that stood still. "I want to shut up shop!"

They looked again at the signs, trying not to feel downhearted. "Ours is the brightest one!" James said. "And it's in the best place!"

Mandy agreed. "I have another idea!"

With the second bright pink card in her hand they shot off ahead of Jean, up the driveway, and down into the village. "It's Friday. Grandma will be playing badminton!" They rode on past the post office and the general store toward the village hall.

"So?" James overtook Mandy. His soccer training was coming in handy for stamina. They headed for the village hall, which was set back from the road, next to the church.

"They have a Women's Club bulletin board in the entrance," Mandy reminded him.

"Right." James nodded and kept up the pace. Lots of kindhearted ladies came to the village hall to do flower arranging and cake icing, besides the Friday evening badminton club. It was a great place for one of their signs.

They almost bumped into Miss Davy from the Old School House as she came out of the hall, racket in hand, and not a silver-blue hair out of place. She turned and called in a shrill voice, "Dorothy, one granddaughter!" She smiled at them and continued on her way.

Grandma emerged, red-faced and breathless. She wore a bright turquoise track suit. "Mandy!" She gave her a quick peck on the cheek. "How nice. But it's thirteen-eleven, final game. I can only spare a second!"

"Sorry, Grandma." Mandy held up her KITTENS IN THE KITCHEN sign. "Can we pin this on the bulletin board?"

Mrs. Hope squinted at it. "Oh, the kittens? Yes, yes, of course. Good idea. 'Bye, honey!" And she dashed back to finish her game.

Mandy opened the glass door of the bulletin board and made space between lists of flower arrangers for the church, dates of Brownie meetings, and a charity drive. She pinned her sign firmly in the center, closed the door, stood back, and admired it.

"That should do it!" James said.

They were pleased with the evening's work as they finally said good-bye and headed home.

After supper Dr. Adam took Mandy into Animal Ark with a secret smile on his face. "Come and see a new admission," he invited.

Near the door of the residential unit was one of the see-through cages, shaped like a cat carrier but made of clear plastic. Dr. Adam picked it up.

"What is it?" Mandy could see the usual newspaper nest and a roll of soft gray cloth, but she couldn't spot any animal in there.

"Squirrel!" her father said. A small black nose peeped out of the newspapers. "A baby. Five weeks old." Two large black eyes appeared, and out it came, the size of a hamster, with a long, long tail. Dr. Adam unlatched the cage door and lifted it out. He handed the little gray squirrel to Mandy.

"Oh!" she said. She was speechless with delight. She felt its sharp little feet. She stroked its soft gray back, while the baby tried to suck the end of her finger. "Where's its mother?" she asked.

"She got run over."

Mandy gasped, and her face crumpled.

"Yes, I know," he said, looking at her. "And this little one would have died if someone hadn't found him."

Mandy shook her head. Life could be so cruel.

"You'll never guess who brought him in."

"Who?"

"Old Ernie Bell from the cottages behind the Fox and Goose."

Mandy looked surprised. She knew Ernie Bell as a grumpy, silent old man who shuffled down the village street with his bag of groceries.

"He came in and handed him over. ''Ere, veterinary,' he says to poor Jean, 'just check 'im over while I fix up a run for 'im in my backyard. I'll be back for 'im in twenty-four hours. Just check 'e's all right!' And he leaves the little fellow with Jean and stomps off to build a wire netting run. Who'd have believed it?" Ernie didn't have the reputation of being soft on animals. Dr. Adam put the baby back in its cage.

"What's the roll of cloth for, Dad?" Mandy bent down to study the squirrel in his cage.

"For comfort; something for him to snuggle up to. Animals need a mother substitute, you know. Something to take the dead mother's place." His voice was warm. He put an arm around Mandy.

"What are you feeding him with?"

"This stuff. It's the bottle food we give to orphan kittens. Why?"

Mandy was making new plans for Walton's

brood. She took the box of white powder and read the list of ingredients and instructions printed on the side. "Can I buy some of this from this week's pocket money?" she asked.

"For your school kittens?" Dr. Adam lifted three boxes down from the shelf. "Go on, take them. You don't have to pay!"

Mandy smiled. "Walton's a little weak right now. We'll have to help her feed the kittens properly."

"Well, this stuff is much better than cow's milk," Dr. Adam said, adding an extra box. "Mix it with boiled water, and use these little bottles with rubber nipples. The kittens can suck these properly. Everything's sterilized, of course."

"How often?" Mandy realized that there was a proper way to do this. The kittens' lives depended on it.

"Every couple of hours for the first week."

Mandy gulped.

"Less if the mother cat can still give milk herself, during the night for instance."

"I think she can. She's just a very small cat, and she's tired." Mandy was still determined to think the best.

"Well, then, this stuff four times a day will do the trick. Breakfast, lunch, after school, supper." He glanced at Mandy's serious face. "You're going to be busy," he said. "Any luck with finding homes for them yet?"

"Not yet." She bent thoughtfully to the level of the baby squirrel in the cage. "Will Mr. Bell have to let him go eventually, back into the wild?"

Her dad shook his head. "He's not allowed to. It's against the law, I'm afraid. That's because he'd never survive out in the wild now. Poor little fellow, it seems he'll have to make do with Ernie's backyard for the rest of his life!"

Mandy nodded.

"Don't worry, there are worse fates," Dr. Adam said.

"Oh, I know." But Mandy was still in a serious mood as she rode over to school with the special kitten food. True, like Ernie Bell and the little squirrel, she was giving the kittens a chance of life. But without homes, would it be a life worth living?

She rode and prayed that the signs in the post office, Animal Ark, and the village hall would work. She wondered, too, whether she could persuade Mr. Williams to give them more time. A week was so short! She leaned her bike against the hedge and went up the steps into the custodian's kitchen.

* * *

Once Walton was happily eating, Mandy showed
Mrs. Williams the new arrangements for Smoky,
Patch, Amy, and Eric. To her surprise, the custodian's wife actually offered to help. "Don't tell my
husband!" She pressed her thin lips tightly together.
"He wouldn't approve!" She took Amy out of the
basket and gingerly snuggled her up against her
flowered apron, complete with feeding bottle.
"Poor little scrap!" she murmured.

Mandy smiled. "She's fine. Look, she's hungry!"

Mrs. Williams sat happily when the kitten fed. "You mustn't mind my Eric," she confided. "I know, he must seem like a grumpy old nuisance to you, but he's not so bad, really."

"No." Mandy tried to believe it. All she could think of were Mr. Williams's big boots and his loud voice. Hands as big as shovels. Temper like a volcano.

"You must think he's a stubborn old mule."

"No!" Mandy knew she didn't sound sincere.

"Yes!" Mrs. Williams looked down into the kitten's face. "Yes, you do. But he loves his garden!" She bent sideways toward Mandy. "Do you know, he keeps a squeeze bottle full of water out there on the porch. If a cat comes anywhere near his roses looking as if it's going to dig, Eric pulls out the bottle. You should hear him when he scores a direct hit!"

"One wet cat!" Mandy joined in the laughter. "I was thinking he might give us a little longer than a week," she said. "Even when we find homes for the kittens, Walton will have to go on looking after them for quite a while. The less we need to move them around the better." She looked pleadingly at Mrs. Williams. "Maybe you could persuade him?"

"Hope by name, hopeful by nature!" Mrs. Williams said. But she was shaking her head. "No, I know Eric. He's made up his mind!"

"Can't you just try?" Mandy was busy cleaning up the bottles and saucers.

But this time Mrs. Williams wouldn't bend. "No, it's not fair to him. He won't come into his own kitchen as it is. I know, I know," she interrupted Mandy's protest, "it's not sensible. But Eric's not always a sensible man. Who is? I'll tell you something else. He has a lot of pain, bending and kneeling and such. Arthritis. In the knees. Very painful." She lowered her voice. "To tell you the truth we don't mention it in case the school happens to hear. He's worried about his job!"

Mandy nodded. Suddenly Mr. Williams seemed human after all. "I'm sorry to hear that."

"Well, don't say I told you," Mrs. Williams warned. They were standing out on the porch. Walton was perched on the rim of the laundry basket licking herself clean. "He's out playing darts this evening. It cheers him up."

Mrs. Williams stared up at the pebbled clouds. "But Eric's a worried man. It's the job, the house, everything. And the pain, of course. I can't even get him to go to a doctor." She glanced at Mandy. "So, you see, I can't ask him to do any more, can I? He's done enough already."

Mandy agreed and smiled sadly. She rode home slowly. She understood more about Mr. Williams's bad temper now, that was certain. But it didn't stop time passing. The sand was running steadily through the hourglass. They had five days left!

Five

"Hello, Welford 703267?" a woman's voice asked.

"This is it!" Mandy yelped, then lowered her voice to speak into the phone. "Yes, this is Welford 703267." She held her breath. "Who's speaking, please?" She gave her mother a hopeful thumbs-up sign.

"Hello?" The voice sounded shy and cautious. There was a long pause.

"Hello, this is Amanda Hope. Who's speaking, please?" Mandy made a face of pretend panic at her mom.

"Hello, I want Welford 703267." The voice

seemed strange and not used to talking on the telephone.

"Can I help you, please?" Mandy said firmly. What was going on here? Her mom had paused over the washing up and was trying to listen in.

"Did you put a sign in the post office?" the woman on the end of the phone asked. "Are you the person with the kittens?"

"I am!" Mandy said with a grin. "I take it you're looking for a kitten?" Dr. Emily winked and continued washing the breakfast dishes.

There was a long, crackly pause. "My name is Miss Marjorie Spry. I live at The Riddings. Please come to see me at two o'clock precisely."

Then the phone went dead.

"Well?" Dr. Emily said.

Relief swept over her as Mandy realized that their plan was beginning to work. It was only nine o'clock on Saturday morning, and they'd already gotten a response! "Yes!" she yelled, nearly jumping for joy. "I'm going over to tell Grandpa!"

"Mandy, what if there are any more phone calls?" Dr. Emily was drying her hands, following her out.

"Write down the numbers on that pad, will you, Mom? I'm so thrilled I can hardly wait!" She rushed up the lane without a jacket. It was drizzling, but she didn't care.

Her grandparents were stacking cans of soup inside the tiny cupboard aboard their camper. "Tomato, minestrone, cream of chicken!" Her grandmother handed them up to her grandfather and ticked them off her list.

"Can opener?" Her grandfather popped his head out of the sliding door. He saw Mandy. "Hello, sweetie!"

"It worked! It worked!" she greeted them. "Your brilliant sign, Grandpa, it worked!"

He rubbed his hands. Mandy's grandparents both stood there in their twin knit sweaters, the drizzle wetting their gray hair. "It has? You have a response then?"

"Of course she has a response, haven't you, Mandy?" Grandma put in. "Come inside. We're all getting wet."

"Who is it?" her grandpa asked as he put on the kettle. "Anyone we know?"

"It's someone called Spy. No, Spry. That's it, Miss Marjorie Spry!"

Grandma shut the kitchen door firmly and wiped her feet. Her head went to one side. "The Riddings, right?"

"Yes, The Riddings. Why, what's the matter? Do you know her?"

Her grandmother straightened herself up and bustled with the cups and saucers. "Yes. She lives at the big house out on Walton Road. Set back from the road. You know, the big old house."

"I know!" Mandy said. They passed it every day on the way to school. It was well away from the traffic, with a huge lawn and garden. The perfect place for a cat to live! "She wants me to go and see her there at two o'clock this afternoon."

"Does she now?" her grandmother said. "That'll be one for the record book!"

"Why? What do you mean?" Mandy was nearly bursting with impatience. "I thought you'd be pleased!"

"We are, sweetie," her grandfather soothed.

"They don't usually like visitors, that's all," Grandma explained. "In fact, I believe the last person they had over their threshold was Mr. Lovejoy, the old pastor before Mr. Walters, and that must be over five years ago!"

"No!" Mandy couldn't believe it.

"Yes, when their father died, the two sisters went into a sort of hibernation. It's true!" Grandma insisted. "Still, that won't make any difference to you,

I don't expect. If Miss Marjorie Spry wants to see you about a kitten, and she's asked you to come over, you go see her." She patted Mandy's hand. "They're harmless. A bit peculiar, but harmless enough."

"Anyway, it's best to check these places before you send these precious kittens off to their new homes," her grandfather agreed. "You have to see if they're the right sort of thing!"

Mandy nodded, but she refused to give up hope.

"Take someone along with you," her grandfather suggested. "Just to be on the safe side."

"James will come with me," Mandy said. She lifted a cardboard box full of bread, cornflakes, milk, and margarine. "Where do you want me to put these?"

Together they finished packing for "the great trial run," as her grandfather called it. He meant their first expedition in their new camper. Finally they were ready.

"Map?" Grandpa said, climbing into the driver's seat.

"Map!" Grandma produced it from the glove compartment.

He turned on the windshield wipers. "Rubber boots? Raincoats? Rain hats?"

Grandma flipped the map at him. "Ready?" she laughed. They waved to Mandy. "To sunny Scarborough!" she cried.

Mandy watched them disappear into the drizzle. There were still four hours to go before the visit to The Riddings. She would call James to arrange to meet him, then fill up the morning with little jobs at Animal Ark, and of course by riding over to feed Walton and the kittens.

Two o'clock came at last. They arrived to find the front lawn of The Riddings spread out like a soccer field. James and Mandy decided to leave their bikes at the gate.

"I wonder who cuts this grass?" James said. It went in neat strips, light and dark. The edges were neatly clipped.

"I do!" An ancient man in corduroy trousers growled at them from behind a laurel hedge. He was bent almost double, probably from years and years of clipping the edges of huge lawns, Mandy guessed. "Have you come about a kitten?" he growled again.

They nodded.

"Miss Marjorie warned me about it. 'Geoffrey,' she said, 'show the girl up to the door!' So I'm following orders. This way!" He trudged ahead of them up the gravel driveway.

The house was as big as a hotel, built of stone, with pointed towers at each corner. It was covered in ivy. Though they passed it every day, James and Mandy could truly say that they'd never really paid much attention to it before. It had arched windows, stone pillars, and massive steps up to a wide front door. "Like a setting for a horror film!" Mandy whispered nervously.

Just when they felt they needed him most, their guide left them. "This is as far as I ever go. Ring three times," he said. "Nice and loud, now. You might have to wait." And he went off, bowed and grumbling, to mow the lawn.

They looked at each other, shrugged, then James rang the bell. Silence. He rang again. And again. Finally someone began rattling locks on the other side of the massive door. "Wait!" a tiny voice ordered.

"What do you think we're doing?" James whispered to Mandy, trying not to laugh.

"Shh!" Mandy said. They had to be on their best behavior.

But even Mandy couldn't stop her jaw from hanging wide when the door finally creaked open.

The hall was the size of a ballroom, all in pink marble, with dark wood panels and glass chandeliers. But it was dull with age and gray with years of neglect. What had once been as splendid as a fairy tale had now decayed.

"Yes?" A lady stood before them. Her sticklike arms and legs poked out from the moth-eaten cream silk robe. She peered at them like a bat in the light.

"Miss Spry?" Mandy said uncertainly. A loud voice would have knocked the old lady down flat, she was sure.

"Yes!" She blinked her watery gray eyes. A skinny hand clutched the neck of her robe. "We don't see visitors!" she chattered.

Mandy's grandmother had been right. No one had come to this place for years. Curtains were closed to keep out the daylight. A collection of old blue-and-white china ornaments cluttered the window-sills. Great piles of yellow newspapers were heaped on shelves. "Miss Marjorie Spry?" Mandy repeated, her heart sinking as her eyes took in the mess.

"Joan! I'm Joan!" the woman shrieked. She began to close the door in their faces, but it was big and heavy. They saw the figure of another thin little woman come hurrying downstairs.

"Come in, come in," this second person ordered in a thin voice. She was beckoning to them, half running across the hall. "They've come about the kitten, Joan. Now open the door at once!"

And there they stood, two ladies thin as sticks, wild-haired, in matching silk robes. They had the same sharp face. They had movements that mirrored each other and voices that echoed and mocked. Identical twins! Miss Joan and Miss Marjorie Spry!

"We don't want visitors!" the first one, Miss Joan, repeated with a birdlike twitch of her head.

"Yes, we do. I invited them!" Miss Marjorie argued. "I want a kitten for this dreadful old place. I want to bring some life in here!"

Miss Joan stared stubbornly, silently back at her sister. Her hand stayed poised to slam the door shut.

"I do, Joan! I'm tired of living in this old museum of a place. I want some life. We're not old yet; let's make a fresh start!" Miss Marjorie pleaded. "Look, this girl is advertising kittens. So let her in!"

At last Miss Joan gave way. Fascinated, Mandy and James stepped inside. To them it seemed like actually stepping into the past, into a kind of prison. Miss Joan pushed the door closed after

them. It shut with a dull, heavy click. "What kittens?" Miss Joan challenged. She looked her sister in the face. "Who told me anything about a kitten?"

"I told you!" Miss Marjorie snapped. "The sign in the post office. Welford 703267!"

"But I don't like kittens!" Miss Joan protested. "You know that!"

Mandy stood in the middle of their argument, her heart sinking right into her shoes by now. Miss Joan would never give in over this. Anyway, who'd want to leave a kitten where it wasn't wanted one hundred percent by everyone in the house? She looked at James and could tell that he thought the same. They both sighed.

They watched as Miss Marjorie grew more and more angry. "How do you know you don't like kittens?" Her eyes seemed to spark. "Have you had one? Have you ever owned a cat in your entire life? Have you? Have you?"

She turned to face Mandy and James, smoldering with rage. "*I* like cats! Joan likes cats, though she says she doesn't! She only says it to be difficult. Yes, you do!" she snapped at her twin. "She's just a spoilsport. It's because it's *my* idea to bring a kitten to The Riddings, to help bring the place back to life a bit. She says no to all my ideas!" She nearly cried with exasperation. The tiny twins stood face to face like featherweight boxers.

"Anyway, I'm the older twin!" Miss Marjorie said grandly. "And I have decided. Don't listen to her!"

"Well, they're still very young," Mandy began to explain. "We're only trying to find suitable homes for them in the future, you see." Still she couldn't settle those doubts about this being a good place to bring one of her precious kittens.

"Where is it?" The older twin began poking at Mandy and James as if a kitten might be hidden in one of their pockets.

"She's still with her mother. We're just starting to look, as I said."

"Not here? You haven't brought it with you?" Miss Marjorie said sharply.

"Ha, ha, ha!" Miss Joan sang out. She did a little dance of delight. "Ha, ha, ha!"

Miss Marjorie's thin patience finally snapped. "Quiet!" she bellowed. She picked up an old black umbrella from the stand and launched it like a javelin at her noisy sister. It missed by miles, but Miss Joan froze on the spot. Then she grabbed a newspaper from a shelf and rolled it up like a baseball bat. James and Mandy stood with their mouths open. Who would believe this?

"Joan!" Miss Marjorie warned.

"You threw something at me first!" Miss Joan retaliated.

"Get out!" Miss Marjorie cried. "Get out, get out!"

James and Mandy didn't know if she meant them or her sister. Everything was chaos. Mandy was growing sure of just one thing, though: This was no place for a tiny kitten.

She knew this once and for all when Miss Joan raised her rolled newspaper and began to chase Miss Marjorie from the hall into the study, a room at the front of the house. In a panic to stop them from injuring each other, Mandy and James hurried after.

Mandy stopped short. The room was lined from ceiling to floor with old books. But on the many tables scattered about the room were glass cases, dozens of them. Inside the dusty cases, perched, poised, and perfectly preserved, were . . . stuffed animals!

A heron stood on one leg, forever fishing. An otter bared his teeth at an invisible enemy. A wildcat stared warily out, as if he knew he was about to be made extinct. Mandy squealed. Both hands flew to her cheeks.

"Let's go!" James said. For once, he took the lead.

He grabbed her hand and made a run for it, back through the littered hall. They didn't turn to see if they were being followed. They just ran.

"Hey, you two!" Miss Marjorie called.

But they covered the distance to the gate in record time, ignoring the grinning gardener as they fled. Outside the gate they paused for breath. "Well?" James gasped.

"No good," Mandy said, almost in tears. The door was closed; the ivy still smothered the walls. The house seemed empty and grim. It would be another five years before anyone dared to disturb it.

"I agree." They were both too shocked to think straight.

It was only the routine of riding over to look after things in the Williamses' kitchen that saved them. They fed the kittens and rode back home to news from Mandy's mom.

Dr. Emily smiled across the treatment table, where she was giving Snap the terrier an anesthetic to make him sleep. "A Mrs. Parker Smythe called," she said. "She's interested in one of the kittens!"

Six

Mandy was up early the next day. She'd done her chores, been over to feed Walton, and was back before her mom had finished breakfast.

"I'll take you up to the Parker Smythes in the car, if you like," Dr. Emily offered. "The appointment is for nine-thirty." It was the only other phone call about the kittens since the Misses Spry disaster, so Mandy felt glad her mother was coming along to give moral support.

"It's way out of the village, up by the Beacon." Dr. Emily opened the passenger door of their big four-wheel drive. "Hop in," she said. "Do we have to pick up James?"

"No. He came over earlier to feed the kittens, but he has a soccer game today, and his mom told him to take Blackie on an extra long walk, so he can't come."

"Do the Hunters still have that cat of theirs?" Dr. Emily fastened her seat belt.

"Benji? Yes, of course. Why?"

"He's getting a bit old, that's all."

They took the high road out of Welford. Soon a steep hill loomed ahead of them. On top there was a stone pillar, visible for miles around: the Beacon.

"I guess James is still recovering from yesterday?" Dr. Emily said, her eyes set firmly on the road ahead.

Mandy nodded. "We both are." Mandy was brave, but even she was rattled by the Spry sisters. She knew she was the least squeamish person around; she'd watched operations on stomachs, intestines, legs, and hearts. But she shuddered at the thought of the poor stuffed creatures in the library at The Riddings, glass-eyed, covered in dust.

"You have to remember it was the fashion a hundred years ago. Most people have thrown those glass cases full of birds and animals away by now. But don't blame the twins too much. Poor things." Dr. Emily spoke quietly. She pushed a stray strand of hair behind her ear.

"Yes," Mandy agreed. "Animals look so much better alive and out in the wild, not stuffed inside some rotten case!"

"I meant the sisters!" Her mom glanced across at her. The hill was beginning to flatten out now. They could see the Beacon just ahead. "They don't mean anyone any harm."

"What, those two horrible old things? Nobody ever goes near them, and all they ever do is argue!"

"Exactly," Dr. Emily said softly.

And Mandy had to sit and think about that as they pulled up outside a high hawthorn hedge with double iron gates, electronically controlled. BEACON HOUSE was written in big gold letters. And NO PARKING. TRESPASSERS WILL BE PROSECUTED.

Dr. Emily put on the parking brake. "Anyway, this looks more normal." She spoke into a little security box on the gatepost, then the gates opened as if by magic.

Mandy turned and took in the long-distance view of the valley: its odd-shaped patchwork fields, scattered hillside farms, the road and river running parallel along the bottom, and Welford's two main streets crisscrossing in the far distance.

Then she turned again and followed her mother up the drive. They went on foot through a small patch of trees, up to the big white house.

"What's that?" Mandy whispered. She pointed to a flat paved area the size of a tennis court, but marked with large white circles. It wasn't a tennis court anyway, because *that* was on the other side, to the right of the house.

"Helicopter pad?" Dr. Emily suggested. She rang the doorbell.

Mandy gulped. A very blonde, very smartly dressed woman opened the door. She wore a white shirt and trousers, and gold necklaces, rings, bracelets. A lot of gold. Even her shoes had gold decorations sewn on.

Mandy felt her mother give her a little shove forward to speak. "Mrs. Parker Smythe?" she asked nervously.

The woman nodded. Her blonde hair stayed put. Not a highlighted strand moved. Her smile revealed two rows of perfectly even, perfectly white teeth between shiny pink lips. "Come in!" she said, like you heard it said in posh films, usually with "darling" on the end.

They went in, and she closed the door. "Come this way!" she said, all teeth and lipstick and gold things dangling. Through the white hall with Italian tiles and rugs, into the kitchen. "You must be Mandy? You put the nice pink sign in the village hall? I was picking up Imogen from the

Brownies and we saw your ad!" she gushed.

Mandy nodded. She was finding it hard to fit in a word. Anyway, the kitchen made her feel that being there in her jeans and T-shirt and talking out loud in her ordinary voice was a mistake. It wasn't a bit like the old pine table and quarry-tiled floor of her own kitchen. This kitchen had shiny blue glass bowls and white gadgets everywhere, and no food anywhere to be seen.

Mrs. Parker Smythe didn't seem to notice Mandy's shyness. "Imogen is my little girl. She's seven!" she said proudly, as if Imogen being seven was like winning the Olympic Games singlehanded.

"And this is Ronald, my husband. He's in satellite television!"

A balding man walked in, nodded, and walked out again. He wore the palest yellow V-neck sweater and tan checked trousers.

"He's going to play golf," Mrs. Parker Smythe told them. She shared another confidence: "With Jason Shaw! You know, Jason Shaw, the actor. They're very good friends, Ronald and Jason."

Mandy risked a glance at her mother but didn't dare ask, "Jason who?" Her mother was looking steadily out of the window, trying not to smile.

"We first met Jason when he came to film here, you know," Mrs. Parker Smythe rattled on. "For an episode of *The Swallows in Spring*, this time last year. They used our swimming pool!"

Mandy gulped again. She couldn't help it. Maybe tough little Smoky would be the right kitten for the Parker Smythes. The rough-and-tumble one. He'd bring them down to earth.

"Yes, our swimming pool was used as a set for the program. It belongs to the right period for the series. So Jason and the crew came up. That's how we met!" Mrs. Parker Smythe bubbled on. She seemed to have forgotten all about the reason for their visit.

"Did you want a kitten for your little girl?" Mandy managed to fit in at last. Mr. Parker Smythe wandered in and out again, apparently looking for something.

"Yes, well, we have so much space here." Mrs. Parker Smythe spread her arms and her jewelry jangled. "And such a big garden! And of course we have security cameras out there, so there's no danger of the poor little mite getting lost or anything."

Mandy noticed her mother's eyebrows shoot up a fraction of an inch.

"And when we're away at our house in Italy, we still have Mrs. Bates, our housekeeper, to come in and look after the kitten, feed it, and so on." Mrs. Parker Smythe looked at her gold watch. "Would you please excuse me a moment?" She dashed off after her husband.

"I wonder what he's lost?" Mandy whispered.

"His helicopter?" her mom said. But no; they heard huge blades begin to whir out on the pad. Clearly it had been wheeled out from its hangar and prepared for takeoff.

They grinned. Mandy felt more relaxed. "What if Smoky doesn't fit in here because he's only a plain, ordinary tomcat?"

"Let's meet the little girl first, before we make any decisions," Dr. Emily said.

Mandy nodded. She had to admit, once again, the signs were not all that promising.

"Oh, good, you're still here!" Mrs. Parker Smythe floated back in after a few minutes. "Now you must come and meet Imogen!"

She led them out of the kitchen across a giant sunroom full of artificial palms and pink-flowered cane furniture. But this was only a link to the house's main attraction, its indoor heated pool. This opened up from the sunroom through wide double doors.

The poolside was dazzling white and the water was deep blue. There was a fountain at one end, and windows from ceiling to floor all down one side. And there in the water, swimming like a walrus with just its nose and whiskers out of the water, was Imogen Parker Smythe.

"Imogen!" her mother called out, clapping her jeweled hands smartly.

Imogen ignored her.

"Imogen, we have visitors!" her mother called again.

No response. Imogen swam around and around the fountain at the deep end. Mandy was amazed by her rudeness. *I'd never get away with that!* she thought.

Mrs. Parker Smythe sighed. "Come along, we'd better go down." She went along the poolside carrying an apricot-colored bathrobe and a towel for her daughter. Mandy and Dr. Emily followed.

"Imogen!" Mrs. Parker Smythe said in a coaxing voice. She crouched beside the water. "Now come along, darling. Come and talk to Mommy about a sweetie, itsy-bitsy kittie for Immikins!"

Mandy swallowed hard. She stuck both hands into her jeans pockets. *Yuk!* she thought. She just hoped no one could read her mind.

"Won't!" Imogen retorted, swimming in smaller circles.

"Oh, come on, darling! Remember, we talked about a sweet little furry kitty for you just this morning at breakfast. Remember?"

"No!" Imogen spat out water like a whale.

"Immie!" Mrs. Parker Smythe was getting wet. "Now come along out of there immediately, or I'll call your daddy!"

With a great sigh and much splashing, Imogen Parker Smythe heaved herself out of the water. She was a mousy-haired, slightly overweight little girl with a constant scowl. She squirmed as her mother wrapped her in the bathrobe. She pushed away the towel offered for her dripping hair. Instead she shook her head from side to side like a dog.

"Hello," Mandy said. She forced herself to take the lead in this conversation.

Imogen tossed her head and sniffed up great drips of water.

"I hear you want a kitten?" Mandy went on.

Sniff. Sniff.

"I've got four kittens. Four tiny ones just a few days old. But soon their mother will finish feeding them, and after that they'll need really good names and somebody to look after them!" Mandy explained in what she thought was a clear, sensible way.

"I know that!" Imogen snorted. "Everyone knows that!"

"Immie!" Mrs. Parker Smythe chirped.

"They'll need good homes, and someone very kind and careful to look after them!" Mandy said in a much cooler voice.

"What color are they?" Imogen demanded, eye to eye with Mandy. "I want a white one!"

Mandy paused. "Well, the color isn't that important, really, is it? I mean, a kitten isn't a kind of toy, is it? It's a real live animal, you know. Soon it'll grow into a big cat that will still need to be fed and taken to the vet and somewhere clean and airy to sleep. In fact, it will need lots of looking after!"

Imogen turned to her mother. "I only want a white one!" she whined.

"But Immikins!" Mrs. Parker Smythe looked helplessly at Mandy.

"You said I could have a white one!" The child stamped her foot. "A white kitten! A fluffy white one with long fur! I want one! I want one!"

Mandy was furious. She felt like stepping right up to the revolting girl and pushing her back into the swimming pool. "Kittens are not toys!" she repeated. "And they don't have to match your color scheme!"

"Mandy!" Dr. Emily warned under her breath.

But Imogen was equal to the fight. She took a long look at Mandy, then she screwed her face tight and whined loudly. "O-o-oh, Mommy, make the horrible, nasty girl go away! I don't like her! Make her go away, Mommy!"

Mrs. Parker Smythe fell for it. "There, there, Immikins, don't cry!" she said. She cuddled her daughter at a distance, so as to keep dry. "You don't have to have a kitty if you don't want one, darling. There, there!"

Mandy saw Imogen's face peep out at her from behind pudgy little fists. Imogen sneered up at her. "That got you!" she seemed to be saying.

Dr. Emily was pulling at Mandy's arm. "Time to go," she urged.

But Mrs. Parker Smythe had stopped cuddling Imogen and came toward them. "Pay no attention," she whispered. "Imogen's in one of her moods. You can bring the kitten anyway. I'll talk her into it."

But Mandy stood her ground. She was determined to have her say. "Mrs. Parker Smythe," she announced, "I'm afraid this would never work!"

Mrs. Parker Smythe's gold jewelry trembled as she went back and bent over her daughter.

Mandy continued. "To keep a pet you have to be a sensible, caring person. Animals have rights, you know, and one of those rights is to belong to a good, responsible owner!" She paused for breath, but there was no stopping her now. "And I'm afraid Imogen just doesn't qualify! I can't imagine anyone *less* suited to look after Smoky, Patch, Amy, or Eric!"

She glared down at them as they hugged each other by the side of their swanky pool. She turned on her heel. Her sneakers squeaked on the wet tiles all the way down to the French doors, but she didn't care. She swung through the sunroom, the designer kitchen, the hall. Dr. Emily caught up with her halfway down the driveway.

"Sorry, Mom, for being rude," Mandy said. But her mother didn't seem to mind as they marched out to the car, shoulder to shoulder.

"No good," Dr. Emily sighed and opened the door.

Mandy sank back in the passenger seat. She felt bitter about spoiled little rich kids and their soft mothers. And she was panicking about the kittens. Two replies to their ads so far, and two disastrous results! "No, no good again!" she said.

Tears of disappointment threatened to burst out, but she bit them back. She had to keep on looking. She had to succeed!

Seven

The weekend was almost over, and still the kittens were homeless. Mr. Williams would kick them out of his kitchen on Thursday or do something dreadful. For him, they weren't creatures with feelings. They were just nuisances to be gotten rid of.

"That's how some people think," Mandy's dad explained. "Especially some older people around here. You don't get sentimental about animals when you live on farms or in the villages. When Mr. Williams was young, they drowned unwanted kittens in the rain barrel behind the barn. I don't suppose they even thought it was cruel."

Mandy shuddered. As far as she was concerned, it was murder.

"Come on, help me take this young fellow over to Ernie's!" Dr. Adam suggested. He picked up the plastic cage containing the baby squirrel. "I've checked him over and he's as right as rain. He can go into the run at the back of Ernie's house and we'll see how he gets along."

They set off on foot down their lane to the main street. It was a sunny afternoon, with blossoms everywhere. Gardeners were out with their trowels and pruners, making the flowers stand at attention. "Good afternoon," people said pleasantly. Some stopped to look at the squirrel and pass the time of day.

Mandy liked the fact that everyone knew her father. He'd been born up at Lilac Cottage and had lived in Welford all his life, except for his college days in York. The older villagers still called him "young Adam" or "Tom Hope's lad." They knew he was a brainy boy, he'd been to college, and he was known as a decent vet. At any rate, he was one of them.

The women came out of their houses and made a fuss over Mandy, while the men described problems with moles on their lawns or a sheep stuck in the cattle fence at the back of the Janekis' farm.

The squirrel scampered in its cage, accepting offers of peanuts through the bars.

At last Mandy and her father reached the Fox and Goose. "It's only taken us an hour and fifteen minutes!" she remarked.

Dr. Adam laughed and went into the tavern for lemonade. They spent another fifteen minutes in the last rays of sunshine, sitting on a bench, gossiping.

"Right!" Dr. Adam wiped his beard and stood up. He sounded purposeful at last. "You bring the squirrel, Mandy."

She followed him across the cobble stone courtyard of the pub. The squirrel scuttled in its cage.

"That used to be the forge," Dr. Adam said. He pointed to the plush restaurant at the side of the pub.

"I know, Dad, you've told me!"

He carried on regardless. "My own grandfather had the place in the 1920s."

"I know, Dad!" Boy, was he embarrassing sometimes. Mandy shuffled from one foot to the other. Soon she'd have to ride over to Walton for the regular evening feeding. The kittens were doing well on the special liquid food, and Walton herself was looking sleeker. Mandy was pleased with their progress. "Come on, Dad, let's go!"

He turned and grinned. "Sorry, sweetie!" And he led the way again, down the side of the pub to a row of tiny two-story stone cottages that had seen better days. There were five cottages, all with broken-down doors, unruly ivy, and great stone slabs making a path along the length of the row. Most of the front doors stood open in the sunshine.

"Now then, young Adam!" a gruff voice said.

Mandy and Dr. Adam stopped at the first house. She might have known they wouldn't make it to Ernie's without at least two more interruptions.

"Hello, Walter. Lovely day!" Dr. Adam stopped and leaned in at Walter Pickard's door. "How are things?"

"Mustn't grumble," the old man said. "Hello there, young miss!"

Mandy smiled hello. Walter never remembered the name of anyone under thirty. It was just "young miss" or "young sir." He was a retired butcher, a Wednesday evening church bell-ringer alongside her grandfather, and, what's more, a cat lover! Two lovely old ginger cats sunned themselves on his front doorstep.

"What have we here?" Walter said, bending and tapping the cage. Inside, the squirrel sat up and begged. "Hey, look at that!" Walter said, half laughing. He went off down the dark, narrow hallway and came back with a piece of cracker, which he fed to the squirrel.

Mandy liked Walter. He was a big man, but his deep voice was gentle, and his lined face under its flat cloth cap was always smiling. His wife had died last year, but Walter's three cats still kept him company. Mandy liked him because of his smile and his cats. What she couldn't understand was how he'd spent his entire working life in a butcher's shop. All those cold sides of beef hanging on their hooks. All those dead chickens. Mandy shuddered. She was glad she was mostly a vegetarian. These days she hardly ever ate meat.

Dr. Adam glanced at his watch. "Do you know if Ernie's in?" he asked.

Walter nodded. "Most likely."

"In that case I'll just get this little fellow over there." Dr. Adam picked up the cage, saw Mandy was busy stroking the ginger cats, and said, "You stay, Mandy, and tell Walter the story of Ernie Bell and the orphan squirrel!" Then he wandered off down the lane.

Mandy recounted the sad story of the squirrel.

"Ernie Bell!" Walter said, shaking his head. "He's adopting a squirrel, that miserable old devil!" It was like saying he, Walter Pickard, had won the soccer pools.

Mandy had her hand deep in the soft, warm fur of one of the old ginger cats when an idea struck her. She looked up from her cross-legged position on the path. "Walter, how many cats do you have?" she asked casually. But the excitement of the idea was beginning to make her heart beat faster.

"Three," he said. He sat down heavily on an old wooden stool just inside the doorway. "That one's called Scraps because she feeds on any scraps I give her. She's not the least bit fussy." He pointed to the one Mandy was stroking. "And that's Missie over there, because she's a proper little madam and only eats the best fish and chicken breast." This other ginger cat was contentedly purring in the sun. "Then there's Tom. He's indoors."

Mandy listened quietly, but she thought furiously.

"We used to have another one, you know," Walter went on. "My Mary loved cats, and it was her favorite, Susie, that passed away just after Christmas." He sat with his own memories for a while, then pulled himself together. "Susie was a dainty little cat, just like my Mary. That's why she was her favorite." He smiled. "Yes, indeed."

Mandy nodded. She knew it was now or never.

"Why not get another?" she said. "It just so happens I'm looking for homes for kittens right now, and there's one little dainty one, a little tortoiseshell called Amy, who'd be just right for you, I'm sure!"

Walter listened. He seemed to like the idea. "A tortoiseshell?"

"Yes. They're only a few days old, and we're partly having to hand-rear them, James Hunter and I, because the mother's too weak. She was a stray. But we'll need homes for all of them. Good homes!" She stressed the "good" and looked up at Walter.

He blew out his cheeks like a trumpeter. "A tortoiseshell?" he repeated. Mandy pictured a young kitten scampering about on the warm flagstones all summer long, jumping up at his wallflowers, tumbling in over the step.

"A really lovely little tortoiseshell!" she insisted. She held her breath.

"Aye, I'd love one," Walter sighed.

"Oh, it'd be a perfect home for Amy!" Mandy told him. "It's nice and quiet back here, off the road, and the older cats would look after her, and you know all about kittens. It would be ideal!"

Say yes, she prayed. *Say yes!*

But a shadow crept down the hallway. A big

bruiser of a shadow padding up to the doorstep in the sinister shape of Tom.

"Hello!" Mandy said to the barrel-shaped cat. He stood foursquare in his doorway. He bared his teeth and hissed. "Hello there!" She ran her fingers up and down the flagstones. "Come here!" she coaxed. He ignored her game. Sulkily he padded across the step, back and forth, strong shouldered, wide mouthed. He was a black-and-white bully with a pirate's black patch over his left eye, a chewed left ear, and ragged whiskers.

"Ah, Tom!" Walter said with a sigh of regret.

Tom arched his back at Mandy and spat. He padded around the two ginger females, just checking up on them. Then he stood and stared again at Mandy.

"There's Tom to consider, you see," Walter explained. "Scraps and Missie would be fine. But not Tom." The old man shook his head. "Just take one look at him. He'd eat a new kitten for breakfast!"

Mandy could believe it. Never had she seen a cat like Tom; a heavyweight, a bouncer, a sumo wrestler of a cat!

"No," Walter said sadly. "Much as I'd like to, I'm afraid old Tom wouldn't be happy with a stranger around the place. You can see my problem?"

Mandy nodded. Though she was desperate, she had to agree.

"Never mind, Thomas, no one's going to come upsetting you." Walter bent forward to scratch the chewed-up old ear. "Just relax, old man!"

The cat blinked and tilted its colossal head in victory. He'd staked out his territory and won.

Sadly, Mandy got to her feet. Such a missed opportunity! But her dad was returning with the empty cage. "Ready?" he asked.

They said their good-byes to Walter and set off

across the pub yard. The old man continued to sit on his stool, cats at his feet.

"You know," Dr. Adam said, glancing backward, "old Walter's fond of cats. Why don't you —"

"It's all right, Dad," Mandy interrupted, "I already have. I asked him, and he says he'd like another kitten, but Thomas the Terrible wouldn't appreciate it." She joked, but she was feeling very low. "In the end he said no."

"Ah, well," Dr. Adam said, swinging the empty cage, lost in his own thoughts.

All the gardeners had gone inside for tea, so their walk home was much quieter and quicker. Dr. Emily had prepared their own evening meal, knowing that Mandy would want to ride over to school before it got dark. No one mentioned the kittens. If they had, Mandy felt she might have broken down. And her mom and dad knew when not to make a fuss. She ate, then packed her bag. She met James at the post office and together they rode to Walton.

Mr. Williams was in a very bad mood.

"It's Sunday night," Mrs. Williams reminded them. "He always gets like this on a Sunday night."

He'd been stamping about the kitchen when they arrived, but as soon as he saw them, he grunted, took his Sunday newspaper, and headed out of the room.

"It's because it's Monday tomorrow," Mrs. Williams explained. "W-O-R-K! The dreaded four-letter word."

Then Tuesday, then Wednesday, Mandy thought with a lurch. She wanted to stop the clock or at least to stretch the days. The trouble was, as each visit to the kittens came and went, she grew fonder of them. They were about five inches long and weighed just three or four ounces or so. They hadn't yet struggled to their feet, and their eyes were still closed. Smoky was strongest, but Patch put up a good fight for food. Amy and Eric were patient, more content.

Now was the time to ask Mrs. Williams if they could gently tip the laundry basket onto its side so the kittens could begin to get a feeling of the outside world. "And then Walton might be ready to move them to a new nest," Mandy suggested.

"What, tip it over and leave it there?" Mrs. Williams asked. She looked doubtful. "It'd make the place look a terrible mess!" But in the end she agreed. The basket could be tipped onto its side.

As James and Mandy fed each of the kittens in turn, Mr. Williams stamped back in. He was wearing a very clean, very stiff white shirt and a maroon tie. He looked smart in his dark suit, but he walked awkwardly, Mandy noticed for the first time. He frowned at the turned-over laundry basket.

Mrs. Williams leaped to her feet. She was ready for the evening service at church, in her beige dress and silk scarf. "Now, Eric!" she warned. She saw him glaring at the two kittens who happened to be pulling by mistake at the sleeve of his best blue shirt. They were seeking out Walton, but getting tangled in the shirt instead. "It's only till Wednesday night!" she promised.

He didn't even grunt. He just stamped out onto the porch.

"Good thing it's Sunday!" Mrs. Williams whispered.

"Why?" James asked.

"Eric never swears on a Sunday," she said. She raised her eyebrows. "Otherwise the air in the kitchen would be blue as that shirt!" She sighed as she picked up her shiny brown handbag. She checked her keys. "Lock the door when you go," she reminded them. Then she followed her husband down the road to church.

Mandy shook her head. The kittens were all safe for the night. James was washing Walton's food bowl and saucer, and the mother cat was coming to Mandy for a final grateful stroke before she settled down with her kittens. "I wish . . ." Mandy said. But she never finished the sentence.

James felt helpless, too, as they checked the kitchen, turned off the light, and locked the door. "That's what I like about computers," he said out of the blue as they got on their bikes.

"Huh?" Mandy said. "What are you talking about?" James sometimes came out with these odd things.

"Computers. That's what I like about them. They're straightforward and simple, and they never make you feel bad."

"Not like people and animals, you mean?"

He nodded. "And you can just switch them on and off, no problem."

They rode along for a while in silence.

"But they break down!" Mandy objected. You shouldn't prefer machines to live things, she thought.

"So do animals," he said. Another silence. "Like Benji."

"Oh, what's wrong with Benji?" Mandy asked. James had had Benji for as long as she could remember; he was a beautiful, docile black tomcat.

"Dunno," James said. "My mom has to bring him into the Ark tomorrow morning to see if your mother can find out."

Mandy nodded and sighed. "Well, see you tomorrow, early?" she said by way of good-bye.

"Tomorrow early," James promised, as they each rode their separate ways.

Eight

One little victory would be enough, Mandy thought. One home for one kitten. It wasn't asking much, and it would be a start. She went through the names they had so far, just to make sure that none of them would do.

Thinking hard, she handed Simon a thermometer to take the temperature of a Border collie who was just recovering from parvovirus. It was only because she was so young and strong that she'd survived.

Simon stroked the dog's long, black coat. "At least they'll remember to have her vaccinated from now on," he said.

Mandy nodded, but she was thinking of Miss Marjorie Spry. Surely even she could remember to open a can of cat food each day. The kitten could be given a quiet, cozy corner in the garden shed if that old gardener would clear a space. Mandy stopped scooping meat into the dog bowls and stood, fork poised.

"A penny for them," Simon said with a smile. He was looking at his watch.

"What?" Mandy was imagining Amy snugly curled up behind the old flowerpots and garden shears.

"A penny for your thoughts!" Simon took the fork and went on preparing bowls of food for their resident cocker spaniel and two black Labradors. "You don't usually daydream on the job," he said.

"Oh, sorry!" Mandy gave a sigh. Of course, The Riddings was hopeless. Simon had broken her dream. She recalled the frozen snarl of the stuffed wildcat, the glass stare of the heron. All those dusty cases with dead animals in them. She was afraid it would never work to send Amy there, and the poor kitten was still homeless.

"Best get a move on," Simon said. "Here, you do the hamster dishes next, while I clean out the cages. And remember Flopsy and company out back!"

Mandy took the scoop full of rabbit food out into

the backyard. There was always the Parker Smythe mansion for Smoky, she told herself. She knew she was clutching at straws, though. How long would it be before the kitten lost its novelty there? Two days? Mandy sighed again. And that was only if Imogen would accept a gray cat. No, she wouldn't wish Imogen Parker Smythe on her worst enemy, let alone on precious Smoky.

If only Walter Pickard's old tomcat had been better tempered! Mandy stood there with a handful of oats and sunflower seed mixture, deep in thought.

When she went inside, Simon had finished the hamster cages. He took a last look at her and in his quiet way took charge. "Look," he said. "I'll finish here, so you can get off to school early again."

"What? Oh, yes, thanks!" Mandy dusted off her hands and scrambled out of her white coat. "Is that the time? I must run!"

She was out of Animal Ark and in her school uniform when she bumped into her mom on the stairs. "Any phone calls?" she asked, hoping for more responses to the signs.

"No," Dr. Emily said.

"Right." She hadn't really expected any this time. Her hopes were not high.

Then she was out of the house, up the lane on

her bike to meet James outside McFarlane's. Her mind was still working overtime. *I suppose I could always try Walter again*, she thought as she screeched to a halt. James was already there.

"Sorry I'm late!" she said.

James was quieter than usual as they rode to school, but Mandy had a lot on her mind, too.

School went by in a semidaze. She got two questions wrong in history and a lecture from Mr. Holmes. "What's wrong, Amanda? This isn't like you. Watching too much television, I expect. Now just pay attention, please!" Mandy's face felt red and hot, and she tried to concentrate.

She was thinking of the kittens when a group of friends asked her if she was going to the dance on Friday. Mandy didn't answer. "Oh, be like that!" one said. They were all giggling about something or other. "Don't think we care whether you come or not! You're not the center of the universe, Mandy Hope!" And they flounced off.

Mandy shrugged. It was time to go and feed the kittens.

And she was still thinking of them when James met her after school and told her quietly that he had to go straight home tonight. He'd promised his mom.

Mandy nodded. "See you tomorrow then," she

said. She had a plan in her head; not much of a plan, but she'd decided she would visit Walter again. She'd feed the kittens first, then she'd drop by the cottages. Anyway, it couldn't do any harm. She'd invent an excuse; maybe she'd visit Ernie Bell's squirrel and just "happen" to call on Walter. He mustn't think she was pestering on purpose.

"Hello, young miss!" Walter greeted her from his open door. "Where's that grandfather of yours gone? I haven't seen him around here lately."

Mandy propped her bike against the end wall. "Hi, Walter." She tried to sound casual. "He and Grandma are off on a camping trip in their new van." She gave him one of her cheeriest smiles. It was an effort, but she wanted to be bright and breezy.

"Camping!" Walter said with a low whistle. "At their age!"

"Not exactly." She explained the luxuries of the modern mobile home. "It has a fridge, electricity, everything!"

"Hmph! Don't they have a fridge and electricity at their house?"

"Yes."

"Well, then, what's the point?" Walter said. His ginger cats came padding elegantly down the hall.

Mandy gave in and changed the subject. She stroked Scraps and Missie. "I just popped over to see Mr. Bell's squirrel," she said casually. "To see if he's settled in okay."

Walter nodded. "Yes, if he'll see you," he said. "Ernie doesn't always answer his door!"

"I'll be back in a minute," she said.

She walked up the flagstone path to the end of the row. She knocked hard. The green door was faded and flaking; it needed a good coat of paint. And it had an old lion knocker that hadn't been cleaned for years. It was stiff with disuse. She knocked again.

"Hold your horses, hold your horses!" Ernie grumbled from inside. She heard bolts sliding, locks turning. Finally Ernie opened his front door.

Mandy heard Walter mumble and turn back inside his own house. She was left to face Ernie alone.

"Yes?" Ernie snapped. He was a small man with a shock of white hair rising back from his lined forehead. There was something birdlike about his sharp nose, his bright, dark eyes. He wore an old vest and a shirt without a collar. "Yes?" he said again, peering at Mandy.

She introduced herself as the vet's daughter. "My

dad brought the squirrel yesterday. How is he?" she asked.

Ernie frowned. "Fine, fine. What do you want now? You can't have him back, you know. I've paid the bill!"

"No, I don't want to take him back," Mandy tried to explain.

"Good. It cost me a fortune just to have him checked over, I can tell you. But I paid!" he insisted. He stood there, frowning.

"No, I —" Mandy hesitated, then changed tactics. "What's his name?" she asked.

Ernie paused. "Sammy," he said, as if he didn't want anyone to hear. "All right?"

"Yes, it's a nice name. I was just wondering, could I take a look at him, please?"

She waited until Ernie made up his mind. He stared at her, thought a while, then nodded. "This way," he said at last.

He led her down a dark hallway, through his kitchen, and out into the backyard. Four cottages away, Walter was out in his garden. He leaned his forearms against his fence top. "Hello there, Ernie!" he greeted his unfriendly neighbor.

Ernie grunted. He stood by, watching suspiciously as Mandy inspected the squirrel run.

"Sammy!" Mandy called gently. There was a sturdy hutch at the far end of the run, with a small hole for an entrance, which only something as tiny and agile as a squirrel could use. The little creature poked out its round gray head.

"Here," Ernie said. "Tempt him with these!" He handed Mandy a few peanuts from his trouser pocket.

And Sammy bounded out of the hutch. He clung upside-down to the netting, swinging like a trapeze artist toward her. His feet never touched the ground.

Mandy held out the nuts in the palm of her hand. Delicately Sammy watched, reached out a paw, and snatched the food. He swung away to a safe distance, then nibbled.

Mandy studied him. This was only the second time she'd been this close to a squirrel. The run was ten yards long, made of timber and fine mesh. Very safe. "This is great!" she told Ernie, tapping the framework.

"Hmm." Ernie nodded. "It should be." He, too, was watching the squirrel, and his face had lost its frown. "I've had a fair bit of practice, you know. I was a carpenter for more than fifty years!" Then, as if he'd given away top secret information, his mouth clamped shut, and the frown returned.

"Well, it's great," Mandy said. "Really sturdy and safe. I'm glad Sammy's found such a good home!" It was almost enough to take her mind off homeless kittens. But she could see Walter over in his own yard, and she was desperate to talk with him. She remembered her real purpose: to persuade Walter and old Tom to change their minds. "Can I come and visit Sammy again?" she asked Ernie.

He swallowed hard, but he nodded slowly. "You can come again," he agreed. "It might not always suit me to answer the door, you understand. But you can always try."

He followed her out to the front of the house. "Well, Mr. Bell —" Mandy was about to turn and thank him again for showing her the squirrel, but the shabby green door was already closed. And like a figure in a Swiss cuckoo clock, Walter was already out at his own front door. As usual, he was not minding his own business.

Mandy wandered toward him. She was going to ask, "How's old Tom today?" and then gently add that perhaps Tom would take to a new kitten, if they introduced him to the idea gradually.

But Walter must have been a mind reader. She never got any further than "How's old Tom?" before he cut her short.

"It's no good you wheedling away, young miss!" Walter laughed at her surprise. "I know what you're going to ask, and Tom's answer is still no!"

As if to confirm this, Tom came barreling around the corner at top speed and rammed right into Mandy's bike. Down it crashed. Tom wailed loudly, leaped over the spinning wheels, and vanished across the pub yard.

"See?" Walter said, laughing again. He picked up the bike. "Nothing's safe with our Tom on the scene!" He turned to Mandy, then he looked down the row to Ernie's end house. "But you know something, I think we've just had an idea!"

"We have?" To Mandy it didn't feel as if anything was going right.

"Yes. You hit it off with old Ernie, didn't you?" Walter scratched his head, a sure sign that he was thinking.

"I suppose so," Mandy said doubtfully. "Listen, you don't think I should ask him?" Her eyes lit up. "I mean, you mean I should ask him to take a kitten?" She felt the idea light up all the dark corners of her mind.

But Walter was shaking his head. "No, no, I don't think you should ask him exactly."

Mandy's face fell again. "Why not? He likes animals. He rescued little Sammy, didn't he?"

"Yes, but Ernie would say no if you asked him directly. On principle, he always says no. He's a grumpy, cantankerous old so-and-so — that's Ernie."

Mandy had to agree. "So what's our idea?" she asked.

"It's this!" Walter got into a huddle with Mandy around the corner, out of sight.

The idea involved taking a very big risk. But then Mandy had forty-eight hours to solve four very big problems. She listened to Walter, she nodded, she considered it. She thought of Sammy snug in his custom-built hutch. She decided to risk it.

So she called home and said she'd be late. Then she rode back over to Walton.

Mrs. Williams watched with concern as Mandy gave Amy a special feeding and tucked her into a specially lined cardboard box. Amy peered up, unseeing, sniffed, then settled down. Walton came over, glanced in, looked up at Mandy, then retreated to the laundry basket. She sat quietly inside with her other three kittens, looking out.

"She trusts you!" Mrs. Williams said. "Poor lamb, she trusts you with her babies!"

Mandy nodded. It was a hard thing to do, to take

the kitten from her mother, but it was a hard thing Mr. Williams was threatening to do, and Walter's plan made it necessary. "Good girl, Walton," she said. Carefully she folded down the flaps of the cardboard box.

"I hope you know what you're doing!" Mrs. Williams whispered.

Mandy looked her in the face. Her heart was in her mouth as she nodded and went outside. She strapped the box onto her bike, nodded again at Mrs. Williams, tried not to think about Walton and the three kittens cozy in their basket, and set off across the field.

It was the most heart-stopping bike ride she'd ever made. Every bend, every hill she took at a snail's pace. She came down into Welford holding her breath. She stopped at the pub, out of sight of Walter and Ernie's row of cottages. Then she un-strapped the box and crept with it in through Walter's open door.

"Got it?" Walter asked.

Mandy nodded. She opened the box. Amy mewed at the light. "Are you sure this will work?" she asked again.

Walter's head went to one side. "Not sure," he said. "Not one hundred percent." He gazed down at tiny, helpless Amy. "She's just a skinny little thing!" He tickled her head.

"Ernie's got a mind of his own. You can bet he'll do exactly the opposite of what you ask. Always has. You say to him, 'Ernie, do me a favor, fix the latch on this back gate for me,' and he'll say straight back, 'What do you think I am, the handyman around here?' and he'll stamp off in the other direction. But if he thinks it's his idea and he sees your gate's broken, he'll make a point of coming up and he'll say, 'I saw your latch was broken, Walter, so I just got out my toolbox and fixed it for you.' Just like that!"

Mandy understood. "Like rescuing Sammy, you mean? It had to be his idea." She lifted Amy out of her box. "So if he finds a tiny kitten abandoned on his doorstep, he'll take her in?"

Walter nodded. "As long as he does think it's his idea! Then he'll want to keep her and look after her, just like the squirrel. He'll come along to me for advice because he knows I've got the three cats, and I'll suggest, very cunning, how much better it'd be to find a feeding mother until the kitten's properly on its feet. That's where you come in, little miss!"

Mandy looked hard at Amy. "Are you sure?"

He nodded again. "Ernie's got a heart of gold underneath it all!" Walter smiled. "Go on, young miss, what have you got to lose? That kitten will have a foster home and be back with her mother before you can say Jack Robinson!"

So Mandy took the precious bundle down the path. Amy squirmed in her hands, mewing piteously. "Shh!" she whispered. Could she do it? Mandy felt as if her heart would stop. Could she leave the poor little thing on a cold doorstep?

She almost stopped to retrace her steps. But what was the alternative? She had less than two days left. Forcing herself to go on, she stooped down by Ernie's front doorstep. She closed her eyes, backed away, and fled back to Walter's house.

"Now we just have to wait," Walter said. They stood inside his doorway, listening to Amy's tiny wail.

"Oh, quick!" Mandy breathed. "Please hear her and come quickly!"

But Ernie's door stayed shut.

Amy mewed her high-pitched sound. Would he hear it? They waited. Mandy leaned forward, desperately wanting to see if Amy was all right. But Walter pulled her back. "You mustn't let him see you!" he warned.

The wait seemed endless. Minutes went by. Amy's tiny howling continued.

Then finally they heard the metal bolts of Ernie's door. They heard the latch turn. The door scraped open. "What the — !" Ernie said. He grunted as he stooped. "Oh-aagh!" They heard him sigh as he picked up the kitten and straightened his old back. He stepped out onto the path. He took time to look up and down. He even carried Amy a few steps toward Walter's house, then he turned and went indoors, carrying the kitten.

"Well?" Mandy was still holding her breath. She looked at Walter.

Walter listened. He considered carefully. Then he brought up one hand in a thumbs-up sign. "I reckon it's worked!" he said.

They had to wait half an hour, maybe more, drinking tea and eating cookies, before they heard Ernie shuffling down the path to Walter's door.

"Say nothing!" Walter warned. "And stay here!" Mandy nodded.

"Now then, Walter," Ernie said. He poked his head inside the front door. "You know about cats!"

"I do, Ernie," Walter said. "I know something about them, at any rate." Mandy sat out of sight in the kitchen as Walter went down the hall to greet Ernie. "Why, what have you got there?" He managed to sound genuinely surprised.

"Kitten," Ernie said. "What's it look like?" He had wrapped Amy in an old gray sweater. "It's shivering." He showed the little bundle to Walter.

"Yes, it would," Walter said. "It's only a littl'un."

"It just turned up out of the blue," Ernie said. "I was just washing up when I heard it making a racket on my doorstep! I reckon its mother dropped it there; one too many to look after in the litter."

"Well, it must be your week for it," Walter said, keeping his voice flat this time. "First the squirrel, now this."

"I dunno about that. It just turned up." Ernie

stood there looking helpless. Peeping, Mandy could see the two old men head to head against the square of light in the doorway.

"Ah, well, I reckon you'll have to get rid of this one," Walter said. "Two orphans to look after is more than you can manage."

Mandy gasped and bit her lip. How could he? How could Walter take such a risk?

But Ernie gave Walter his eagle stare. "What do you mean, more than I can manage?" He wrapped Amy up carefully. "I've no intention of getting rid of it, Walter Pickard! No, this little kitten is here to stay!"

Mandy cried. She cried tears of silent joy.

"Aye, but how will you feed it? Look at it, poor little scrap. It needs feeding already," Walter insisted.

Ernie thought about this for a while. "That's why I'm coming to you, Walter. You know about cats."

Now it was Walter's turn to stand there looking awkward and sullen. "It's too young for me to handle. It needs a mother cat," he said. "One that's still feeding her own youngsters."

Ernie squared his shoulders and asked how they would set about finding such a thing; a mother cat that would feed his kitten until it was weaned? He'd like Walter to call the vet right then and there, on his telephone, and get the vet's young girl over there as quick as possible. "I reckon she'll know of just such a cat," Ernie said, hugging Amy to his chest.

"Oh, she'll know," Walter confirmed, giving a little smile.

Back in the kitchen, Mandy grinned. Walter's plan had worked perfectly!

"Then you go ahead and give her a call. You tell her I want her down at my cottage in fifteen minutes sharp!" Ernie instructed. "And tell her to bring something to carry a tiny kitten in. We need a mother cat right away, or my little kitten will starve to death!"

"Right!" Walter agreed.

"Right!" And Ernie marched on back home with Amy.

Walter came back grinning all over his face. Mandy sat on the kitchen stool and smiled through her tears. They'd found a home for Amy. At last they'd found one good home!

Nine

Mandy paid a visit to Ernie's, complete with her lined cardboard box. She fed Amy quickly and expertly, mixing the powdered food in a miniature feeding bottle. She held Amy in one hand, then stroked her abdomen with a forefinger to help her digest the food and get rid of the waste. Ernie didn't bat an eyelid at that.

"You have to do it, otherwise they hang on to it and get constipated," Mandy explained. "That's why the mother cats lick them."

"And how often will this mother cat have to feed it?"

"*She* needs feeding every couple of hours. And the mother will keep her warm, too," Mandy said.

Ernie picked up his kitten and said an awkward good-bye. His fingers looked broad and clumsy against Amy's tiny head, but he held her calmly. He gave her every scrap of his attention. He bent his white head, making encouraging little chucking noises with his tongue. Then he looked up. "I'll call her Twinkie!" he said.

Mandy started to protest, then bit her tongue hard. She couldn't tell Ernie that Amy already had a name. She swallowed and nodded. "Good idea." She took the kitten from Ernie and put her carefully in the box. "She'll be ready to come home in six or seven weeks," she promised.

So Amy became Twinkie. "Brilliant name, isn't it?" She greeted James with the news when they met in the village early next morning. But Mandy was so thrilled that the name hardly mattered. "Three more to go!" she said, full of new enthusiasm for the task. The morning was sunny. Things had begun to go right.

James nodded. He was looking pale and tired.

"What's wrong?" Mandy asked. She was peering in through the post office window to make sure that their sign was still up there on the bulletin board.

"Nothing." James shook his head and started to set off for school. He refused to look Mandy in the face as he mumbled, "Let's go."

"No, there is something wrong!" Mandy insisted. James was always shy and only got visibly excited about soccer. But today there was something making him even quieter than usual. He hadn't really reacted to the news about Amy. He hadn't said, "Great. Well done. I knew you could do it, Mandy!"

James shook his head again. He was staring down at his sneakers.

Mandy put one hand on the handlebar of his bike. "It's Benji, isn't it?" she said softly.

And James nodded.

"Oh, James, what's wrong with him?" She could have kicked herself. She'd been so full of her own news that she'd forgotten all about poor Benji being ill.

But James couldn't speak. He just sighed.

"He's going to be all right, isn't he? I mean, they'll fix him up at the Ark. It isn't anything serious, is it? What did my mom and dad say?" Mandy was beginning to sense something really awful. She'd never seen James look so sad.

And finally he came out with it. "Benji's dead," he said. "We had to have him put to sleep."

Mandy gasped. She expected the whole sky to come crashing down. Benji was dead. "Why?" She couldn't believe it.

The story came pouring out now. "He had some kind of tumor on his brain. We didn't know it was anything serious, only over the weekend he was a little groggy. No appetite, either." James paused to take a deep breath. "He kept staggering. My dad laughed and said he must have been out on Saturday night drinking. He looked pretty sorry for himself, so my mom said we'd take him into the Ark." He paused again and glanced at Mandy. "I think my mom knew," he said.

She nodded. "Then what?" No more Benji, she was thinking. No more Benji curled up on a seat in the Hunters' sunroom. No more Benji leaping from the sloping roof up through the bathroom window. Benji had always been there. He was part of the Hunter family.

James shrugged. He stared hard at his feet again. He was standing astride his bike, head down, miserable. "My mom took him in yesterday. By that time he could hardly stand. It was your mom who looked at him." Mandy realized that nothing in James's life had ever been so difficult for him to say. "Anyway, she said he had this growth on his brain. And there was nothing to be done in this kind of case."

"So?"

He sniffed. "So your mom explained that he'd be in a lot of pain."

"And *your* mom agreed to have him put to sleep?"

James nodded. "It would have been cruel to let him live."

For a second Mandy's hand touched James's. "That's true," she said.

Then there was a big silence. They both thought of Benji. Patient old Benji who'd grown up with them, who'd always let you pick him up any old way, and who always sat on your lap and let you tickle his chin. He'd put up over the years with all their rough treatment, and he'd never put in a cross word. He was a great cat.

"Let's go," James said. He glanced around at Mandy. "I told my mom to ask your parents not to say anything to you about it. I wanted to tell you myself."

Mandy nodded and followed on. Life, like the road over to Walton, was full of ups and downs.

It must have been hard for James, she thought, to help with the kittens this morning. He did the jobs as usual, before school and during lunch break. He listened as Mandy told Mrs. Williams how Amy, alias Twinkie, was safely back with Walton. And her future was secure.

"I hope this Ernie Bell person knows what he's doing with this kitten!" Mrs. Williams said primly. "I mean, men! They don't know how to look after things properly. They're not made that way!"

Mandy raised her eyebrows and glanced at James. He was busy with Smoky's feeding. "Oh, I don't know about that," she said.

"Not my Eric, at least," Mrs. Williams blundered on. "He's a bit old-fashioned in that respect."

As if on cue, Mr. Williams tramped in for his lunch. He ate in silence, glancing sullenly at the kitten activity in the far corner of the kitchen. "Tomorrow's D-Day!" he reminded them as he reached for his cap. "And don't you forget!"

D-Day. Death Day. Destruction Day. Deadline Day. Mandy didn't think it was possible to hate someone as much as she hated Mr. Williams just then. He stamped off down the garden path, tweaking a rose bush, perking up a primula.

"He's got to go see the headmaster!" Mrs. Williams whispered to Mandy. "He's been summoned!"

Mandy raised her head. She couldn't help that,

she thought. And all she really cared about right now was the kitten problem.

"Do you want to go right home after school?" she asked James, on their way into afternoon classes. She thought there was only so much she could ask him to do, considering Benji.

James looked up at the school shield in the entrance hall. Underneath there was a list of names of men who'd died in two wars, and underneath that was the school motto: "Through Suffering We Succeed."

"No," he said to Mandy. "I'll be there as usual."

James must have been thinking about poor Benji all through his game that afternoon. Mandy had glanced out of the science lab window down onto the soccer field, and she'd spotted him hanging about miserably on the goal line, most unlike him.

But when they met up after school, his face looked composed, even calm. "I just want to call my mom," he told her. "I'll be there in a minute."

So Mandy went on ahead. As usual, the routine of caring for the kittens took over, and she managed to push away the worry about James. She watched with delight their fluffy, wriggling little bodies, their ears beginning to unfold and perk up into position, their bruising battle to feed and to survive.

James came in just as she lifted Eric out of the basket for his feeding. She handed the kitten to him. "Here, you feed Eric," she said.

They worked in silence for a few minutes. Then James pushed his glasses up the bridge of his nose, sat back, and made an announcement. "I'd like Eric!" He said it quite straightforwardly, just like, "I'd like a candy bar!" or, "Tea with milk but no sugar, please!"

Mandy stared. "What did you say?"

"I'd like Eric," he repeated. "I've thought about it, and I'd like to adopt Eric!"

"Are you sure?" Mandy put Smoky back into the basket. "I mean, you're sure it's not too soon after . . . I mean, well, are you *sure*?"

"Yes. I called my mom. She agrees. If we're going to get another cat after Benji, we should do it right away." He looked down, half sad, half happy at the new scrap of life on his lap. "And I'm sure Benji wouldn't mind!"

Mandy waltzed around the kitchen. "Oh, great!" she said. "You hear that, Walton? Oh, wonderful! Oh, James!" She smiled and smiled.

Walton mewed.

There were practical things to arrange. When Mr. Williams threw the kittens out the next day, should James take Eric home then, or could they work out a way to keep Walton and the kittens together until they were weaned? A halfway house. That was the thing to work on, Mandy told James. She looked at Mrs. Williams, who was hovering in the doorway with her shopping basket.

"Don't ask me!" she muttered darkly. "Eric is in with the headmaster this very minute. Lord knows what's going to happen to any of us!" She went out tight-lipped, shaking her head.

"It's something we can work on," Mandy told James as they went out to their bicycles. "A halfway house. Anyway, we have two good homes. Two wonderful homes!" Mandy could have sung for joy as they rode home.

"Two to go!" Mandy told her mom as she flung her backpack in the corner of the hallway. She told her about James's decision to take Eric. "He's probably the grumpiest kitten of them all, like the person he's named after," she joked. "But James seems to like him!"

Dr. Emily smiled. "He's a good boy." Then she asked Mandy to help in the kitchen. "Your dad's out on an emergency call. One of Mrs. Janeki's sheep. But your grandfather called while you were out, just to let us know they're back."

Mandy nodded. "Did they have a good time?"

"He didn't say. But he said your grandma had gotten a reply from the prime minister." Dr. Emily looked puzzled. "Could that be right?"

"Yes. But that was quick." Mandy asked if she could run up to see them.

"After supper," Dr. Emily said. She always had to remind her daughter to slow down enough to eat. "What's the point of me preparing all these vegetarian meals for you if you won't even sit down and eat one!" she complained.

Mandy gave her a hug. "Okay, Mom, after supper!"

The camper sat in the driveway, splashed but splendid. "Hi, Grandma! Hi, Grandpa!" Mandy burst in on them. She reported the good news about Twinkie ("What a name!") and Eric. She said James was a hero, a real hero!

"Oho!" her grandfather raised his eyebrows.

"No, Grandpa, not like that!" she said.

"That's what they always say. I think Mandy's got a soft spot for young James."

"Stop teasing, Thomas!" Mandy's grandmother warned. "Anyway, she's come to see my letter from the prime minister, haven't you, honey!"

Mandy nodded and laughed. "Sorry, Grandma. It's just that the kittens have been taking up all my time. Did you have a good vacation?" she remembered to ask.

There was a small silence. "Yes," Grandma said. "But about this letter from 10 Downing Street. See, official notepaper!" She waved the reply in Mandy's face.

"'Yes' means 'Yes, but,'" Grandpa put in. "And then we quickly change the subject!"

"Why, what happened? Did the camper break down?"

"Break down!" he exclaimed. "You must be joking!"

"Of course not," Grandma said. "The camper was perfect. But Scarborough wasn't."

"Not sunny?"

"Sodden," Grandma conceded. "Forty-two hours of solid rain. We counted!"

"Ah," Mandy said. "What a shame."

"Yes, but this letter here, see!" Grandma waved it before starting to read:

"Dear Mrs. Hope:

   The Prime Minister acknowledges receipt of your letter. While he recognizes your concern about the continued existence of your local sub post office, he wishes me to point out that government policy on the issue is the concern of one of his junior ministers.

Accordingly he has asked me to pass on this matter to the relevant department.

Yours sincerely,
E. B. Whyte
(Assistant private secretary to
the Prime Minister)"

"There!" Mrs. Hope flung the cream-colored letter onto the table.

"What does it mean?" Mandy asked. "Are they going to close the post office or not?"

"It doesn't mean yes, it doesn't mean no. It doesn't mean anything!" Grandma said indignantly.

"It means they've passed the buck," Grandpa said. "As usual."

"They won't get away with it!" Grandma insisted.

Grandpa muttered in a stage whisper, "Watch it, Mandy, she's on the warpath!"

Grandma ignored him. "We'll have a campaign. Save our post office!" She stood up and strode across the room.

Mandy was enjoying this, her grandmother on her high horse.

"I'll have to organize everything, of course!" There was a glint in Grandma's eye.

Bells began to ring in Mandy's head. In fact, they set up a giant racket! Did this mean her grandparents would have to put their feet firmly back on Welford ground?

"This'll take a lot of time and energy, Grandma," she pointed out.

"Who cares?" Grandma swept around the room. "It's important! In fact, it's vital! We'll design a logo for our campaign. A heart shape, to show our post office is at the heart of the village!" Her hair was coming loose from its comb, and she was looking very fiery.

"I'm glad I'm not the poor little prime minister!" Grandpa laughed.

"Does this mean you might not go to Portugal?" Mandy asked. "I mean, you might have to stay at home more to run this campaign."

Grandma stopped in her paces. Grandpa said, "Ha!"

"We-ell," Grandma said. "We might not go quite so far afield as we thought." She gave Mandy a little grin. "The fact is, we missed you all terribly; you and your mom and dad, and this old place!" She sighed. "We're a pair of old softies, after all!"

"And then there's my tomatoes to consider," Grandpa said thoughtfully. "I'll have to talk nicely to my tomatoes!"

Mandy looked at them, bursting to ask the question. She took a great, deep breath. "Does this mean you might be willing to take a kitten after all?"

They broke into smiles, both of them. They hugged her. "We thought you'd never ask!" They looked at each other. Clearly they'd been thinking about it all the time they'd been away in soggy Scarborough.

"Smoky!" Mandy said, breathless.

"On two conditions," Grandma added.

"What?" She glowed with happiness. A home for the third kitten. A home just up the hill from Animal Ark. Mandy couldn't believe it.

"First, you've got to agree to come up and feed him whenever we do go away for a couple of days," Grandma said. "When we go off in the camper to lovely Wales, or wherever."

This was hardly a condition! Mandy nodded, speechless. She'd love to feed Smoky. Then he'd be half hers, wouldn't he? She just sat there nodding.

"Second!" Grandpa said, frowning and trying to look serious. "You must swear to water my tomatoes!"

"Oh, yes," she said. She'd even talk to them. "Oh, yes, yes!"

Ten

Thursday came, and Mandy woke three quarters happy, one quarter sad. Her heart felt pulled apart over Patch; poor little Patch, the only kitten still left homeless.

Dr. Emily looked at her across the breakfast table. "Problem?" she asked.

"You realize what day it is," Mandy said miserably.

"Thursday," her father said helpfully over the top of his newspaper.

"Yes, Thursday. And I've found homes for three of the kittens, but there's still one left over! Today's the deadline!" The word "deadline" had an awful hollow ring.

"Hasn't the mother cat decided to move off to a new nest site yet?" Dr. Adam asked.

Mandy shook her head. "No, she's still there in the kitchen, in the laundry basket. And today's the day *he* throws them out!"

"You mean Mr. Williams," Dr. Emily corrected her. "Not 'he.' So what next?"

"Grandma and Grandpa say they don't mind if the kittens and Walton move in with them until the kittens are weaned in about six weeks." Mandy managed a smile of relief. It had been a close call all around.

"But?" her mother asked.

"But they say the same thing as you. They say I have to find a home for Patch. Otherwise it's cruel to keep him alive!" Her eyes filled. "Poor Patch!"

"It's true. You can't just turn him out to fend for himself when the time comes. He has to have a home!" Even her softhearted father was telling her the same thing; the thing she didn't want to hear.

"Dad!" she cried.

"There's no 'Dad!' about it," her mother said firmly. "Look, Mandy, you've done brilliantly to find these three homes. We think you're wonderful!"

"Don't!" The tears brimmed over and down her cheeks.

Dr. Emily looked across at Dr. Adam. Mandy thought she spied a glimmer of hope through her tears. "Listen, sweetie, I'll come over and see you at school this lunchtime, all right?"

"What for?" Mandy said, sniffing and drying her eyes.

"Wait and see. I can't promise anything yet." Dr. Emily smiled and patted Mandy's hand. "Just wait and see."

That lunchtime Mandy fed Patch with an aching heart. James was busy with little Eric, and the other two kittens were already snuggled down in the basket, when there was a knock at the door.

"Hello. Is Mandy here?" a voice said to Mrs. Williams.

She recognized her mom, but the misery of looking down at Patch's little face, his eyes nearly open now, was too much. She couldn't bear to think about what might have to happen to him.

"Mandy?" her mom's voice repeated.

She looked up.

"I've brought someone with me." Dr. Emily was gentle but firm, as always. "Come in, and let's have a look at this little fellow."

Mandy felt suddenly surrounded by people and dragged back to the present from fears of the future. She pulled herself together. "Sorry," she said, standing up with Patch cupped in her hands. Her eyes focused on the visitors: Miss Marjorie and Miss Joan Spry!

What on earth was her mother up to? Mandy stood, ready to protest, but her mom gave her a meaningful look.

"This is the kitten Mandy came to see you about," Dr. Emily explained calmly. "And I'm sure she apologizes for running off so rudely." She smiled encouragingly at Mandy, who turned red and nodded without saying anything.

The two sisters nodded back and peered down at Patch. They poked their thin faces toward him curiously. They looked silently at each other.

Mandy had gotten over her shock. She trusted her mom to know what she was doing. And today the Spry twins didn't look so strange. Their untidy hair was combed back underneath straw hats, and their pastel summer coats made them look like quaint wedding guests.

"This is the only kitten left without a home," Mandy said. She offered Patch to one of the twins, not knowing which one.

The twin shook her head. "No, give him to Joan. See if she likes him," Miss Marjorie said. "She did promise to try to like him!"

Mandy held out the kitten again. With shaking hands Miss Joan took the little fur scrap and cradled him. She brought her face close to the kitten's and felt him lick her finger. "What is his name?" she breathed.

"Patch," Mandy said, holding her own breath. "He's just one week old!"

Joan looked up at her sister. The silence held them all like a net. Would she say yes? Would she give Patch a home and a future?

"Yes," she said at last. "I think I like him!"

"Of course you do! What did I tell you!" Miss Marjorie said.

And they all smiled and congratulated one another. They listened to Mandy's instructions about how a kitten should be treated: "Don't poke him, don't press him too hard, don't disturb him too much!" She said they should put him back with his mother now. "The excitement's too much for him," she said as she returned a squeaking Patch to his warm, dark nest.

The Spry twins smiled and thanked Mandy and went happily down the porch steps, arm in arm.

"See!" Dr. Emily said, head to one side. "Didn't I say they were harmless? You have to learn that all people are different, but that doesn't make them wrong. This kitten will be the best thing that's happened to the twins in an awfully long time!"

Mandy laughed and hugged her mom. "Oh, thanks!" she said. A great weight had lifted off her chest. She sighed and looked in on the kittens. They were curled up, snug and warm against Walton's sleeping body. "Four homes! We did it!"

"You did it," her mother said. "You and James!"

They looked at each other with huge grins on their faces. James turned red, even before Mandy hugged him.

When Miss Marjorie came back in for a moment, James stepped aside. Dainty as a canary in her pale yellow coat, Miss Marjorie headed straight for Mandy. "Thank you, my dear!" she said, patting her hand. "Thank you for bringing life back into our dark, dreary house. It's all due to you!" She beamed, nodded to James. "I'd best get back to my sister. We'll wait for you in the car," she told Dr. Emily before walking off again.

"Happy now?" Mandy's mom asked.

Mandy's eyes shone with tears again. She nodded, and they nearly spilled over. This time Mandy could say nothing at all!

* * *

School was coming to an end, and the great move began. "It's time for a new nest, Walton," Mandy told her gently. "And you don't even have to do it yourself, you lucky cat!"

"You're sure it'll be all right now?" Mrs. Williams fussed. There was no sign of her husband. It was a hot, humid day, threatening rain when Mandy's grandparents' camper pulled up in the playground. "Walton won't desert these kittens now?" She stood at the kitchen sink, grasping a dish towel.

"No, it'll work out okay, Mrs. Williams. Don't worry!" Mandy looked up and realized the old lady would miss Walton and the kittens after all. She smiled. "Honestly, Walton would fight to the death for them now. She's made a good strong bond with them. Thanks to you, of course!"

"Oh!" Mrs. Williams raised her hands and smiled modestly as Mandy's grandfather joined them in the kitchen.

"Yes, you gave them a good start," Mandy went on. "Now my grandmother and grandfather will keep a close eye on them up at Lilac Cottage!"

"Then what?" Mrs. Williams folded her dish towel into a precise rectangle. She laid it down on the drain board and smoothed it carefully.

"Then James will take Eric and give him a home," Mandy said, handing the kitten to him.

"And me and my wife will keep this little fellow," Grandpa said, lifting Smoky in one hand.

"Ernie Bell is waiting to have Amy — er — Twinkie. And now Patch has found a home at The Riddings!" Mandy counted them off on her fingers.

Mrs. Williams sniffed and nodded. "And what about Walton?"

Mandy looked at James. "We haven't gotten that far!"

He shrugged. "We have a little time to think of something."

"Well, I'll have to have a word with my Eric," Mrs. Williams said. But she would say no more.

So they drove off in triumph in the silver camper; cat and kittens, James, Mandy, and her grandpa.

Walton quickly regained her strength in the sunny warmth of Lilac Cottage. After three more weeks Smoky, Patch, Twinkie, and Eric began to bounce and tumble. They chased anything that moved. On Mr. Hope's lawn they sat in wait for butter-flies to land on the rosebushes. Still as statues, they watched and waited. Then they bounced and pounced and tumbled. They always missed. They turned endless somersaults. Mandy would give them scores from one to ten like they were international gymnasts doing their floor exercises.

James came often to check on Eric. He lay propped on his elbows out on the lawn, with a computer magazine spread out in front of him. He pretended to read, but really he watched Eric's every move; the kitten's grumpy swipes with his front paws at mischievous Smoky and Patch, his sulking under the shade of the rhubarb leaves.

"Don't worry," Mandy said. "After a week in your house he'll be as sweet-tempered and patient as

poor old Benji was. It's the Hunters' magic way with cats!"

James looked up from his magazine and smiled.

Mandy went down regularly to the village to report to Ernie on Twinkie's progress. Ernie would ask endless questions about his kitten and waited with utter impatience for the day when he could have her home. "Hey!" he warned Sammy, flipping the squirrel off his shoulder. "Stop nipping my ear, you!" The squirrel, who had free range of Ernie's kitchen, scampered down his back and around his waist, to cling on to his belt buckle.

Mandy laughed. "He'll be jealous when Twinkie comes!"

"He should be," Ernie said. "I can't wait to get that kitten home!"

At Lilac Cottage, Walton fed the four kittens less and less, watched them take to solid food, and grew rather bored with motherhood. These days she preferred a quiet corner in the kitchen underneath the vegetable bin, with a bit of peace and quiet. Her job was almost done.

Vacation time arrived. It was a green world; everyone at school was packing up and going home.

"Hey, there," Mr. Williams grunted at Mandy by

way of greeting. She was unlocking the padlock on her bike.

She glanced up. It was unusual for the custodian to talk to her at all these days, and it was weeks since she'd seen his wife. "Oh, great!" she muttered.

She hadn't forgiven him for hanging that dreadful threat over their heads, even though things had worked out fine in the end. The best she could do was to avoid the custodian whenever possible. She hastily got ready to push off for home.

"How are those kittens of yours?" Mr. Williams grumbled in his low, gravelly voice. "Getting pretty big and strong by now, I should think?"

Mandy nodded.

"And I hear you've found folk willing to take them," he persisted. One hand was on his precious garden gate, but he looked like a man with something on his mind.

Oh, go away, just go away! Mandy thought to herself.

But instead he said, "Come here a second," and looked around furtively at the lace curtains of the kitchen window. "I want to have a word with you!"

It involved Mandy riding back to school on the first day of her vacation. She had the basket strapped carefully to the back of her bike. *Who would have believed it?* she thought to herself as she lifted the basket, reached in, and gathered Walton gently into her arms.

"Come on, Walton, come on, girl!" she murmured.

"Shh!" said Mr. Williams, gesturing toward the porch. "This is still a secret!"

Mandy nodded and set Walton down. Immaculate, ladylike, and elegant as a model, Walton sniffed the logs, tested the doormat, pushed the door with her paw. It swung open.

"Eric?" Mrs. Williams called from inside the kitchen. Mandy grinned at the custodian. Then, "Eric!" Mrs. Williams said again, her voice high-pitched and surprised. "Eric, this cat has just walked back into this kitchen as if she owns the place!"

They went inside to see, and there was Mrs. Williams staring down at the familiar black-and-white shape. "How did she get here? Did she run away?" Mrs. Williams demanded.

Her husband gave a self-conscious little laugh. "No, as a matter of fact, Amy, I asked this young lady here to bring her back home for you!"

Mrs. Williams looked up at him, her eyes filling with tears. "Oh, Eric!"

"Yes, well!" He looked embarrassed. "I knew you were pining for the darn cat." He half turned toward Mandy. "She pestered me to death about it! She's too soft by half, my wife!"

Mandy watched Walton wrap herself around Mrs. Williams's legs, purring like mad. She peered in her corner for food and looked up as if to say, "Where is it?" They laughed, gave her a saucer of milk, and made a great fuss of her homecoming.

"And will we take her with us?" Mrs. Williams asked, still unable to believe her husband's change of heart.

"Why, where are you going?" Mandy asked.

"Eric's leaving his job."

"He's not . . . ?" Mandy looked anxiously at the old couple. Had Mr. Williams's arthritis finally beaten him?

"No, he hasn't been fired," Mrs. Williams said. "No, in fact the headmaster only wanted to see him to ask him to stay on beyond retirement age. He said he'd never find another custodian as good as Eric!"

Mr. Williams tut-tutted.

"Yes, he did, Eric! But he came home and we talked about it, and we decided of our own accord that we'd call it a day. We're getting on, and we want some peace and quiet in our old age."

Mr. Williams nodded. He watched Walton grooming herself after her drink. She was sitting on the windowsill, using her front paw to clean behind her ears. "Well!" he said, taken aback.

"I told you they're nice clean animals!" Mandy laughed.

"So we've decided to retire!" Mrs. Williams announced. "We've got our eye on one of the new houses just up the road!"

"A quiet little street, plenty of garden!" Mr. Williams said.

"Perfect for Walton?" Mandy could hardly keep the smile from spreading all over her face.

The custodian looked at his wife and broke into a grin. "I suppose so," he said, shaking his head.

"And will it be all right if I make an appointment at Animal Ark for Walton's operation?" Mandy asked, trying to be tactful.

"Operation?" Mr. Williams repeated slowly.

"Yes, so she won't have any more kittens."

"Oh," he said, very old-fashioned. "*That* operation!"

"Yes, you don't want any more little ones cluttering up your kitchen, getting into your best shirts!"

Mr. Williams turned bright red. He looked sheepishly at his wife, then his face broke into a broad grin again. "I should say not!" he agreed.

So Mandy made the arrangements. She wouldn't hear of them having to pay for Walton being spayed. She knew her mom and dad would want that, too. So she said she would schedule Walton for the following Monday. Mandy took the hand offered by Mr. Williams and shook it warmly.

"No hard feelings?" he asked.

"None!" she said.

Mandy rode home along the field road. She felt on top of the world. The road crested the hill. Lapwings curved overhead in the clear sky, the fields rolled in every direction. Perfect!

She headed downhill to Welford and Animal Ark. She'd go in to see who else needed rescuing; maybe a lost hedgehog who'd found its way to the examining room or a "male" hamster who'd just produced six babies! ("The pet shop said it was a boy, they did really!")

The wind caught Mandy's hair. She tilted her head back and stuck her legs out sideways to freewheel down the hill. And she laughed out loud.

ANIMAL ARK®

Kitten in the Candy Corn

Ben M. Baglio

Illustrations by Ann Baum

Special thanks to Lucy Courtenay

**Thanks also to C. J. Hall, B.Vet.Med., M.R.C.V.S.,
for reviewing the veterinary information
contained in this book.**

One

"Well, what do you think?" Mandy Hope demanded. She held up a cardboard cat mask. It was painted black and had sharp ears. Its long white whiskers were made from pipe cleaners. "It's taken me ages to stick the whiskers on. I'll wear a black sweatshirt top and leggings as well, and Gran's making me a belt with a tail."

Mandy's best friend, James Hunter, looked up from his piece of buttered toast. He squinted in the bright morning sun that was slanting through the Hopes' kitchen window. "It's great," he said, impressed. "You'll make my costume look really boring."

"I'm glad I invited you over for breakfast now!"

Mandy joked. It was Tuesday morning, the second official day of their vacation, and she and James had
planned an early start to make the most of their week
off. Most important of all, they had a Halloween party to
plan. They were going to hold it at the end of the week.
"You'll look fantastic as Harry Potter, James," Mandy
continued, remembering what he had told her about his
costume. "Everyone will know who you are. Do you
think they'll realize I'm Catwoman?"

"Catwoman!" Emily Hope, Mandy's mother, swung
around from pouring herself a cup of coffee and
clapped one hand to her forehead. "Of course! We've
been scratching our heads all weekend about your Halloween costume."

"Come on, Mom," Mandy teased. "Since when have I
ever dressed up as anything but some kind of animal for
Halloween?"

Dr. Emily laughed. Everyone knew that Mandy was
animal crazy. Her parents ran Animal Ark, the veterinary
clinic in the town of Welford in Yorkshire, and Mandy
loved every hectic second of it. Whatever the problem,
whatever kind of animal, she was always eager to help.

Her dad, Dr. Adam, looked up from a list he was making at the other end of the table. "What about last year,
Mandy? That wasn't an animal costume, was it?"

"Of course it was, Dad!" Mandy was indignant. "OK,

so I got the tail wrong, but everyone knew I was a squirrel."

"With the straightest, dangliest tail ever to decorate a squirrel," said Dr. Adam solemnly.

Mandy made a face at her dad, then reached for another piece of toast. "I can't wait for Saturday," she said, and sighed. She turned to James. "Is Blackie going to wear a costume this year?"

James's black Labrador had been sniffing under the table for crumbs. He stopped and pricked up his ears when he heard his name.

"I thought maybe a bat," said James, rubbing his glasses on the bottom of his sweatshirt. "He's the right color and everything, and his ears would be a great shape if I could figure out how to stop them from flopping over."

"We can't possibly let Blackie join in," said Dr. Adam, shaking his head. "Those sharp canines of his would give him too much of an advantage in the apple bobbing."

Mandy and James exchanged a grin at the thought of Blackie with his head in the washtub, chasing apples.

"Come on, you two," said Dr. Adam, rapping the table with his pencil. "I'm stuck here. We're supposed to be making a list of party games, and I only have bobbing for apples so far. The clinic opens in fifteen minutes. Brainstorm time!"

"Identifying slimy things in jars," James said promptly, peering over Dr. Adam's shoulder at the list. "That's always a good one. Peeled grapes, spaghetti, jelly — stuff like that. It's really gross when you put your hand in and have to guess what you're feeling."

"How about fishing jelly beans out of flour with your teeth?" Mandy suggested.

"Powdered sugar would taste nicer," Mandy's mom pointed out, placing the breakfast plates in the dishwasher.

Maybe it was the excitement of knowing that the Halloween party was only four days away, but the ideas suddenly came thick and fast. Eating chocolate with chopsticks. Halloween Pictionary. Pin the hat on the headless horseman.

"What about doughnuts on strings?" James suggested enthusiastically. "Cookies, too."

"Don't mention doughnuts and cookies." Dr. Adam groaned, putting his hand on his stomach. "I feel hungry just thinking about them."

"Dad's on another diet," Mandy explained to James. "Mom insisted. He's getting a bit of a stomach."

"Just enough to make me cuddly," Dr. Adam protested. "What I wouldn't do for a cookie right now!"

As Dr. Emily flapped a dish towel at him, there was a

quiet knock at the kitchen door. There was only one person Mandy knew who knocked as politely as that.

"I bet that's John!" she said, getting out of her chair and running to open the door.

John Hardy lived with his father and stepmother at the Fox and Goose in Welford. He was away at school for much of the year, but he was good friends with Mandy and James and saw them whenever he came home for vacation. Mandy enjoyed spending time with him and his rabbits, Brandy and Bertie. They got along so well that sometimes she found it hard to believe John didn't live in Welford all year-round.

Mandy opened the door and beamed at the boy who was standing there. He had neatly brushed brown hair and clean, ironed jeans, and he was shifting from one foot to the other as if he was trying to make up his mind about coming in.

"Hello, John!" Mandy exclaimed. "We were expecting to see you yesterday. Didn't you get out on Friday, like us?"

"We got out on Sunday, actually," said John. "Sorry I didn't come over before now. I've been sort of busy."

"Playing with Brandy and Bertie, right?" asked Mandy. "It must be nice to see them again." A little girl in town named Imogen Parker Smythe looked after

John's rabbits while he was away at school, and Mandy knew that John missed them a lot.

John's solemn face lit up. "It was great," he agreed. "Imogen has looked after them really well. They're much bigger. I came over to see if you have any of those chewy sticks for them, for cleaning their teeth."

"I'm sure we'll find some for you, John," said Mandy's mom. "Come in. I think these three could use your help."

John carefully stepped over Blackie, took off his coat, and hung it neatly by the back door. "What are you doing?" he asked.

"Thinking of Halloween games for the party," James replied.

John looked surprised. "What party?"

"Our annual Halloween party," Mandy explained, picking up her cat mask and waving it with a flourish. "It's a costume party, and it's on Saturday. Can you come?"

"And do you know any good party games?" James added.

John looked delighted. "I'd love to come," he said. Leaning over, he studied the list of games with the air of a botanist studying a rare plant. "What's this one?" he said, pointing at James's suggestion of cookies on strings.

"Dad's favorite," said Mandy. "You hang doughnuts

and cookies from the ceiling on pieces of string, and you have to eat them without using your hands."

John's eyebrows shot up. "Don't you get very messy?" he said cautiously.

"Very," Mandy agreed. "It's great."

John frowned. "How does it work?"

Dr. Adam clapped his hands. "It seems we need a demonstration!" he said with a gleam in his eye.

"Dad," Mandy said warningly, "don't forget your diet!"

Dr. Adam produced some string and reached for the cookie jar. "We all need to make sacrifices in the name of research," he said, picking up the lid and removing two fat, crumbly chocolate chip cookies. "Mandy, James, tie these two for me, would you? Then we have to hang them from something."

"I'll hold them," Mandy offered. She hopped up on a kitchen chair and held out her hands for the cookie strings.

"Hold them up high," Dr. Adam advised. "We've got to be on tiptoe for this. Now, on your mark, get set, GO!"

Mandy got a terrible attack of the giggles as her dad gobbled down the first cookie at lightning speed. Then he and James dueled over the second cookie, with James having to jump up really high to compete. Breathless with laughter, they soon had cookie crumbs all over their faces and clothes. Blackie ran back and

forth, gobbling up the cookie crumbs that littered the floor.

"So much for the diet, Adam," said Dr. Emily, sighing.

"What do you think of the game, John?" Mandy asked once she'd gotten her breath back.

John grinned. "Excellent!"

Dr. Adam looked at his watch. "We just have time to take a look at the guest list. You are in charge of making the invitations, Mandy, OK? They have to go out by Thursday or no one will know about it in time. So who do we invite?"

"Mom, Dad, me, Gran and Grandpa, James, Blackie, and John. That makes" — Mandy counted on her fingers — "eight."

"What about trick-or-treating?" Mandy's mom wanted to know. "Who are you going to visit?"

"Ernie Bell usually likes to see our costumes," Mandy said. "And Walter Pickard —"

"He's just arrived with Flicker," came the voice of Jean Knox, the Animal Ark receptionist, who was standing at the door to the waiting room. "He says he has the first appointment this morning. Of course, I can't find the appointment book anywhere, so we'll just have to hope that he's right, won't we?" She sighed and disappeared back into the clinic without waiting for a reply.

"Hey, wasn't that weird!" said Mandy after a moment. "Just when I said Walter's name."

John leaned forward. "That's Halloween for you," he said seriously. "Expect the unexpected!"

Walter smiled broadly when Mandy, James, and John came into the clinic waiting room. "Hello there," he said. "On vacation, I take it?"

"Yup," Mandy replied. "Is Flicker all right?"

Walter looked down at the cat basket by his feet. "Not really. She's got a nasty cough," he answered.

"We have another cat in for observation with the same thing," said Mandy sympathetically. "I think there's a bug going around."

A quiet cough floated up from the basket. Mandy knelt down to see Flicker curled at the very back of the basket, staring up at her with wide, fearful eyes.

"Hello, sweetheart," she said softly. She looked up at Walter. "May I pick her up?"

"Of course you may," Walter nodded. "Got to get her out of her basket sometime. But it won't be easy. You know how she can be when she's scared."

The little cat flinched into the corner of the basket as Mandy reached in and petted her fine black ears, talking soothingly all the time. Gradually, Flicker began to relax, though her green eyes remained wide and distrust-ful. After a moment or two, Mandy moved her hand around to tickle the cat's chin. When she finally scooped the cat out of her basket, Flicker was still and relaxed. A gentle rumbling sound came from deep in her throat, and she rested her neat black-and-white head in the crook of Mandy's neck.

Walter shook his head in amazement. "You've got quite a touch there, Mandy."

Mandy grinned at Walter. "All part of the Animal Ark service."

Walter scratched the little cat between her ears. "She still remembers you," he said. "She knows if it weren't for you, she probably wouldn't be alive."

"Mandy rescued Flicker when Welford had those bad floods," James explained to John. "The poor thing floated right up to the door in a barrel! She was washed away from the farm where she lived when the river burst its banks."

Dr. Emily came over. "Let's take a look at this cough then, young Flicker," she said with a smile. "Mandy, could you bring her into the examining room for me?"

Mandy carried Flicker into the examining room, closely followed by Walter. Dr. Emily examined the cat swiftly and gently, looking down her throat with a small flashlight and listening to her chest with a stethoscope. The cat mewed plaintively, and Walter petted her with one huge finger.

"Is it the same thing that Misty has?" Mandy wanted to know. Misty was the cat in the residential unit.

"I think so," Dr. Emily replied, washing her hands. "We've caught it earlier in this case, though, so she doesn't need to stay here. I have some cough medicine you can give her, Walter, twice a day. Just keep her warm, and she'll be good as new in a few days."

"Is chocolate the latest hair accessory?" Walter suddenly asked Mandy as they returned to the waiting room. He pulled a chocolate chip from Mandy's hair.

Mandy laughed. "Nope!"

Sitting on one of the waiting room chairs, James looked up from the wildlife magazine he was reading. "We were practicing one of the games we're having at the party on Saturday," he explained.

"I love Halloween," Walter said, setting Flicker back into her basket. "There's something about the dark evenings and autumn leaves and the bare tree trunks — all black and orange and Halloweenlike. Do you know what I mean?"

Mandy nodded.

"Did you have Halloween parties when you were young, Mr. Pickard?" John wanted to know.

"We certainly did," Walter said. "Apple bobbing, pumpkin carving, all that stuff."

"I've carved a pumpkin this year," Mandy said proudly. "It's on the kitchen windowsill. It looks really spooky when I put a candle inside it. Mom made some soup with the insides on Sunday."

"We used to have pumpkin-carving competitions in town," Walter went on, "until one year, the minister banned it. Someone's goat got into his garden and ate the prize pumpkin he'd been growing especially for the competition."

"A goat in the minister's garden? Sounds like a bit of early trick-or-treating," James suggested.

Mandy leaned forward. "It was you, wasn't it? Who let the goat in? Come on, Walter, you can tell us."

Walter laughed. "That's for me to know!" he said. "Anyway, it was harmless enough. Not like some of the tricks they pull these days. You won't be playing any silly pranks this year, will you? The town has enough to worry about at the moment."

Mandy frowned. "What do you mean?"

"Haven't you heard?" asked Walter, surprised.

"Heard what?"

Flicker mewed and scratched at the side of her basket, and Walter reached down to reassure her. "I'd better be getting this young lady home," he said, picking up the basket. "I'm sure you'll hear all about it before long."

Mandy reached through the basket opening with her finger and tickled Flicker's neck. She loved all the animals who came to the clinic, but the little black-and-white cat had a special place in her heart. Not for the first time, Mandy wished that she had a cat of her own.

Maybe that's why I'm dressing up as Catwoman this year, she thought with a sigh. *It's the closest I'm going to get to the real thing.*

Two

Because the sun was shining, Mandy, John, and James decided to walk into town with Walter and Flicker. It wasn't long before they were strolling down the narrow road, Blackie leaping at the end of his leash, John clutching a handful of chewing sticks for his rabbits, and Walter carrying Flicker as carefully as if she were a carton of eggs. As they approached the town crossroads, a cold breeze tugged at Mandy's coat, making it flap and startling Blackie into a volley of barking.

"Don't frighten Flicker, Blackie," Mandy scolded. "She's had a bad morning already."

Blackie whined and retreated behind James's legs, staring suspiciously at Mandy's coat.

"I think Blackie's more scared than Flicker," Walter observed. "Ah, here we are. So I'll see you on Saturday night for trick-or-treating?"

"Will you have some candy, Mr. Pickard?" John asked hopefully.

"You'll have to wait and see," Walter said and grinned.

Mandy, James, and John waved at the elderly man as he made his way down the path beside the Fox and Goose to his tiny white house, which nestled behind the restaurant.

"Tom will be pleased to see Flicker back home," Mandy said. Tom was Walter's other cat, a big black-and-white cat. He was famous for his bad temper, but he had grown very fond of Flicker after his other friend, Scraps, had to be put down.

"Sara will be pleased to see *me* back home," John remarked, looking at his watch. "I promised I wouldn't be too long, and it's already nine-thirty. I haven't fed the rabbits yet."

"Don't worry, I have," said a voice from behind them.

They turned to see Sara Hardy, John's stepmother, getting to her feet. She was holding some broken pottery pieces that Mandy recognized as part of a flowerpot that usually stood outside the door of the restaurant.

"Don't look so worried, John." Sara smiled. "I thought Mandy would keep you for a while."

"What happened to your flowerpot, Mrs. Hardy?" Mandy asked curiously.

"This?" Sara asked, holding up one of the pieces. "Heaven only knows. The wind must have knocked it over. It's been pretty blustery today."

Blackie was sniffing around the flowerpot pieces that were still lying on the ground.

"Hey! Look at his fur," James said suddenly.

On the way to town, Blackie's fur had been blown in all directions by the wind. Now it lay sleek and neat against his skin.

Mandy guessed at once what James meant. "The wind couldn't have blown over the flowerpot," she said with a frown. "It's too sheltered by the door. I wonder what really happened."

Sara sighed and looked down at the mess of pottery, dirt, and flowers at her feet. "All I know is that this is going to take a while to clean up. I don't suppose you could lend a hand, could you?"

With four pairs of hands (plus a less helpful four paws and a tail), the cleanup took less than five minutes. Soon, Mandy, James, and Blackie were on their way back to Animal Ark, having promised to come over later and see the rabbits using their new toothbrushes.

"Don't you think it's odd?" Mandy said as they walked back to the clinic.

"What?" asked James, busily tugging Blackie away from an interesting smell at the side of the road.

"That business with the flowerpot and the wind." Mandy stopped for a moment. "If the wind didn't blow it over, it must have been something else — or some-one else."

"Who'd knock over a flowerpot?" James asked.

"Someone with nothing better to do," Mandy replied thoughtfully. She thought back to the interrupted conversation she'd had with Walter, about there being some kind of trouble in the town.

Blackie gave a sharp bark, interrupting Mandy's train of thought. She looked up. "James!" she said, entranced. "Look at that beautiful dog!"

About fifty yards farther down the road, a red-haired boy was coming around the corner with a golden retriever. The dog's long fur rippled like barley in the wind, and its ears pricked up when it saw Blackie. The boy was fiddling with the zipper on his jacket, so he hadn't seen Mandy or James.

"It's Matt Burness," James said. His voice was strangely flat. "I wondered when we'd be seeing him."

"Who?" Mandy asked, her eyes fixed on the retriever.

"A boy at school. He's just moved to town. Come on."

To Mandy's surprise, James tugged at Blackie's leash and started walking hurriedly in the opposite direction.

Mandy was confused. "What's the matter?" she asked, breaking into a trot to keep up with her friend. "Don't you like him?"

James shrugged and kept walking. "What's to like?" he said. "He's a bully. He always hangs around with these tough guys who act like they rule my class. He's just moved from Walton to Welford. I've heard his pals teasing him about being a country bumpkin and having no friends here. Well, big deal! I'm not going to talk to him."

Mandy put out a hand and caught James's arm, slowing him down. "We could try being friendly," she insisted. "If he's just moved to town, he may be lonely."

James snorted. "Trust me, Mandy," he said. "He's trouble."

Mandy stood in the middle of the road, undecided. The boy didn't look too bad. His red hair fell almost to his shoulders, and he wore baggy jeans and a green baseball cap with the brim slanting to one side. And she really wanted to meet his dog. What should she do?

Blackie made the decision for her by pulling free from James and bounding up the road, his tail wagging joyfully. The boy looked up to see the black Labrador racing toward him and gave a half smile. But when he

noticed Mandy and James, the smile was replaced by a sullen frown.

James stayed well back, but Mandy followed Blackie. "Hello," she said when she came up to the boy. She looked down at Blackie, who was frisking around the retriever as if they were the best of friends. "You have the most beautiful dog," she said in a rush. "What's his name?"

There was a brief silence, and for a moment Mandy thought that the boy wasn't going to say anything at all.

"Biscuit," he muttered at last. "Because of his color."

Mandy crouched down in front of the retriever and held out her arms. "Hello, Biscuit," she whispered. "You're gorgeous, aren't you?"

Biscuit grinned at her, his long pink tongue lolling out of his mouth.

"I'm Mandy," she said, standing up again and smiling at the boy. "You're new in the town, aren't you?"

The boy said nothing and fiddled with Biscuit's leash.

"It's just that I've never seen you before, and I'd remember you," Mandy continued. "And I'd definitely remember Biscuit."

"That's small-town life for you," the boy said scornfully. "Everyone knows everyone." He jerked his head in James's direction. "I'm sure he's told you all about me, so there's no need to act like you want to be my friend. I don't want to be here, so just leave me alone, OK?"

He tugged sharply at the retriever's leash. "Come on, Biscuit. Let's go home."

Mandy felt puzzled and hurt as the boy walked down the road with his shoulders hunched, past the cross-roads and out of sight.

"Told you," said James, walking up to her.

"And you're always right, I suppose," said Mandy, still staring after the boy.

"In this case, yes," James said firmly. "Come on. Let's get back."

James tied Blackie in a sheltered spot outside the clinic when they got back to Animal Ark, in case there were any small animals inside. The waiting room had filled up since they had left. Mrs. Parker Smythe was sitting in one corner with her daughter Imogen's rabbit, Button, on her lap. John's rabbits had come from one of Button's litters, and Imogen was the girl who looked after Brandy and Bertie when John was away at school.

"Hello, Mrs. Parker Smythe. What's the matter with Button?" James asked.

Mrs. Parker Smythe was a tall, elegant woman with shining blond hair pinned into a French twist on the back of her head. She petted Button and indicated a small nick on one of her ears. "Button had a little accident with a piece of loose wire in her cage," she explained in her light, silvery voice. "Darling Immi was far too upset to come with me today. It's been simply dreadful for her."

Button, who seemed fairly cheerful, shook his head and butted James's outstretched fingers as if to say hello.

A loud, bossy voice drew Mandy's attention to the reception desk, where another of her mom and dad's clients, Mrs. Ponsonby, was talking to Jean. Pandora, Mrs. Ponsonby's spoiled Pekingese, was lying on the floor by her owner's feet with her head between her paws.

". . . terrible pain," Mrs. Ponsonby was saying. "We really must see the vet immediately."

"I'm sorry, Mrs. Ponsonby," Jean said apologetically, "but we're very busy today, as you can see. You will have to wait your turn, I'm afraid. If you'll just take a seat, Dr. Emily will see Pandora as soon as she can."

Mrs. Ponsonby heaved a sigh and settled her blue-rimmed spectacles a little straighter on the end of her nose. "But Pandora can't *walk*," she said, her bottom lip wobbling. "This toenail is causing her the most dreadful agony. It's terribly cruel —"

"Hello, Mrs. Ponsonby," Mandy broke in cheerfully,

bending down to scratch Pandora in the spot she liked best, right between her shoulders. Pandora gave a whine of pleasure and wriggled under Mandy's hand.

"Ah, Mandy." Mrs. Ponsonby turned toward her, beaming. "Pandora's always pleased to see you, aren't you, my darling little girl?" She puckered her fuchsia lips at the Peke and made kissing noises. "You have such a way with animals, dear," she told Mandy, scooping Pandora up and tucking the little Peke under her arm.

Mandy led Mrs. Ponsonby to a seat by the waiting room window, not far from Mrs. Parker Smythe and Button. Jean gave her a grateful glance and turned to answer the phone.

"You will follow in your parents' footsteps here at Animal Ark, won't you?" Mrs. Ponsonby asked Mandy, settling herself in a chair and placing Pandora on her lap. "I can't imagine anyone else looking after my treasures. You simply can't trust strangers these days."

Mrs. Parker Smythe looked up. "You are quite right, Mrs. Ponsonby," she said earnestly. "Have you heard about those dreadful vandals in town?" She lowered her voice. "Strangers, of course."

"Vandals?" Mandy echoed. "Here in Welford?"

"Oh, yes!" Mrs. Parker Smythe exclaimed. "The worst kind. Scribbling graffiti in the town phone booth and hanging around the restaurant, though goodness knows why, because they're far too young to go in there alone."

The broken flowerpot, Mandy thought suddenly.

"I've seen one of them, I'm sure of it," Mrs. Ponsonby chipped in importantly. "A ruffian if ever there was one. Red hair down to his shoulders! They say you have to watch the red-haired ones. They have such terrible tempers."

"We're not all bad," said Dr. Emily with a grin, standing at the door of the examining room and twirling the end of her dark red ponytail around her finger. "Provided you don't feed us after midnight. Now, who's next?"

Mrs. Ponsonby blushed and bent down to fiddle with Pandora's collar. As Mrs. Parker Smythe carried Button across to the examining room, Mandy glanced across at James, whose eyebrows had shot up under his hair. Mrs. Ponsonby's description fitted Matt Burness almost exactly. It seemed that James was right after all.

Matt was trouble with a capital *T*.

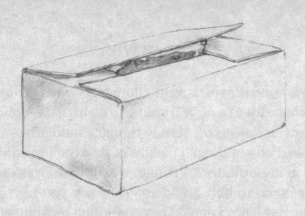

Three

Halfway to the examining room, Mrs. Parker Smythe suddenly stopped dead in her tracks and looked out the window. "Who on earth is that?" she asked.

Mandy and James both ran to see. Coming up the Animal Ark driveway, with a large cardboard box tucked under one arm, was the most extraordinary-looking person Mandy had ever seen. The tall woman had iron gray hair in a long braid that hung down from beneath the brim of a battered black hat, and she was draped from top to toe in an enormous black cape. Each of her long strides made the cape billow out to reveal a pair of

178

red-and-black-striped tights that ended in two sturdy black lace-up boots.

"It's *her*!" Mrs. Ponsonby said and gasped, peering over Mandy's shoulder. "Araminta Greenwood. I haven't seen her in town for a while. Whatever does she have in that box?"

Araminta Greenwood. The name sounded familiar to Mandy. Where had she heard it before?

"I've heard people talk about her," James whispered dramatically, his eyes wide and a little fearful. "They say that she's a *witch*."

Araminta Greenwood certainly looked the part. The only thing missing was a broomstick. Mrs. Parker Smythe looked a little frightened and hurried into the examining room with Button.

It was coming back to Mandy now. "She's the woman who treats wild animals in the woods!" she said in excitement. "Mom and Dad told me she set a doe's broken leg once, and it healed as good as new." Her heart began to pound with expectation. "She must have a wild animal in that box. Maybe a rabbit? Or a fox cub?" She hoped the animal hadn't been hurt by a snare or a trap. It was always horrible to see an injured wild animal, but even worse when its injuries had been caused by humans.

James pushed his glasses up on his nose. "The box

looks too big for a rabbit or a fox cub," he said. "Maybe there's a full-grown fox in there. Or maybe," he whispered, "it's her — what do you call it? — you know, the animals that witches have to help with their spells?"

"Familiar," Mandy said absently.

"Exactly," said James. "Her familiar. Maybe one of her spells went wrong and she turned her cat into a toad or something!"

Somehow it wasn't difficult to picture Araminta Greenwood stirring a cauldron and muttering magic words with a black cat or a toad by her side.

Mandy grinned. "I can't see Mom or Dad being able to solve a problem like that," she said. "I think your first idea was better, James. A full-grown fox."

James didn't look convinced. "I'd better go and see if Blackie's OK," he muttered.

"Ms. Greenwood isn't going to turn Blackie into a puff of smoke!" Mandy exclaimed.

"You can't be too sure," James replied darkly, and hurried outside.

"She lives alone in the woods near Bleakfell Hall," Mrs. Ponsonby told Mandy with a theatrical shiver. "I've heard the most extraordinary noises coming from her house when I've been walking my darlings in the woods. I wouldn't be at all surprised to learn that what they say about her is true. After all, where there's smoke . . ."

The half-finished sentence was left hanging in the air as the door opened and Araminta Greenwood swept in on a draft of chilly October air. Up close, she looked even taller, and her cape seemed to fill the whole room in a swirl of black. Mrs. Ponsonby shrank back against her seat and pulled Pandora closer to her. Ignoring the curious glances, Araminta Greenwood walked straight over to the reception desk and put the box down.

"May I help you?" Jean asked politely.

"Badger," Araminta Greenwood said. She had an odd, abrupt way of speaking as if she were unused to conversations and wanted to use the fewest words possible. "Injured. Can't fix him on my own."

As she spoke, she opened up the flaps on the top of the box.

Mandy caught her breath as a pointed black-and-white snout appeared, warily sniffing the air. "How wonderful!" she said, and gasped.

Araminta Greenwood looked around. "Not so wonderful for the badger," she said drily.

Mandy went over to the reception desk and gazed into the box. The badger was shifting restlessly from side to side, hampered by a thick woolen blanket that Ms. Greenwood had wrapped around him. He gave a few deep, unhappy growls and sniffed the air again. He looked young but fully grown. Mandy guessed that he was searching for the cool, woody smells of his forest home; the antiseptic smell of the clinic must have seemed very strange and frightening.

"Poor thing!" she exclaimed. "What happened?"

"He fell," said Araminta Greenwood. "There's a steep bank near the house. Seen him hunting there a few times. Went out this morning, and he was lying at the bottom. Poor creature tried to get away from me, but that leg stopped him."

"What do you think he was hunting?" Mandy asked.

"Worms." Araminta Greenwood gave a glimmer of a smile. "Rather him than me."

Mandy grinned. Even if the woman *was* a witch, she had a good sense of humor.

Just then, Dr. Emily stepped out of the examining room with Mrs. Parker Smythe. Button had a neat white dressing on her ear and was flicking her head in annoyance, trying to dislodge the offending bandage.

"Just keep that ear clean, and the cut will heal," Mandy's mom said, ushering Mrs. Parker Smythe through the waiting room and toward the door. "And tell Imogen not to worry. Button is going to be fine."

She glanced across at the reception desk. "Hello, Ms. Greenwood," she said with a smile, walking forward and holding out her hand for the woman to shake. "What brings you here?"

"It's a badger, Mom." Mandy's words tumbled out in her eagerness to explain. "He's hurt his leg."

"This is my daughter, Mandy," Dr. Emily explained. "She often helps in the clinic."

Araminta Greenwood smiled at Mandy. "Chip off the old block, I see," she said. "Interested in animals, are you?"

"Crazy about them," Mandy agreed. "Especially wild animals. Did you really mend a doe's leg?"

Araminta Greenwood looked surprised. "Where did you hear that?"

"Come along," Dr. Emily said hurriedly. "Mandy, can you give me a hand? Simon's busy in the residential unit at the moment."

"Ahem!" Mrs. Ponsonby cleared her throat and cautiously glanced at Araminta Greenwood. "I believe I was next, Dr. Emily. Pandora is in a *great* deal of discomfort."

"Adam!" Dr. Emily called to the kitchen. "Can you see Mrs. Ponsonby and Pandora for me?"

Mandy's dad appeared, holding a cup of coffee in one hand and shrugging his white coat on with the other, and swept Mrs. Ponsonby into the second examining room. A crumb of chocolate chip cookie was clinging to his chin. Mandy rolled her eyes at her dad's lack of willpower, before following her mom and Ms. Greenwood. She put on her white coat and washed her hands at the sink in the corner of the examining room, then turned to see what her mom needed her to do.

"I wrapped him in a blanket to stop him from scratching me," Ms. Greenwood said. "He's strong as an ox, and not very happy."

The badger growled again and shuffled around, trying to free himself from the folds of the blanket.

"I can see that," Dr. Emily replied. "Mandy, could you pass me the gloves?"

Mandy handed over a pair of heavy-duty gloves. Her mom carefully lifted the protesting badger from his box, speaking reassuringly to him as she unwrapped the blanket and set the animal down on the table. The badger kept up his warning growl, and Mandy felt sure he had very sharp teeth.

Simon, the veterinary nurse, poked his head around the door. "Do you need me, Dr. Emily?" he asked. "I've finished in the residential unit. Jean said something about a wild animal."

"Perfect timing," said Dr. Emily, putting the blanket to one side and holding the badger down with her other hand. "Meet Brock the badger. We'll have to sedate him to get a good look at that leg."

Sedating an animal was a tricky job and too specialized for Mandy. She helped Simon wheel out the gas

tank, and he fitted the mask to the badger's snout. Soon the only noise to be heard was the quiet hiss of the gas and the badger's gentle breathing.

"OK," said Dr. Emily. "Let's take a good look at him now."

The badger seemed oddly bigger when he was asleep. Mandy figured he was almost a yard long from his snout to the tip of his tail. There was something bearlike about him, with his broad, brindled back and short legs. His tail was very short, and his claws looked wickedly sharp.

Araminta Greenwood leaned over Dr. Emily's shoulder. "The bone isn't too badly displaced from what I could see, but old Brock is having trouble putting his weight on it. Hairline fracture, perhaps?"

"Why do you all call him Brock?" Mandy wanted to know.

"It's the old country word for badger," Dr. Emily explained, gently palpating the wild animal's leg. "I agree with you, Ms. Greenwood. We'll need to splint that leg for about three weeks. How are you doing with the anesthetic, Simon?"

"Fine," said Simon. "Go ahead."

Dr. Emily looked across at Mandy. "Get me some orthoboard, would you, dear? It's over there, second drawer down." The clinic often used orthoboard to splint broken limbs instead of the more traditional plaster cast. It was easy to apply and only took five minutes to set.

Mandy took a piece of orthoboard from the drawer. It looked like a sheet of thin brown cardboard. She put it in some hot water for a minute to soften it, then passed it to her mom, who measured it against the sleeping badger. Mandy helped to cut it to the right size before her mother tucked it underneath the badger's foreleg and wrapped it tightly around, pressing and molding it with her fingers.

"Good." Dr. Emily straightened up from the table after a minute. "I think we're done. By the time Brock wakes up, he'll be able to walk on that leg just fine. We'd like to keep him in our wildlife unit overnight, just to make sure he has no side effects from the anesthetic."

Araminta Greenwood nodded. "I'll come pick him up in the morning."

As Mandy removed her white coat and hung it on the peg by the door, she couldn't help feeling worried. The badger was a wild animal, and she knew that too much interaction with humans was a bad idea. Would Ms. Greenwood really be looking after a wild animal for three whole weeks, until Brock's cast came off? She wondered how to ask without seeming rude.

Ms. Greenwood glanced at her. "I'll keep him fed and warm just until the cast comes off," she said, "but that's as far as I'll go. He's a wild animal, and I won't forget that." She smiled. "If that's what's worrying you."

Mandy blinked in surprise. "How did you know I was thinking that?"

Ms. Greenwood's eyes twinkled and she tapped the side of her nose.

Maybe she is a witch, after all, thought Mandy, feeling a shiver of fear and respect for the unusual woman.

In order to avoid crosscontamination with the domestic pets, the wild animals were kept in a separate residential unit. Mandy followed Simon and the sleeping badger over to the wildlife unit, where she filled an empty cage with clean straw. She was longing to pet the badger's rough, peppery fur, but she knew she wasn't supposed to touch the wild animals. Instead, she watched as Simon gently placed the badger into the cage.

"He'll wake up in half an hour or so," said Simon, shutting the cage door. "Then I bet he'll be hungry."

"What are you going to feed him?" Mandy asked as they washed their hands.

"Cat food," Simon said. He laughed at Mandy's expression. "Honestly! It's not as good as earthworms, but we aren't going to be digging up any of those for Brock tonight."

Ms. Greenwood was in the waiting room putting on her long black cape when Mandy returned. The cape smelled of moss and mushrooms and made Mandy wonder about the elderly woman's life in the middle of the woods.

Standing in the doorway of the second examining room, Dr. Adam was giving some instructions to Mrs. Ponsonby. Pandora's foot had a bandage on it, and Mrs. Ponsonby was cooing sympathetically and rubbing her face against the Peke's head.

"Come in and see us on Saturday, Mrs. Ponsonby,"

said Dr. Adam. "We'll check on that infection and change the dressing."

"Witch hazel," Araminta Greenwood suddenly remarked.

Mrs. Ponsonby turned pale and clutched Pandora tightly. "Don't you cast your spells on my little dog," she warned, sidling across the waiting room. "You and your witch . . . witch . . ."

"Hazel," Ms. Greenwood repeated, looking amused. "Good for taking care of infections. Only trying to help."

"Well, we don't need *that* sort of help," Mrs. Ponsonby said. She turned and walked extremely fast out of the waiting room, muttering something about magic under her breath.

"Don't mind Mrs. Ponsonby," Mandy said, worried that Ms. Greenwood was upset.

"Oh, I don't mind her," said Ms. Greenwood, picking up her hat and ramming it on her head. "Though it's clear that she does mind *me*. A lot. Until tomorrow, then." She marched out the door with her cape flowing behind her like water.

After a second, the door banged open again and James came running into the waiting room. "She's gone!" he said, panting.

"What are you talking about?" Mandy asked.

"That witch woman," said James. "She's gone already.

I was in the garden playing with Blackie, and I saw her come out of the clinic — and the next minute, I couldn't see her *anywhere*. Now look at me, and tell me she isn't a witch!" he concluded triumphantly.

Mandy put her hands in the air. "OK, she's a witch!" she said and laughed. After all, it *was* Halloween.

Four

"A *badger*?" James was amazed when Mandy told him about Ms. Greenwood and the contents of the box.

"He's beautiful," Mandy said enthusiastically. "Come and see." She dragged James off to the wildlife residential unit, where Simon was preparing the badger's lunch.

"Is Brock awake yet, Simon?" She peered into the cage, trying to see if the animal's eyes were open. The badger had his back to her, and it was impossible to tell.

"He'll be coming around shortly," Simon replied, mixing the cat food in a bowl. "If he doesn't wake up on his own, the smell of food should do it."

Because the badger was asleep, Mandy was able to

examine him more closely. She saw how the animal's fur darkened from its silvery tips to a deep browny-black close to the skin, and how his tiny ears were almost invisible, folded flat against his furry head.

The badger began to stir. He lifted his head and sniffed. At last, hampered by the bulky wrapping on its injured leg, he turned his large wedge-shaped body around in the straw and stared at them sleepily with a pair of dark, deep-set eyes.

"He's enormous," James murmured. "I didn't think they grew that big."

"Yes, this one's a record breaker all right," said Simon. He slipped the bowl of food through the bars of the cage and the badger began to eat right away.

"Mandy?" Dr. Emily poked her head around the unit door. "Your gran's on the phone. She wants to know something about this tail she's making for your Catwoman costume."

"Tail? Catwoman?" echoed Simon, raising his eyebrows.

Mandy grinned. "You'll have to come to our Halloween party to see," she said. "But only if you come in a costume."

"I'd better go," said James. "Mom's expecting me back for lunch."

"See you later, Brock," Mandy whispered to the badger when James had gone. "Don't worry, I promise it won't be long before you're back in the woods, eating yummy earthworms again."

The badger shook his broad head at her as if to say that cat food wasn't bad in the short term, and continued eating his food.

James came over first thing the next morning on his bike.

"Still worrying about Ms. Greenwood putting a spell on Blackie?" Mandy teased when she noticed that he hadn't brought the Labrador with him.

James didn't quite meet her eyes. "Just thought I'd come on my own today," he said. "It's really difficult keeping him on the leash when I'm on my bike." He quickly changed the subject. "Can we go and see the badger?"

Mandy's dad was just closing the door to the badger's cage when they came in. "Good news," he said with a smile. "Brock's doing well and showing no signs of stress or shock. I think we'll be handing him over to the capable hands of Ms. Greenwood this morning, as planned."

The badger started scratching his shaggy back on the wire mesh of his cage.

"Oh," Mandy said, feeling disappointed that the badger's stay at Animal Ark was over so soon. *Stop thinking like that*, she told herself firmly. *The badger needs to go back to the forest, and you know it.*

"I'm glad he's going home," said James sincerely. "It's wonderful to see him up close, but it doesn't feel right, seeing him in that cage. Do you know what I mean? He's just too . . . *wild.*"

James was right. Mandy started to feel more cheerful at the thought of the badger snuffling through the leaves in the woods again, hunting for worms.

"He'll be in good hands while his leg gets better," said Dr. Adam. "Ms. Greenwood knows more about healing wild animals than any vet I know."

"I'm looking forward to seeing Ms. Greenwood again," Mandy said as her dad closed the door of the wildlife unit behind them.

"I'm not," said James.

Mandy rolled her eyes. "She's really nice, James. You'd like her if you just gave her a chance. She knows lots about animals."

"Hmm," James replied. "Snakes and newts and bats, too, I bet."

"All very topical, given the time of year," said Dr. Adam as they made their way back into the clinic. "How's your costume coming along, Mandy?"

"Gran called last night to tell me she's almost finished," Mandy said happily. "She's done something clever with a coat hanger inside my tail, so it curls up."

"An improvement on last year's squirrel, then," joked Mandy's dad, and Mandy punched him gently in the arm.

Ms. Greenwood was already waiting at the reception desk. She looked pleased when Dr. Adam gave her an update on how Brock was doing. "Half the battle with the wild ones is dealing with the shock," she said. "It can shut them down, stop them healing themselves. Sounds like he's made a good start."

"He shouldn't give you too much trouble," said Dr. Adam, handing her a bottle of painkillers and a set of feeding instructions. "Come back and see us in three weeks, when we can take that cast off."

Ms. Greenwood tucked the painkillers and the instructions somewhere deep in her black cape. Mandy noticed that her tights were striped yellow and green today. Then Simon emerged from the wildlife unit, carrying the badger in a traveling box. Mandy could just make out a pair of bright eyes looking through the small airholes in the side.

"I'll give you a hand loading him, Ms. Greenwood," said Simon. "Do you have some kind of vehicle?"

"A broomstick, probably," James whispered to Mandy.

"It's outside," Ms. Greenwood replied. "Follow me."

Mandy was a little disappointed not to see a neat,

twiggy broomstick leaning up against the wall outside the clinic. Instead, Ms. Greenwood marched up to a gleaming red mountain bike with a large basket attached to the handlebars.

James stepped forward, his mouth open. "Cool!"

"Glad you like it," said Ms. Greenwood while Simon strapped Brock's box firmly inside the basket. "Twenty-one gears, aluminum wheels, front and rear suspension." She gave James a wink. "Not exactly witchy, but very useful in the woods."

James blushed.

Ms. Greenwood tugged her hat on. "Got to run an errand or two in town, then we'll go home," she said. "Thanks for the help." She patted the box, making doubly sure that it was secure. Then she swung one yellow-and-green-striped leg over the saddle, pushed down on the pedals, and was out of sight within moments.

"No wonder Ms. Greenwood disappeared so quickly yesterday," Mandy remarked. "That bike looks really fast."

"OK, OK," James muttered. "But I still think she's a witch."

"I wish *I* were a witch," Mandy sighed as they walked around to the kitchen door. "I could do with some magic right now. I haven't even *started* the Halloween invitations, and the party's on Saturday. If we don't get them done today, no one will come."

"Don't worry," said James. "With two of us, it won't take long. Are we using those?" He pointed at the pile of black cards lying on the kitchen table.

Mandy nodded. "I thought we could use these, too," she said, and opened a plastic container that held two metallic gold pens, an orange gel pen, a tube of orange glitter and a small pot of glue.

"Great!" James said. "Come on, let's get started."

They settled down at the kitchen table and started planning the wording on the invitation. Then they wrote out several practice versions to see which one looked best.

Dr. Emily came into the kitchen for a quick cup of coffee. "Thank goodness you're starting those," she said, flicking on the kettle and scooping some instant coffee into her favorite mug. "I thought we might have to telephone everyone this year instead."

"It's all under control, Mom," Mandy assured her. "We're just deciding exactly what to write. Which of these sounds better? "Come and join the party in our spooky lair. Wear a groovy costume, spiders in your hair. That's the first one."

"That was mine," James put in proudly.

"And the second one is: 'Party fright and party shock, party starts at seven o'clock,'" Mandy read. "That's mine."

Dr. Emily took a sip of her coffee. "They're equally great," she said. "Why don't you use them both?"

They all looked around when the phone rang. Mandy was closest so she leaned over and picked up the receiver. It was John Hardy.

"You've got to come over!" he said as soon as Mandy had said hello.

Mandy blinked. "Right now?"

"Yes!" John insisted. "We've just gotten a package from Sara's sister in the States. They take Halloween really seriously there, and she's sent us some great American candy. I want you and James to come over and try it."

Mandy looked at the pile of black cards on the table. "We're supposed to be making the party invitations," she said.

"You can play with Brandy and Bertie, too," John said temptingly. "If you want."

That sealed it. *We can do the invitations later*, Mandy decided.

John didn't wait for Mandy's answer. "See you in fifteen minutes," he said, and put the phone down.

Mandy looked at James, who was staring expectantly at her. "John wants us to go and try these American candies his aunt sent him," she explained.

"Don't be too long," Dr. Emily warned. "The invitations won't make themselves."

"OK, Mom," Mandy said, grabbing her coat. "We'll see you later."

"And don't eat too much of that candy!" her mom called after her as she and James went into the yard to get their bikes. "You haven't had lunch yet!"

Mandy had to admit that it was much easier to ride without Blackie leaping around beside them. The road whizzed past beneath their wheels, and the sharp October air bit at their faces and made their noses red.

"Car!" James warned as they reached the crossroads outside the Fox and Goose. Mandy braked and brought her bike to the side of the road as a large green car drove past. Biscuit the golden retriever was looking out the back window. Mandy caught a glimpse of Matt Burness's face staring out beside the dog, and she raised her hand and waved. But Matt looked away, sullen and unresponsive.

John was waiting impatiently at the door of the Fox and Goose when Mandy and James dismounted. "I thought you'd never get here," he said.

"You only called us ten minutes ago!" Mandy protested.

John sighed. "Well, you're here now," he said. "Come in."

Mandy knew that John didn't mean to sound bossy. He just wasn't very good at chatting. *Sort of like Ms. Greenwood*, she decided.

They followed John around the back of the restaurant to the kitchen, where Sara Hardy was making a large pot of tomato and pepper soup for the lunchtime customers. The smell of warm rolls from the oven made Mandy's stomach rumble.

"Come to try the candy corn?" Sara asked.

Mandy was confused. "The candy what?"

"Candy corn," Sara smiled. "That's what this American candy is called. The box is over there, on the windowsill. Help yourself."

James peered inside the brightly colored box. "They look like little teeth!" he said, picking up a piece of candy corn and examining it.

"They're supposed to look like kernels of corn," John explained. "They're a great color for Halloween, aren't they?"

The candy corn was striped yellow, orange, and white. Mandy took a piece and bit into it. The sweet, fudgy taste was delicious. She closed her eyes, savoring the taste. "Perfect," she agreed. "Your parents can give

them out to trick-or-treaters. Once word gets around, the Fox and Goose will be really popular!"

"Do you want to take some for the party?" John offered.

"Thanks. We can fish them out of the powdered sugar instead of jelly beans," said James happily.

"Are you sure you can spare them?" Mandy asked.

"Oh, please take as many as you like," said Sara, wiping her hands on her apron. "The fewer there are in the house, the fewer I'll be tempted to eat."

"Do you want to come and see Brandy and Bertie?" said John. "I've put them in their run. Come on."

Mandy and James eagerly followed John out to the yard, where Walter Pickard's neighbor Ernie had made a large, roomy run with wire mesh stretched over a wooden frame. Weeds and lettuce leaves lay at one end, and a bowl of drinking water was at the other. Brandy and Bertie were running up and down, munching the leaves, and enjoying the pale October sunshine.

John's eyes shone as he scooped them both into his arms. "I'm sure they missed me," he said confidently. "Imogen looked after them really well, but it's not the same. Is it, guys?" He cuddled the two little rabbits under his chin. "Here, Mandy. You take Brandy," he said generously. "James, you can hold Bertie if you like."

They played with the rabbits, tickling their tummies and petting them while they talked about the party. When a bicycle-shaped shadow fell across the grass, Mandy looked up to see Ms. Greenwood pedaling past, the traveling box still strapped firmly into her basket.

"Ms. Greenwood must have finished her errand," she said, shading her eyes and watching the back of the woman's cape flapping in the wind like the wings of a giant crow. "I hope the badger's OK in that box."

"What badger?" John asked curiously.

Mandy and James told him about Brock while they put the rabbits back into their run.

"And you think she's a witch?" John asked with interest.

"*James* thinks she's a witch," Mandy corrected, laying her cheek on top of Brandy's soft brown head before putting him down next to the lettuce leaves. "I just think she knows a lot about herbs and animals and things like that."

"I bet she is a witch," John mused, shutting the mesh door of the run. He made his voice sound deep and spooky. "I bet she casts spells that make you go —"

"AAAAAHHH!"

A piercing scream echoed around the yard, and they all jumped out of their skins.

"That was Sara!" said John. He turned and ran back inside, with Mandy and James close behind.

In the kitchen, John's stepmother looked like she'd seen a ghost. Her face was white, and she was leaning against the kitchen table with one hand on her chest. "I've just had the scare of my life," she declared when they all rushed in. "Look at the candy corn! I swear it's moving!"

Mandy stared at the box on the windowsill. Sara was right. The candy was rustling and shivered as if it were alive. Then, like a small volcanic eruption, two black ears and a furry black head rose out of the orange-and-yellow candy. A pair of wide orange eyes blinked at them.

Mandy was so surprised she could barely speak. There was a *kitten* in the candy corn!

Five

The kitten tipped its head to one side and looked at its openmouthed audience. Several pieces of candy slid off its head and landed back in the box with a quiet *plop*.

"What on *earth* is a kitten doing in a box of candy?" Sara said at last.

The kitten shook its head and yawned, showing a pale pink mouth and a set of tiny sharp teeth.

"It's gorgeous," Mandy whispered.

"Do you think maybe it came all the way from the United States?" James asked in astonishment.

"The box was taped shut when it arrived," John told him. "A kitten wouldn't have survived the plane trip sealed in a box like that. It must have come through the window a couple of minutes ago." He pointed to the kitchen window, which was open slightly to let out the steam from Sara's soup.

"But the window's practically closed!" said James. "I know cats can squeeze through small spaces, but that's crazy!"

"Not as crazy as coming by mail," Mandy said. She walked slowly over to the box of candy without taking her eyes off the kitten. The little cat stared at her as she approached but didn't try to scramble out or burrow back into the candy corn. Mandy reached carefully into the box and tickled the kitten's head. The jet-black fur was warm and very soft. The kitten closed its eyes and let out a tiny rasping purr. Feeling encouraged, Mandy dug her other hand into the candy and gently lifted out the kitten.

"Now that's what I call a *black* cat," Sara remarked, coming closer to admire the little ball of fur that now sat cradled against Mandy's shoulder. "Look — not a speck of white on him! Or should I say her?"

Mandy looked at the kitten's tummy. "It's a boy," she said. Then she looked over the rest of the kitten, feeling for injuries the way her parents had shown her. There was a long scratch on his shoulder, which Mandy thought was probably a result of squeezing through the narrow window, and he was a little thin, but otherwise he seemed fine. Mandy guessed his age to be about six weeks, just old enough to leave his mother.

"So where did you come from, little fellow?" she asked, nuzzling him.

The kitten wriggled and gave the most extraordinary wailing meow that Mandy had ever heard. It wasn't so much a meow, she decided, as a yowl. Long and loud, it sounded like it should be coming from an animal twice the kitten's size.

"Whoa," said James, stepping back. "That's a spooky noise."

The hairs rose on the back of Mandy's neck as the kitten yowled his deep, mournful sound once again. "It's OK, little pussycat," she murmured. "You're safe with us."

"What's going on in here?" John's father, Julian Hardy, asked as he came into the kitchen. "First a scream, then a wail. Do we have ghosts?"

Mandy held out the kitten. "He just popped out of the candy corn! Isn't he sweet?"

"He's certainly a handsome little fellow," Mr. Hardy said with surprise. "But what's he doing here? He couldn't have come in the box of candy?"

Mandy felt the kitten tense. Before she could react, he sprang out of her arms and dug his tiny black claws into the sleeve of Mr. Hardy's sweater. Quick as a flash, he scrambled up Mr. Hardy's sleeve, ran across his shoulder, and came to rest on the top of his head.

"Wh-wh-," Mr. Hardy spluttered, waving his arms. The kitten clung on like a neat black wig, his ears pricked and his mouth slightly open as if he were laughing.

"Stay still!" Mandy grinned. "You'll frighten him."

"*I'll* frighten *him*?" Mr. Hardy echoed. "What about *me*? I'm not used to being treated as a pole to climb. And — ow! My head's not a pincushion! What are you doing up there?"

The kitten seemed to be enjoying the view and didn't want to come down.

"Take him into the restaurant like that, Dad," John begged, his eyes sparkling with laughter. "See if anyone notices."

Mr. Hardy obediently turned around and walked out of the kitchen. The kitten remained perfectly balanced on his head, crouched and steady. "Hey, does anyone recognize my hat?" Mandy heard Mr. Hardy ask. There was a burst of laughter and she peered through the door to watch what was going on.

It was nearly lunchtime, so the restaurant was almost full. Mr. Hardy stood with the kitten still clinging to his head. Ernie Bell was sitting at a table with a glass of juice in front of him and a broad grin on his face. "Suits you, Julian," he said.

"It's the fashion these days, Ernie," said Mr. Hardy with a grin. He looked upward. "You don't recognize this little fur ball, do you?"

"He's not yours?" Ernie said with surprise.

"Nope," said Mr. Hardy. "He just showed up in the kitchen. Can any of you help?"

Mandy saw people shaking their heads. No one seemed to know where the tiny black kitten had come from.

Suddenly, the kitten got bored. He took a flying leap

from the top of Mr. Hardy's head and landed in a blur of black fur on a table, where he raced up and down and batted at a couple of coasters. His paws shot out from beneath him as he skidded in a small puddle of water. With a look of great surprise on his face, he tried and failed to grip the table with his claws, slid gracefully along the polished wood, off the edge and straight into Ernie Bell's lap, where Ernie caught him like a ball.

"Well!" said Ernie as the laughter subsided, holding the small black cat up close to his face. "You're a feisty one, aren't you?"

The kitten curled up in Ernie's fingers and shut his eyes.

John's dad lifted the kitten out of Ernie's hands and brought him back into the kitchen. "No one out there could help, I'm afraid," he said sympathetically.

Mandy took the kitten from Mr. Hardy, and the huge orange eyes flew open. He yowled his peculiar yowl again as she cuddled him up against her sweatshirt. "It looks like we'll have to take you to Animal Ark," she said.

The kitten stretched and daintily pushed and pulled at Mandy's palms with his claws. Then he shot out of her hands and straight into the pouch at the front of her sweatshirt. Mandy felt him creep into the soft darkness, curl around on himself a couple of times, and settle down.

"You're even wearing your kitten-carrying outfit," Sara observed with a smile. "I'm sure your mom and dad will know what to do." She held out her hands apologetically. "I'm just sorry we can't help."

"Don't worry," said Mandy, putting one hand into her pouch and resting it on the kitten's back. He felt warm and cozy, his breathing quick and light. "We'll work something out."

"Let me hold him, Mandy," John begged. "Just for a minute."

Sara had given them all some soup for lunch since the kitten had seemed happy to stay in Mandy's pouch for a while. Then John insisted on coming back to Animal Ark with Mandy and James. Because of the kitten, Mandy was wheeling her bike with one hand while keeping the other one inside her pouch, petting her sleeping passenger. John was walking beside her, and James was riding as slowly as he could, wobbling precariously as he tried to keep pace with Mandy.

"He's still asleep," Mandy began. "Ouch!" She felt a sudden attack of tiny teeth on her thumb. She instinctively pulled her hand out of her pouch. The kitten came, too, his little body wrapped around her wrist and his teeth biting playfully at the fleshy part of her hand.

"Stop it, you little monkey!" Mandy protested, laughing. She stopped wheeling her bike and gently took hold of the scruff of the kitten's neck to detach him from her hand. He stopped biting at once and hung quietly from her fingers, curled into a tight ball.

"Doesn't that hurt?" John asked anxiously.

"It's how his mother would carry him around," Mandy explained, putting the kitten into John's outstretched palms.

The kitten began to knead vigorously at John's hands, first with one paw and then with the other. John flinched, laughing.

The three friends made their way slowly to Animal Ark, taking turns carrying the kitten. The little black cat was endlessly entertaining. One minute he was completely still, and the next he was scrambling up a sleeve or burrowing under a sweater. It was almost as if he had a tiny switch of energy that flicked on and off in an instant.

At last they walked into the Animal Ark kitchen, where Mandy's parents were clearing away their lunch.

"Wait till you see what we have," Mandy said breathlessly.

Mandy's dad looked wary. "A tarantula?" he asked.

Mandy rolled her eyes. "Where am I going to get a tarantula in Welford?"

"I never know what you're going to produce next, Mandy," her dad replied. "Come on. Show us."

Mandy put her hand carefully into her pocket and took out the kitten. Exhausted from playing most of the way from the Fox and Goose, he had fallen asleep again and didn't move.

"What a darling!" Mandy's mother exclaimed. "Where did you find it?"

"Him," Mandy corrected. "I checked."

"He popped out of a box of candy," John informed them.

Dr. Adam started to say something, then raised his hands. "I won't ask," he said with a grin. "Whose is he?"

"We don't know," Mandy confessed. She quickly explained what had happened at the Fox and Goose.

"We'd better put up a sign in the clinic," said Dr. Emily. "We can see if anyone comes forward when they realize he's missing."

"But did he escape from somewhere, is he lost, or was he abandoned?" Dr. Adam wanted to know. "If it's one of the first two, then maybe there's a chance someone will claim him. But if it's the third . . ."

He didn't need to finish the sentence. With a heavy heart, Mandy knew what he meant. If the kitten had been abandoned, no one was going to claim him and take him back to a loving home. She bent her head and kissed the sleeping kitten between the ears. *How could anyone lose you?* she thought wistfully. *If you were mine, I wouldn't let you out of my sight.*

"May he stay in the residential unit tonight?" she asked.

"Of course," her dad replied. "But you know the rules, Mandy. Tonight, and *only* tonight."

Mandy did know the rules. It was impossible to keep every lost or abandoned animal that came to Animal Ark. It was a rule that seemed really hard at times, but she understood why her parents insisted on keeping it.

The kitten woke up. He opened his eyes very wide at the sight of so many faces peering down at him and started purring loudly.

"He obviously likes people," Dr. Adam said. "That's a good sign."

The kitten gave one of his long, loud yowls.

"That sounds Burmese," Dr. Emily said with surprise, scooping up the kitten and looking closely at him. "The color's wrong, but I bet there's Burmese ancestry somewhere. What do you think, Adam?"

The kitten blinked his wide, jewellike eyes and yowled again.

"He sounds more like a police siren than a Burmese cat," Dr. Adam remarked, looking over his wife's shoulder. "But that would fit with his friendly nature. Burmese cats are very much like dogs in that way — they love to be around people. I haven't seen a Burmese with orange eyes before, though."

"Actually, they can have eyes that color," John said unexpectedly. "I've read about them. They can have any color from green to orange."

The kitten yowled again and struggled.

"He must be hungry," Mandy said. "Can we feed him some of Brock's cat food?"

"He's still very young," said her mom. "I think he'll just need milk for now. Then we'll see if he's still hungry and judge whether or not he needs some solid food as well."

She put the kitten on the floor, where he immediately started chasing his tiny tail. When Mandy set the bowl of warmed milk down beside him, the kitten lapped at it with great concentration, milky droplets trembling on his threadlike whiskers. Then he stopped drinking and gave a huge yawn.

"Up you come," said Mandy, picking up the sleepy kitten and setting him down on a cushion that James had brought from the living room and put on the kitchen table. The kitten curled up with his nose tucked under his tail.

"I could stay here and watch that kitten all day," said

Dr. Emily, smiling. "But we've got work to do. You'll get back to making those invitations now, won't you?"

Mandy had forgotten all about the party invitations since finding the kitten. "Of course," she promised. "There are three of us now, so it won't take long."

John was happy to stay and help and came up with the great idea of carving some potatoes into spooky shapes and using them as stamps. When Mandy asked what they could use for paint, John showed her how to unscrew the end of one of the gold metallic pens and tip out the ink onto a paper plate. Soon they were stamping their black cards with golden ghosts and spiders, trying not to drip the glittering ink on the wooden tabletop.

Mandy was so absorbed in making the invitations that she didn't notice the kitten wake up with a brisk shake of his head and a yawn.

"Uh-oh," said James. "Mandy, you'd better catch him before" — the little black cat jumped down from the cushion and stepped daintily into the paper plate containing the golden ink — "he steps in the ink," James finished.

Mandy reached out to grab the kitten, but she wasn't quick enough. He sprang into the air and landed in a puddle of gold, right in the middle of the table. Then he ran full tilt across the scattered invitations, leaving a trail of tiny golden footprints behind him before bunching up and leaping at the gingham curtains that framed the kitchen window.

"Oh, no!" Mandy said, gasping as she stood up. "Mom's curtains!"

Splidge, splodge — more gold footprints followed the kitten up the curtain and along the top of the curtain rod. Mandy tried to catch the kitten, but he was too quick. He leaped nimbly down from the curtain rod, shot into a saucepan, and then hurtled out again, coming to rest inside the carved pumpkin Mandy had placed on the windowsill a few days earlier. Luckily, there was no candle inside it.

Mandy didn't know whether to laugh or cry. She peered inside the carved pumpkin and saw the kitten staring up at her with his perfect pumpkin-colored eyes.

She turned around and grinned at James and John. "Well, that's one problem solved at least," she said. "I think we should call him Pumpkin. Can you imagine a better name for a Halloween kitten?"

Six

James propped the invitations up on the windowsill so the ink could dry, while Mandy and John cleaned up after Pumpkin as best they could. The gold ink came off the tabletop easily enough, but the curtains were a different matter.

"I'll have to take them down and wash them," Mandy said glumly. "Mom'll be angry otherwise." She glanced at Pumpkin, who was sitting on his cushion and licking himself clean. "You are *trouble*," she said, wagging her finger at the kitten.

Pumpkin yowled, his pale pink tongue glittering faintly with the gold ink he was removing from his paws.

"What are you going to do with him?" John asked.

Mandy sighed. "I'd love to keep him, but Mom and Dad won't let me. So I guess we need to make some posters to put up around town and on the clinic bulletin board."

"Hello! Anyone in?" Mandy's gran came through the kitchen door, carrying an armful of fake fur. "Hello, Mandy, dear," she said, putting the pile of black cloth down on the table. "Here's your costume — oh!" She spotted Pumpkin, who was fast asleep on the cushion. "What a lovely little thing! Where did you find him?"

Mandy explained. Grandma Hope listened and petted the kitten lightly on the head with one finger. Pumpkin didn't move.

"What a shame," she said when Mandy had finished. "Still, I'm sure you'll find his owner soon. Are you using this black paper to make posters?"

"Actually, we've been using that for the party invitations," Mandy said.

"Well, when you finish those, perhaps you can use the rest to make some posters," Gran suggested.

Mandy looked thoughtfully at the pens, glitter, card, and ink scattered over the kitchen table. "We *could* use up the rest of this stuff," she said. "After all, with his black fur and orange eyes, he's a Halloween cat, isn't he?"

"I'll make a potato cutout of a cat, if you like," John offered.

"And we can use the orange glitter for his eyes," added James.

Mandy smiled gratefully. "That would be fantastic," she said. "We can distribute the posters when we deliver the party invitations."

"I'm sure someone will want him," Gran said reassuringly. "He's such a sweet kitten that even if he has been abandoned, you shouldn't have any trouble finding a new home for him."

"I hope not," Mandy said.

"Now then." Gran picked up a long piece of black fur from the pile she had put on the table. "I just need to adjust the fastening for your tail, Mandy. Arms up, like a good girl."

Mandy obediently lifted her arms while her grandmother looped a tape measure around her middle. After a swift adjustment, she put the tail belt around Mandy's waist and fastened it.

"I love it!" Mandy exclaimed, looking over her shoulder at her new black tail. It fit perfectly, curling up at the end just like a real cat's.

"How did you know, Mrs. Hope?" John asked curiously.

Mandy's grandmother turned to look at him, puzzled. "Know what, dear?"

"About Pumpkin," John said. He sounded baffled.

"We just found him today. How did you make Mandy a costume so quickly?"

"I wasn't planning to look like Pumpkin," Mandy said with a grin. "I was going to be Catwoman. But you've given me a great idea, John." She twirled around, and her tail flew out behind her. "From now on, I'm going to be Pumpkin instead!"

The sky was dark and forbidding the following day. Although it wasn't raining, it was the sort of weather where rain looked like it was just around the next corner. Mandy cycled into town with posters inside her sweatshirt, which she had tucked into her jeans to stop the posters from slithering out. James was waiting for her at the post office, ready to take the invitations and posters around to their friends. He had Blackie with him today because they would be cycling slowly with all the posters and invitations to deliver.

Blackie was delighted to see Mandy and wriggled around her legs as she dismounted and leaned her bicycle up against the post office wall.

"No Pumpkin?" James asked.

Mandy reached down and rubbed Blackie behind his shoulders, making him squirm with pleasure. "Pumpkin's keeping Mom and Dad busy today for a change," she said.

James grinned. "I'm glad you weren't late," he said, rubbing his hands together and shivering. "I hate dark days like this. It feels like the middle of the night, and it's only lunchtime. Do you think it'll take long to pass out the posters?"

"I hope not," Mandy said, taking out the first one and smoothing the wrinkles out of it. "I don't want to be out in this weather for long, either."

James tied Blackie up outside the shop. They pushed open the post office door, glad to be out of the cold, and looked around. Mr. McFarlane, who ran the post office, was nowhere to be seen.

"Hello!" Mandy called. "Is anyone here? Mr. McFarlane?"

Mrs. McFarlane appeared at the back of the shop. She was looking uncharacteristically solemn. "You'll find my husband outside," she said. "He's not in the best of moods today. May I help?"

"We were just wondering," Mandy began. Then she paused. "Why is Mr. McFarlane in a bad mood?" she asked cautiously.

Mrs. McFarlane pursed her lips. "Vandals," she said. "They paid us a visit in the night. Scrawled all kinds of rubbish on the wall that my poor husband is having to clean up. Honestly!" She said. "As if we didn't have enough to do."

Mandy thought back to the conversation she'd had with Mrs. Ponsonby and Mrs. Parker Smythe the day that Ms. Greenwood had arrived with the injured badger. First there was the broken flowerpot at the Fox and Goose, and now this. She had an odd, sick sensation in the pit of her stomach, imagining how she'd feel if someone did this at Animal Ark.

The post office door tinkled and Mr. McFarlane came in, looking tired and annoyed. He was holding a bucket of soapy water and a scrub brush, and his shirtfront was wet and dirty. "Please put the kettle on, dear," he said wearily to his wife. "I need a strong cup of tea."

He noticed Mandy and James. "What do you two want?" he asked.

"We're very sorry about the graffiti, Mr. McFarlane," James said.

Mr. McFarlane grunted. "So am I," he said. "I don't suppose you know anything about it, do you?"

Mandy shook her head, hoping her expression wasn't giving anything away. Was it really possible that Matt Burness had something to do with this? The handsome face of Biscuit the golden retriever kept looming in her mind.

"What may I do for you, anyway?" asked Mr. McFarlane, setting down his bucket and brush.

Mandy held out a poster. "We were wondering if we

could put this up on your bulletin board," she said politely. "If it's not too much trouble." She explained about Pumpkin as quickly as she could, while Mr. McFarlane looked at the poster.

"FOUND!" the poster read, its printed gold letters standing out clearly against the black paper. "One black kitten, in need of a good home." Halfway down the poster was a gold potato-stamp of a kitten, with two specks of orange glitter for eyes, followed by Animal Ark's phone number.

"I have more things to worry about than a homeless kitten," Mr. McFarlane grumbled, but he took the poster anyway. "And if you see any brutes hanging around, give them a piece of my mind for me, won't you?" he called after them as they left the shop.

"Poor Mr. McFarlane," said Mandy as they walked toward the Fox and Goose to pick up John.

"I told you Matt Burness was trouble," said James.

"But his dog . . ." Mandy began.

"It's not his *dog* who's been painting walls," James reminded her. "Just because he has a nice dog doesn't mean he's a nice person, Mandy."

Mandy thought about this when they reached the Fox and Goose. She knew James was right, but she felt miserable just the same.

John was waiting for them, stamping his feet in the

cold. "Dad said he'd put a few posters up in the restaurant," he said, walking out to meet Mandy and James on the road. "I know nobody could help last time he asked, but different people come into the place all the time. You never know."

"True," Mandy said, nodding. "Jean let me put two on the bulletin board at Animal Ark. Mom said she'd put up a couple in the town hall at her next yoga class, too. At this rate, we'll get rid of them all really fast!"

They dropped in on Mandy's grandparents at Lilac Cottage first. "We'll take two posters," Mandy's grandpa declared. "One for the front window, and one for the window of the camper. How's that?"

"Thanks, Grandpa," Mandy said. She picked up Smoky, her grandparents' cat, and cuddled him. "Oh, and here's your invitation for Saturday night, too, before I forget."

Mandy's grandmother adjusted her glasses so she could read the invitation out loud. "'Come and join the party in our spooky lair. Wear a groovy costume, spiders in your hair,'" she read. "That sounds marvelous, Mandy. I can't promise any spiders, but we'll dress up a little!"

"We only have two posters left," said James as they walked down the main street toward the church. "Let's put one on the parish bulletin board. Then everyone who comes through town will see it."

Suddenly, Mandy stopped walking. In the park, she could see a group of four boys hanging around the pond.

"Uh-oh," said James, stopping beside her.

Blackie gave a strange growl in the back of his throat as Mandy stepped forward to get a better look at the boys. It was hard to tell in the dull afternoon light, but one of them looked like he was wearing a green baseball cap.

"I think that's Matt Burness," she said, her heart sinking.

James sighed. "Doesn't surprise me," he replied, tucking his chin into the collar of his coat. "Come on, let's go the other way."

There was a splash, followed by a shout. One of the boys had thrown an empty soda can into the pond. The ducks in the middle of the water squawked in alarm, flapping their wings and taking cover on the far side.

"The poor ducks!" Mandy said indignantly. "I'm going to say something."

James caught her arm. "Don't," he pleaded, dragging her back. "I have to see them at school next week. I don't want any trouble."

"They aren't worth bothering with, Mandy," said John. He sounded disgusted. "Let's just do what James says."

Mandy reluctantly followed James and John, looking

back over her shoulder. Matt was talking and laughing with the others and kicking another can along the side of the pond.

They walked on until they reached the woods at the edge of town.

"One more poster to go," said John. "What should we do with it?"

"I thought we could give it to Mrs. Ponsonby," Mandy said. "She invites lots of people to Bleakfell Hall for coffee and things. Come on, we can take the path through the woods."

James looked slightly pale. "Do we have to?"

"What are you worried about, James?" Mandy asked mischievously. "Mrs. Ponsonby or the woods?"

"I'm not worried," James said unconvincingly. "Blackie is."

It was true that Blackie kept close to James as they picked their way along the narrow path under the trees. Dark branches loomed over their heads, cutting off what was left of the dwindling daylight, while shadows stretched down around them, filled with secretive rustlings and the occasional *chack* of a bird.

"Ms. Greenwood lives in these woods somewhere," Mandy said. "I wonder how Brock is?"

James stopped dead. "I wish you hadn't reminded me of that, Mandy," he said nervously.

John's eyes gleamed in the fading daylight. "Where's her house?"

Mandy shrugged. "I don't know exactly."

"She could be watching us now," John whispered. "Dusk is the perfect time for witches."

"Don't talk like that," James said with a shiver. Blackie whined and pressed himself closer to James's legs.

"It's best to be prepared," John went on melodramatically. "Maybe Ms. Greenwood's house scuttles around on little legs so she can follow her victims through the woods and boil her witchy brews at the same time!"

"Don't be silly," Mandy said. Even she was starting to feel scared. "Come on. Bleakfell Hall's just another five minutes farther."

They continued walking, in silence this time. The darkness seemed to press down on them like a thick blanket, and twigs snapped extra loudly under their feet. Mandy was beginning to wish that John would start talking again, when an owl suddenly hooted somewhere above them.

WHO-HOO . . .

Blackie yelped in terror and bolted off the path, his leash tangling around James's legs. James fell over with a crunch and a yell of pain, skidding off the path and into the wet carpet of leaves that littered the forest floor.

Mandy ran over to where he was lying. "Are you OK?" she asked urgently.

James blinked behind his glasses, which were skewed on his nose. "My . . . ankle," he said through gritted teeth.

Blackie came slinking back, his leash trailing through the leaves and his tail tucked between his legs. He started licking James's face apologetically.

"Don't worry, Blackie." Mandy patted the Labrador. "It wasn't your fault."

James heaved himself on his elbows and tried to get up. But he fell back again with another grunt of pain.

"Can you walk?" Mandy asked, concerned.

James shook his head. "Don't think so."

Mandy looked around. The woods was now looking really dark, and she began to feel frightened. James was too heavy to carry back, but they couldn't leave him here. What were they going to do?

Swish. Swish. Swish.

John swung around. "What was that?"

"Just leaves," Mandy said, an icy feeling creeping up her neck.

"You mean, someone walking *through* leaves," James whispered, his eyes round and fearful.

Swish. Swish. The whispery sound was growing louder. Someone was coming. Mandy felt a moment of blind terror as she stared into the trees. It was all she could do not to scream out loud when a tall, dark figure stepped onto the path.

"Dear, dear," said Araminta Greenwood. "Whatever's happened here?"

Seven

Mandy felt faint with relief. "Ms. Greenwood!" she exclaimed. "We were just talking about you!"

Araminta Greenwood's face was unreadable in the darkness. "Yes, I imagine you were," she said drily. She swept her black cape out of the way and knelt down beside James. "What happened to you, young man?" she asked.

James smiled a little nervously. "I hurt my ankle," he said, pointing at his right foot.

Ms. Greenwood felt James's anklebone with firm but gentle fingers. "Hmm," she said, standing up. "No broken bones this time. Nasty sprain, though. Come on. We'll fix you up back at the house."

She suddenly noticed John, who was hanging back in the shadows. "And who are you?" she inquired.

Mandy made the introductions as John stared hard at his feet.

"Pleased to meet you," said Ms. Greenwood, smiling unexpectedly. "You all look frozen half to death. Hot chocolate at the house. Come on."

She lifted James up as if he were a feather, turned her back, and vanished.

"Where did she go?" John asked.

Blackie flung back his head and howled. Ms. Greenwood had been there one minute and was gone the next. It was uncanny.

Mandy grabbed Blackie's leash and ran in what she hoped was the right direction. "Ms. Greenwood?" she called. "Where are you?"

There was a glimmer of yellow-and-red-striped tights as Ms. Greenwood turned around. With her back to Mandy and John, her long black cape had been the perfect camouflage in the dark woods. "The house is right up here," she called. "Follow the light!"

Mandy noticed a faint, ghostly flickering in the trees. It looked like candlelight. She almost laughed out loud, picturing James's face if they'd seen the flickering in the middle of John's spooky storytelling.

"I really thought Ms. Greenwood had vanished just then," John said, panting and appearing beside Mandy.

"Serves you right for telling scary stories," Mandy scolded, with a grin to show she didn't mean it.

They waded on through the damp brown leaves, following an invisible path between the trees until they reached a clearing. In the middle of the clearing sat a neat stone house with a row of carved pumpkins glowing in the windows. Blackie sniffed with interest at the woven willow fence and hazelwood gate that separated the yard of the house from the forest.

Mandy pushed open the gate and stared around at the carefully planted rows of vegetables in the garden and the clumps of fragrant herbs that lined the mossy path. Light flowed like honey through the cracks around Ms. Greenwood's front door, and wood smoke spiraled out of the chimney.

"It's like the gingerbread house in 'Hansel and Gretel,'" said John in a low voice.

"But Ms. Greenwood isn't going to eat us," Mandy pointed out.

"How do *you* know?" John replied darkly.

Ignoring him, Mandy tied Blackie to a heavy boot

scraper that sat on the doorstep, and she pushed open the door.

The house seemed to consist of one large room lit by dozens of candles and a blazing log fire. Herbs and flowers hung drying from the rafters, and misshapen bottles containing leaves and powders lined the long shelves above an old black stove. A tray of warm cookies sat cooling on a wire rack next to it. Ms. Greenwood was stoking the fire, and the flames leaped merrily upward. Mandy couldn't help thinking that it was the perfect witch's house. There was even a pot that looked like a small cauldron hanging on a hook over the fireplace.

John stopped dead on the doorstep and looked wide-eyed at the cauldron.

"Don't be scared," said Ms. Greenwood. She looked smaller and less forbidding without her cape. "Come in and have a cookie."

John sidled in and sat down next to James, who was lying on a long, low sofa. He looked uncertainly at the cookies.

Ms. Greenwood gave a brisk, barking laugh. "They won't poison you," she said. "Mandy? How about you?"

The cookie was warm and chewy, with an odd taste that Mandy couldn't quite identify. "Delicious," she said gratefully. "What's in it?"

"Spiced nettle," Ms. Greenwood said. "My own recipe."

John cautiously helped himself to a cookie. He took a tiny nibble, and then another. Before long, the cookie had disappeared.

Ms. Greenwood straightened up from the fire. "Mandy," she said, "I'm going to need some comfrey for James's ankle. It's growing underneath the window. Could you pick some for me?"

She swung the cauldronlike pot over the fire on its cleverly rotating hook and poured in several ladles of water from a small barrel beside the log pile.

"What does comfrey look like?" Mandy asked.

"Sturdy little thing with gray-green, spearlike leaves. You can't miss it."

After hunting around, Mandy found the comfrey growing in a sheltered corner under the window. She carefully picked a handful of the thick, slightly furry leaves and went back inside, where the warm smell of cookies had been replaced by the distinctive smell of boiling cabbage. Mandy couldn't help wrinkling her nose as she gave Ms. Greenwood the leaves.

"Cabbage and comfrey," Ms. Greenwood explained, noticing Mandy's expression. She stirred the leaves into the pot. "It'll help to bring down the swelling. Country folk don't call comfrey 'knitbone' for nothing."

When the mixture was ready, Ms. Greenwood ladled

the steaming comfrey and cabbage poultice onto a clean woolen cloth and placed it gently on James's ankle.

"That's amazing," James said after a minute. "It feels better already." He wiggled his toes experimentally and winced.

"It won't heal all at once," Ms. Greenwood warned. "But it's a good start."

There was a strange shuffling sound in the corner of the room, and a squat furry figure waddled into view.

"Brock!" Mandy exclaimed in delight. "I didn't know you were there."

The badger sniffed the air with a funny, nodding motion and shuffled around a little more. John, who hadn't seen a badger close up before, was almost speechless with amazement, and Mandy noticed that he lifted his feet off the floor as if Brock might nibble at his toes.

"How is Brock doing, Ms. Greenwood?" asked James.

"Very well." Ms. Greenwood poured out four cups of hot chocolate. "He got used to the cast very quickly. He's out most of the time, hunting as best he can in the garden, but he likes to come in now and then."

"Does he sleep here?" John asked, his eyes fixed wonderingly on the wild animal.

"On and off," Ms. Greenwood replied. She handed out the hot chocolate. Mandy took hers gratefully and cupped it between her hands. The heat spread through her fingers and up her arms, warming her all over.

Araminta Greenwood settled herself comfortably in a shabby green armchair beside the fire and regarded her visitors. "So," she said, "had you planned this visit, or did our paths simply cross by chance?"

"We were on our way to give this to Mrs. Ponsonby," Mandy said. She pulled the remaining poster from beneath her sweatshirt, straightened it out, and showed it to Ms. Greenwood, who read it thoughtfully.

"Kitten, eh?" she remarked. "Never liked cats myself. I've always found them to be rather selfish creatures."

"That depends on the cat!" Mandy protested. "There are as many different kinds of cats as there are people. Like Burmese or Siamese cats — they are really friendly and sociable, more like dogs in some ways. I'm sure you could find a cat to suit you, Ms. Greenwood."

"Hmm." Ms. Greenwood sounded unconvinced. "How do you happen to have this kitten, anyway?"

"It's a really sad story," Mandy began.

Craaaa! A horrible, hoarse screech filled the room from somewhere up in the chimney. Mandy jumped to her feet, her hands over her ears. James almost fell off the sofa, while John gave a yell and spilled half his hot chocolate on his sweater.

"Wh-what was that?" Mandy stammered.

"That's just Cor," Ms. Greenwood said calmly, refilling her mug from the pot. "He's no nightingale, but he doesn't mean any harm."

"Who is Cor?" James asked.

Ms. Greenwood smiled. "He's a crow. Cor's short for his Latin name, *Corvus*. He fell out of his nest and broke his wing as a youngster, and I rescued him." She nodded out the window. "He's never really gotten the hang of flying and lives outside in a hutch. He's a noisy old thing, but we get along just fine."

Another jarring screech floated down the chimney.

"That must be what Mrs. Ponsonby heard," Mandy said. "That time when she was walking her dogs in the woods. No wonder she thinks you're a witch, Ms. Greenwood!" She clapped her hand to her mouth in dismay, wondering if she'd sounded very rude.

Ms. Greenwood reached for a nettle cookie. "I know my reputation," she said matter-of-factly. "Tell you the truth, it suits me. Never cared much for company. Folks leave me alone, and I like it that way."

It was really dark now, and Mandy could barely see the trees outside. Her mom and dad would be worried. "Excuse me, Ms. Greenwood," she said, "but may I use your phone? It's getting late, and I should call my parents."

"Haven't got a telephone, I'm afraid," Ms. Greenwood apologized. "Never needed one."

Mandy's face fell. How were they going to get home? They didn't have their bikes, and James couldn't walk.

Ms. Greenwood saw her concern. "Why don't you borrow my bicycle and go get your parents?" she suggested. "There's a helmet and some lights by the door. The bicycle is outside, by the gate."

"OK," said Mandy, making up her mind. "It'll take me about ten minutes to ride to Animal Ark. I'll get Mom or Dad to come here in the Land Rover."

John looked nervous at the prospect of being left behind with Ms. Greenwood. James didn't look very happy, either. Mandy smiled encouragingly at them. "I won't be long," she promised.

Outside, she glanced hopefully around the garden for Cor, but the crow was nowhere to be seen. Ms. Greenwood fitted the lights to the bike and showed Mandy how the brakes worked. Then she handed her a helmet.

"Go carefully now," she advised. "The path is rough. And don't worry about your friends. We'll be fine until you get back." Her eyes twinkled. "Though it's clear that they expect me to eat them as soon as you've gone!"

Mandy was out of the woods within five minutes, feeling very relieved at how easily Ms. Greenwood's bike negotiated the ruts and puddles on the muddy path. It wasn't long before she was pedaling into town. Steering the bike carefully, she swung around the corner by the park and almost ran straight into Matt Burness, who was standing by the side of the road.

Mandy swerved and put her leg down to stop herself from falling off the bike.

Matt Burness stepped forward. "Are you OK?" he said, sounding concerned.

Matt's friends appeared behind him. "Who's this, Matt?" The tallest of the three boys looked Mandy up and down. His dark, deep-set eyes were unfriendly. "Your girlfriend?"

Matt stepped back from Mandy as if he'd been stung.

"I know that bike!" exclaimed one of the others, a stocky blond boy with a pimple on his chin. "That crazy witch was riding it yesterday!"

The tall boy's eyes narrowed. "It belongs to the witch?"

Mandy glared at him. "She's not a witch," she said.

"She's not a witch," the boy mocked, imitating Mandy's voice. His friends laughed. Matt laughed, too, but quietly, as if he felt uncomfortable. "You must be a friend of hers if you're defending her," the tall boy continued. "We don't like the witch." He leaned forward and thrust his face aggressively toward Mandy. "She's someone who should keep her opinions to herself."

It sounded as if Ms. Greenwood had told the boys off the day before. Mandy felt glad.

"We don't like the witch," the boy continued, "so I guess we don't like *you*." He grabbed one of the gleaming red handlebars of the bike. "Nice bike, though," he added slyly.

"Get out of my way," Mandy snapped. She tried to push past the boys, but they laughed and grabbed at the handlebars. Matt joined in, but Mandy noticed that he avoided her eyes.

Suddenly, two bright headlights swung around the corner. The boys blinked and shielded their eyes. The tall ringleader leaned toward Mandy and hissed, "We know where that witch lives, you know. Tell her to expect a visit from us sometime soon!"

Then they all melted into the darkness as Dr. Adam's Land Rover noisily, wonderfully, rolled up beside Mandy.

Eight

"Dad!" Mandy exclaimed. She'd never been so happy to see anyone in her life.

Dr. Adam opened the Land Rover door and stepped into the road. "Where on earth have you been, Mandy?" he asked. Then he frowned. "And who were those boys?"

"I'll tell you later," Mandy replied. "Come on. We've got to go to Ms. Greenwood's. James has hurt his ankle."

She told her dad the whole story while he loaded the bike into the back of the Land Rover. "Ms. Greenwood's house is incredible," she confided, climbing into the passenger seat. "She even has a pet crow living there!"

"Ms. Greenwood is a law unto herself," her dad agreed.

Just then the glove compartment gave a familiar, yowling meow.

"Is that Pumpkin?" Mandy asked with surprise. She bent down to peer into the open glove compartment and was amazed to see the little kitten curled up on a pair of thick woolen gloves.

"Ah," said her dad, shifting gears as he swung off the road and onto the muddy forest track. "My stowaway has woken up. I was on my way to High Point Farm when he popped up on the backseat. He gave me the scare of my life! He disappeared earlier, and we spent ages trying to find him." He looked down at the kitten, who was stumbling around in Mandy's hands and making her laugh. "It was too late to take him home, so I put him in the glove compartment."

Mandy saw the glimmer of a chocolate bar wrapper lurking under the gloves. "And that's not all you put in the glove compartment!" she exclaimed. "Chocolate, Dad? What about your diet?"

"I need extra energy on cold evening calls," her dad protested. "Don't tell Mom, will you?"

They drove up to Ms. Greenwood's house, and Dr. Adam turned off the engine. The sudden quiet made Pumpkin yowl, so Mandy tucked him quickly into her sweatshirt pouch. She felt the kitten curl around and around several times before settling down for another snooze.

Soon they were all inside, eating Ms. Greenwood's nettle cookies while Mandy told everyone about the boys in town.

"It's disgraceful!" Dr. Adam exclaimed. "Who are their parents? I've a good mind to have a word with them."

"The ringleader sounds like Adam Poole," said James, frowning. "The blond one you described is his sidekick, Ben Stevens. And I'd guess the third one is Liam Collins. They always hang around with Matt at school, making trouble."

"They recognized your bike, Ms. Greenwood," Mandy said, turning to her. "Did you speak to them yesterday?"

"I certainly did," Ms. Greenwood replied. "The wretches were throwing cans at the ducks on the pond. I told them what I thought of their behavior."

"I don't like the sound of that threat they made about paying you a visit," Dr. Adam said.

Ms. Greenwood gave a dismissive snort. "They don't scare me."

Mandy's dad checked his watch. "We should take James and that ankle to see Dr. Mason tonight. We'll catch him if we hurry." He looked around the room.

"And on the subject of injured legs, how is Brock the badger?"

As if in answer to his question, two bright eyes and a striped snout appeared around the side of Ms. Greenwood's armchair. Mandy felt the same thrill of excitement that she'd had two days earlier when Brock had come to the clinic. *I'll never get tired of looking at him,* she thought.

"He's getting better," Ms. Greenwood replied. She stood up and moved to the other side of the fire so the badger wouldn't feel too crowded. He shuffled out from behind the armchair and blinked shortsightedly at them all before heading for a bowl of cat food beside the front door.

Mandy felt a twitch in her sweatshirt pocket. Pumpkin had woken up. "Ms. Greenwood?" she said hesitantly, remembering what Araminta had said about not liking cats. "Do you remember the kitten on our poster?"

"Of course," Ms. Greenwood replied, looking surprised at the question.

Mandy pulled Pumpkin gently from her pocket. Surely Ms. Greenwood would change her mind about cats when she saw how cute the kitten was. "Well," she said, "here he is."

She held Pumpkin out for Ms. Greenwood to admire, but the woman made no move to pet the kitten's soft black fur. "Very nice," she said briskly, "if you like cats."

A little crestfallen, Mandy started to put Pumpkin back in her pocket. But the kitten was in the mood for adventure. He took a flying leap from Mandy's hands and landed in the middle of Ms. Greenwood's rug, where he energetically attacked a loose thread with his claws.

"Don't let him anywhere near Brock," Ms. Greenwood warned. "A kitten would make a fine supper for a hungry badger."

As if in slow motion, Mandy saw the badger shuffling back to his place behind the armchair. Pumpkin looked at the passing badger with interest and pounced on his tail.

Brock whipped around, his jaws wide open. The kitten jumped sideways just in time, his stubby tail bristling with terror. John tried to grab him as he whisked by, but he was off across the sofa and up the curtains in a flash. He flew from the curtain rod to the fringed lampshade that hung from the ceiling, dug his claws tightly into the faded silk shade, and yowled with fear and misery.

"Oh!" Mandy cried in dismay. She reached for

Pumpkin, but the lampshade was just out of reach. Seeing the kitten swinging there with terror in his eyes
made Mandy feel awful. *He's still so young*, she thought
unhappily. *He should be with his mother.* What was she
going to do if no one claimed him? The little cat needed
a good home — not just a pocket in Mandy's sweatshirt
or a cage at the Welford Cat Rescue Center.

Ms. Greenwood calmly reached up and plucked the
coal-black kitten from the lampshade as if she were
picking an apple from a tree. "That was close, little cat,"
she said, petting the trembling kitten with one finger.
"Perhaps that will teach you a few manners. Badgers
don't like to be toyed with."

Pumpkin yowled pathetically and tried to burrow
into Ms. Greenwood's large, furry sweater. Against the
black wool, the only part of the kitten that was visible
were his blazing orange eyes.

"That's quite a noise," Ms. Greenwood remarked.
"Burmese ancestry, I guess." She detached the kitten
from her sweater and held him at arm's length, looking
genuinely interested in Pumpkin for the first time since
Mandy had taken him out of her pouch.

Mandy felt a little more cheerful at the sight of the
kitten settling down in Ms. Greenwood's arms. Maybe if
no one claimed Pumpkin, Ms. Greenwood could take
him and look after him, like she looked after Cor and

Brock. *Except,* said a nagging voice in her head, *Ms. Greenwood doesn't like cats. Remember?*

"We found him at the Fox and Goose at lunchtime yesterday," she explained, resolutely pushing away any thoughts of matchmaking. "We think maybe he escaped from somewhere. But so far, no one in town can tell us a thing."

Ms. Greenwood frowned. "Did you find him around twelve o'clock? I seem to remember seeing a car waiting by the restaurant when I was in town. There was the sound of a car door opening and shutting, but no one got out. Then the car drove off. It was strange. If they were abandoning a kitten, it makes a little more sense. What do you think?"

Mandy closed her eyes as Ms. Greenwood's words sank in. It was suddenly horribly clear that Pumpkin wasn't lost at all. He had been deliberately abandoned — and a hundred posters weren't going to find an owner who didn't want to be found.

Mandy was very quiet as Dr. Adam drove them all back through the woods and into town. She kept thinking about what her dad had said back at Ms. Greenwood's house, about Pumpkin's owners. *They wouldn't be from around here, and having gone to the trouble of abandoning him, they certainly won't be taking him back*. She put her hand into her pocket and rested it on the sleeping kitten. It was a horrible feeling, knowing the friendly little cat was unwanted.

Dr. Adam had called the clinic from his cell phone, so Dr. Mason was expecting them.

In the examining room, Dr. Mason looked disbelievingly at James's ankle. "You say you only did this three hours ago?"

James nodded.

"There isn't much swelling," said the doctor with a frown. "I would have expected this whole area here to be bruised and puffy."

"Ms. Greenwood's comfrey and cabbage poultice must have helped," Mandy offered.

Dr. Mason's brow cleared. "Ah! Comfrey, the healer's favorite. That explains it." He cleaned James's ankle and bound it tightly with an elastic bandage. "You'll need crutches for a week or so," he continued, "but I'm not very concerned."

"Crutches!" James said in dismay. "But I'm going to the Halloween party as Harry Potter! I'll look really stupid."

Dr. Mason produced a pair of crutches from a tall closet beside his desk. "Better to be safe than sorry," he said, passing the crutches to James.

James rolled his eyes and reluctantly took the crutches from the doctor's hands.

"How about making them part of your costume?" John suggested.

"How?" James scoffed, peering at the crutches in disgust. "By turning them into giant wands?"

"That's not a bad idea," Mandy said.

Pumpkin chose that moment to pop his head out of Mandy's pocket and yowl, as if in agreement with Mandy's suggestion.

"I've never had a kitten come to my office before," Dr. Mason remarked, bending down to take a good look at Pumpkin. "He looks like a cat I used to have. Smudge was his name. Lovely nature."

"Would you like him, Dr. Mason?" Mandy asked eagerly. "We need to find him a home."

Dr. Mason smiled and shook his head. "I'm afraid Jigsaw and Puzzle would never forgive me," he said.

Jigsaw and Puzzle were Dr. Mason's pet rats. Mandy sighed and sank back into her seat. It had been worth a try.

James was still looking at the crutches, considering how to make them part of his costume. "I could make them look like wands by wrapping them up with black crepe paper, I suppose," he said.

Mandy forced herself to stop thinking about the kitten. "You could wrap the tips in silver foil," she suggested. "It'll look great, James. Really original."

James stood up and made a few hops with the crutches tucked under his arms. "OK, they aren't too bad," he conceded. He hopped a little farther. "In fact, they're kind of cool. I'll be the most unusual Harry Potter Welford's ever seen, that's for sure!"

The next day, Mandy met John at the Fox and Goose. They were going to visit James at his house to see if his ankle was any better.

John produced a bag of candy corn as they walked through town. "I thought James might like some of this," he said.

Seeing the candy corn made Mandy think of Pumpkin. She sighed, wondering for the hundredth time what they were going to do with the kitten. She'd managed to persuade her parents to let her keep him a little longer, just until she could work out what to do about finding a home for him. But she knew she had to do something quickly.

"Thinking about Pumpkin?" said John, glancing at her.

Mandy nodded. "I can't think of anyone who might take him in," she said sadly. "I've found homes for so many cats that everyone in Welford's got one now. What am I going to do?"

"Did you hear from anyone who saw the posters yesterday?" John asked.

"No," said Mandy. "But I wasn't that surprised after what Ms. Greenwood told us about the car outside the Fox and Goose. When someone abandons a kitten, they don't usually call up and confess." She looked at John. "You don't want a cat, do you?"

"It's hard enough being separated from Brandy and Bertie when I'm away at school, without having a cat, too," John pointed out.

Mandy dug her hands deep into her pockets. "I guess you're right," she said glumly. "At this rate, I'm going to have to take Pumpkin to the Cat Rescue Center in Walton. They're really nice there and everything, but . . ." She trailed off.

"I know," John said sympathetically. "It's not the same as having a good home, is it? Cheer up, Mandy. I'm sure we'll work something out."

Ahead of them, a boy was riding a red bike up and down the road. Mandy frowned. "Isn't that Ms. Greenwood's bike?" she said, shading her eyes to get a better look.

"You'd know better than me," John said. "You're the one who rode it yesterday."

"It *is* Ms. Greenwood's," Mandy said slowly. "I'm sure

of it." A cold feeling swirled around in her stomach. "And that's Adam Poole riding it."

The tall boy she'd seen the previous day swung the bike around and yanked it up onto its rear wheel. There was a shout of encouragement from his friends, who were gathered around the pond again.

"How come he's got it?" John said, frowning.

"He must have taken it," said Mandy. "He must have gone to Ms. Greenwood's last night after we left, like he threatened. Oh, John! We've got to go and see if she's OK!"

"What about James?"

"James can wait," Mandy said urgently. "Ms. Greenwood can't. Come on!"

She started running down the road toward the woods, with John close behind her. Awful thoughts raced through her mind with every step. Was their new friend all right? What else had Adam Poole and his gang taken? She ran, full of terrified energy, hoping that Ms. Greenwood wasn't hurt and vowing that she'd never give Matt Burness the benefit of the doubt again.

Mandy's legs were almost giving out when she turned off the muddy path and stumbled up to the house. She burst into the living room, fearing the worst.

Araminta Greenwood was sitting by her fire, looking pale but calm. "Thought you might show up," she said abruptly. "Must say I'm glad you have. It's good to see a friendly face."

John ran into the house behind Mandy, red-faced and wheezing, and leaned against the door to get his breath back.

"Are you all right, Ms. Greenwood?" Mandy asked, holding her hands to her aching sides. "We saw Adam Poole riding your bike. We came as quickly as we could."

Ms. Greenwood waved her hand out the window. "They've made a mess of my garden," she said. "And I can't find Brock anywhere. But I'm all right. Not hurt or anything."

Mandy looked out the window and was dismayed to see that the neat beds of comfrey and willow herb, parsley, and rosemary had been dug up and the plants flung around as if there had been a small whirlwind. And Brock! When she thought of the injured badger hiding somewhere, scared and upset by Ms. Greenwood's night visitors, she felt dizzy with rage.

Ms. Greenwood poured Mandy and James two cups of chamomile tea. "Have some of this," she said. "It'll calm you down."

Drinking tea was the last thing Mandy felt like doing.

Instead, she wanted to run back to town and shake Adam Poole until his teeth fell out. But she took the mug and tried to calm down.

"John and I can help find Brock," she said. "And we'll help you clean up the yard, too. Oh, Ms. Greenwood, I'm so sorry this happened. I feel like it's my fault."

Araminta Greenwood shook her head. "Nonsense," she said. "Those boys wanted revenge after our little argument the other day. They'd have come whether you'd met them in town yesterday or not." She put her chamomile tea down. "Now let's see if we can find Brock. He couldn't have gone far."

Mandy was glad to have something to do to take her mind off Matt Burness and his friends. She and John scoured the yard, hunting behind the woodpile and under the hedges, but there was no sign of the badger. Mandy tried not to think about the dangers of the forest for an injured animal.

A young crow swooped down and landed clumsily in her path. Cocking its black head, it appeared to wink at her before shuffling from one foot to the other and flapping its wings noisily.

"You must be Cor," Mandy said in delight, forgetting her anxiety for a minute. She reached out her hand, but Cor shuffled backward, gave a harsh croak, and took off again, flapping hard to get off the ground. Mandy looked up to see the crow circling overhead, almost as if he was helping them search for the badger. He really was a very inept flier. She immediately felt more cheerful at the thought of an extra pair of eyes and turned back to the task.

But even with Cor's help, Brock was nowhere to be found.

"Did you look in here as well as outside, Ms. Greenwood?" John asked when he and Mandy went back inside.

The woman nodded. "Though my mind may not have been on it," she admitted. "Perhaps it's worth another look."

They all looked up as an odd shuffling sound came from a tall cupboard beside the stove.

Ms. Greenwood's brow cleared. "He's in the pantry!" she exclaimed.

Mandy ran over and gently pulled the door open. At first she couldn't see anything in the darkness. But after a few moments she made out a striped snout, covered with cookie crumbs.

"How did he ever get in there?" asked Araminta Greenwood, perplexed. "I haven't been in there since yesterday."

"It must have closed after him," John guessed.

"Maybe he never even saw the vandals. Maybe he just got locked in!"

Brock blinked at them all before returning to the cookies scattered on the floor.

Mandy laughed with relief. "What a smart badger," she said. "If you're going to get locked in anywhere, where could be better than a cupboard full of food?"

Nine

The next morning dawned bright and frosty. Perched on a stool in the kitchen, Mandy reached across the table and selected an apple from the fruit bowl. Pumpkin was sleeping peacefully in her lap, tired out after an energetic game of chasing his tail. Looking down at him, Mandy felt her heart ache. He trusted her to find him a new home, and she knew she was letting him down.

"When's Ms. Greenwood coming to borrow your bike, Mom?" she asked.

"She was going to call from town this morning," replied Dr. Emily, checking her watch. "She'll probably be here soon. I can't believe those boys stole her bike and she didn't report it!"

Mandy crunched into her apple. "She said she didn't want to involve the police," she explained between mouthfuls. "We made her promise to get a cell phone, though. She was going to get one in Walton today, so she can call us if anything like that ever happens again."

"I'm sure James was sorry to miss all the drama," Dr. Emily commented.

"He was," Mandy replied. "But I called him last night and told him everything."

"Poor Ms. Greenwood," Dr. Emily said, and sighed. "Those boys need to be taught a lesson, picking on an elderly woman that way." She glanced at Mandy and frowned. "Don't eat any more apples, Mandy. Those are for tonight's apple bobbing!"

"Sorry." Mandy blushed and put the second apple back in the bowl. "I wasn't thinking."

Dr. Emily took her white coat down from its peg and put it on. "And on the subject of thinking," she said, looking meaningfully at Pumpkin.

"I know," Mandy said guiltily. "I'm going to take him around town today and show him off. The personal touch always works better than just a poster. Someone's going to want him." She said this with more conviction than she felt.

"Well, I hope they do," Dr. Emily replied as kindly as she could. "But if you can't find anyone today, then we have to take Pumpkin to the Cat Rescue Center first thing tomorrow. Understood?"

Mandy nodded reluctantly, feeling very glum. She had been successful in the past finding homes for animals, especially cats, but it looked as if this was going to be her first failure. She gently put the sleeping kitten down on his cushion and followed her mother into the waiting room.

Mrs. Ponsonby looked up as they entered. "Dr. Emily!" she exclaimed. "Pandora's toenail is much better, thanks to your husband's marvelous ministrations the other day."

Dr. Emily smiled. "I'm so glad, Mrs. Ponsonby. We'll take a look under that dressing in just a moment and see if it needs changing."

"Excuse me, Dr. Emily," said Jean, looking up from the appointment book. "I have a message here for you. Now, where did I put it?"

Mandy and her mother waited patiently as Jean hunted around for her notepad. Jean was famous for losing things — the appointment book had been found two days earlier underneath a pile of flea-prevention pamphlets.

"Ah, here it is." Jean adjusted her glasses. "Ms. Greenwood called from the phone booth to say she'd arrive at eight-thirty. She should be here any moment."

"Ms. Greenwood again," said Mrs. Ponsonby with a sniff. "I would advise you to have nothing more to do with that strange woman, Dr. Emily. I heard those awful, screeching noises near her cottage again the other day. It sounded like" — she lowered her voice — "like some poor creature being *tortured*."

Mandy was about to explain about Cor when all at once a familiar screech filled the air.

"Oh!" Mrs. Ponsonby squeaked in horror. "That's the noise! That's the awful noise I heard in the woods!"

Ms. Greenwood filled the door of the clinic. Her cape swirled around her orange-and-black-striped legs, and Cor the crow was sitting on her shoulder.

"Ms. Greenwood! You've brought Cor!" Mandy exclaimed in delight.

"He didn't want to be left behind," Ms. Greenwood explained. "I hope he won't make a nuisance of himself."

Pandora the Peke gave a frightened yelp at the sight of the black crow. Mrs. Ponsonby glared at Ms. Greenwood. "Your bird is frightening my poor girl," she said imperiously.

Cor cocked his head to one side and made a chirping noise. Pandora stopped yelping and began to look interested instead. Then she gave a sharp yip and tipped her head playfully to one side. Mrs. Ponsonby's words died on her lips as Cor chirped again and Pandora yipped back. It looked for all the world as though the two animals were having a conversation.

Mrs. Ponsonby found her voice at last. "W-well," she stuttered. "Well, I . . . Goodness me, they seem to like each other!"

"Cor's a friendly fellow," Ms. Greenwood said, smiling. "When you get to know him."

Mrs. Ponsonby gave the woman a curious look, half ashamed and half impressed. Pandora squirmed in Mrs. Ponsonby's arms as Cor fluffed out his wings and looked pleased with himself.

Harmony at Animal Ark, Mandy thought happily.

Out of the corner of her eye, she saw an apple roll slowly through the door to the kitchen. Half a second later, Pumpkin flew after it, paws outstretched and whiskers quivering. Pandora jumped out of Mrs. Ponsonby's arms in a frenzy of barking as soon as she saw the kitten, which made Cor screech and fly up into the air, wings flapping madly.

Dr. Emily bent down and picked up the mischievous kitten. "We have to find you a new home before you drive us all crazy!" she said, and chuckled.

Mandy couldn't bring herself to join in the laughter. A new home for Pumpkin still felt as far away as the moon.

After morning clinic hours, Mandy tucked Pumpkin into her sweatshirt pouch, put on her jacket, and went outside to meet John. They walked happily down the road to Lilac Cottage, where Mandy's grandparents lived.

Dorothy and Tom Hope were delighted to see them. After a cup of hot chocolate and several of Dorothy's homemade ginger cookies, Mandy took a deep breath, put her hand into her pocket, and pulled out Pumpkin. The kitten promptly woke up with a vigorous shake of his head.

"Oh, you've brought that sweet little kitten!" Mandy's grandmother exclaimed. "Imagine taking him on a walk with you!"

"It's not exactly a walk," Mandy replied, trying to choose her words carefully. "You see, we need to find Pumpkin a home, so I thought we'd take him around town and see if anyone wanted him."

Tom Hope picked up the kitten in his big hands and cradled him there for a moment. He glanced at Mandy, understanding in his eyes. "And you hoped maybe we'd consider it?"

"Would you?" Mandy said, her words suddenly tumbling out in a rush. "He'd be no trouble. Well," she amended, "all kittens are a bit of trouble, but it would be worth it, don't you think? I'd love it if he went to someone in the family."

Pumpkin yawned so widely that they were given a full view of his pink, ridged mouth and delicate tongue. Dorothy Hope laughed and looked across at her husband. "He is very sweet, Tom," she said. "Do you think that maybe we could?"

Tom Hope put Pumpkin down on the sofa, where the

kitten immediately attacked a tassel on a cushion. Within moments the tassel was torn to shreds, bits of silk thread strewn across the sofa.

"He certainly has a taste for your cushions," Mandy's grandfather observed humorously. "Yes, I suppose we could consider it."

Mandy half rose from her seat in delight, but her grandfather put his hand in the air. "But there is someone we have to ask first," he said. "Smoky may have a very different opinion on the subject. And we have to be fair, Mandy. Smoky was here first."

On cue, Smoky stalked into the living room and spotted the kitten. Mandy held her breath as the older cat's tail began to bristle. *Oh, Smoky, please give Pumpkin a chance,* she thought, crossing her fingers as tightly as she could.

Smoky started growling at the back of his throat and stepped stiffly toward the kitten. Pumpkin yowled with fright and backed deep into the sofa cushions. Smoky continued growling, his eyes fixed on the kitten. When Mandy's grandfather picked Pumpkin up and put him on the floor in front of Smoky, the older cat's growling got louder. Pumpkin batted a tentative paw, inviting Smoky to play. But Smoky only narrowed his eyes and angrily twitched his tail.

Pumpkin pounced in an instant and latched onto

Smoky's tail. With a yowl of outrage, Smoky lashed out with his claws, making Pumpkin shoot under the sofa in terror.

Dorothy Hope met Mandy's eyes. "It won't work, dear," she said, bending down to pick up Smoky. "Your grandpa's right. Smoky was here first. It just wouldn't be fair to make him share his home with another cat. I'm so sorry."

John had managed to coax Pumpkin out from beneath the sofa and was now trying to soothe the frightened kitten.

Mandy felt crushed with disappointment. "I understand," she said, standing up. "Thanks for considering it. And thanks for the cookies, Gran."

Walking back into the center of Welford with John, she realized just how much she had been counting on her grandparents to adopt the kitten. She couldn't think of a single other person who might take Pumpkin in. The situation was getting desperate.

Pumpkin was half inside the neck of John's sweatshirt, his face peeking out over the top. It would have made Mandy laugh if she'd been in a better mood. "Let's go and see James," John suggested. "He needs cheering up, and so do we. And you never know. Together we might think of something."

*　　*　　*

"About time!" James exclaimed, looking up from a mound of black crepe paper and glitter when Mandy put her head around the kitchen door. "I thought you were never coming." He gestured at the crepe paper. "I've been decorating my crutches. What do you think?"

Pumpkin wriggled out of John's sweatshirt and took a flying leap into the crunchy crepe paper, where he landed with a springy-sounding thump. Like Ms. Greenwood and her cape in the woods two nights earlier, he was almost perfectly camouflaged in the paper, only his bright orange eyes giving him away.

Soon Pumpkin was clowning around, playing with the edges of the paper with his sharp little teeth and making them all laugh. *It's hard to feel worried with that kitten around*, Mandy thought, breathless from trying to catch the tumbling scrap of black fur. She knew they should be planning what to do with Pumpkin, but her mood had lifted so much that she felt completely confident everything was going to work out just fine.

Blackie trotted in from the kitchen to investigate the noise. He took one look at Pumpkin and barked eagerly, leaping forward to play. Caught off guard, Pumpkin tumbled helplessly onto his back. John grabbed Blackie's collar and pulled him backward just in time as Pumpkin scrambled back onto his paws. Mandy picked the kitten up and cuddled him, whispering soothing words.

Sheepishly, James took Blackie from John. "Sorry, guys," he apologized. "Blackie doesn't realize how big he is. He was only trying to play."

Mandy planted one more kiss on Pumpkin's head and tucked him safely into her pouch. "I'm sure Pumpkin wanted to play, too," she said. "He reminds me of a puppy sometimes, the way he wants to join in with everything. Don't worry about it, James. It's probably time for us to keep on walking, anyway."

"May I come?" James asked hopefully. "Blackie could use the walk, and I need to practice on my crutches."

Mandy reached over and punched her friend gently on the arm. "You don't have to ask!" she said. "Of course you may. We have to go to the store at the post office to pick up supplies for tonight's party. We could use an extra pair of hands, even if they do have crutches attached!"

Mr. McFarlane had already put the Hopes' party order into several shopping bags by the time they got to the post office, so all Mandy had to do was arrange who was going to carry what.

"James, you take the heavy ones — the lemonade and fruit juices," she instructed. "We can loop the bags over your crutch handles. That will save them from cutting into your hands."

James tried hopping across the shop with the shopping bags and found that the best method was to swing the crutches a little more than usual. He picked up speed as he neared the door and managed to stop just before cannoning into a stack of baked beans.

"You'll fizz up the soft drinks if you do that too much," Mr. McFarlane warned.

James hastily dragged his laden crutches out of the way as the post office door gave its familiar tinkle and swung open to reveal Araminta Greenwood. She was looking extremely agitated.

"Mandy!" Ms. Greenwood looked relieved to see her. "I — oh, dear."

Mandy guessed in an instant that the boys had returned to the house in the woods. She was alarmed to see Araminta Greenwood sway very slightly. Mr. McFarlane pulled a chair out from behind the counter so she could sit down.

Mandy knelt down beside her. "What happened this time?"

"An overturned garbage can," said Ms. Greenwood with a shake of her head. "It's a little thing, I know, but . . . Well, it did scare me."

Mandy felt furious. "That's enough!" she cried fiercely. "We can't let those boys do this anymore!"

Deep inside Mandy's pocket, Pumpkin gave an extremely loud and eerie yowl of displeasure.

"Oh!" Mr. McFarlane clutched at his chest, his eyes wide and shocked as he looked around the store. "What in the world was that?"

Mandy brought Pumpkin out of her pocket. "He's the one on the poster in your window, Mr. McFarlane," she said, trying to bring her temper under control so she wouldn't frighten the kitten. "We're trying to find a home for him."

"A home!" Mr. McFarlane echoed, staring at the kitten in disbelief. "That animal sounds like he should be out in the jungle! His meow is enough to frighten the daylights out of anyone — particularly at Halloween."

There was a pause. Suddenly, Mandy's eyes were full of fire.

"I've just had the most fantastic idea!" she said. "I know how to stop those boys from bothering Ms. Greenwood. It's Halloween. Why don't we give them the fright of their lives?"

Ten

At five-thirty that afternoon, Mandy stood by the fire in Ms. Greenwood's house and adjusted her Halloween mask. It was time for Operation Howl. If everything went according to plan, Matt Burness and his friends would never bother Ms. Greenwood again.

"Your mask looks fantastic," John said approvingly. "When those boys see you in the woods, they'll think they've gone crazy!"

"Tell me," said Araminta Greenwood as she adjusted the back of John's ghostly white sheet, "is this luminous paint?"

"Yes, it is," John replied. "I'll glow in the dark. And if that doesn't frighten them, I don't know what will."

James twitched unhappily at his cape. "I'm sure my crutches are going to get in the way," he grumbled. "It's not very scary, is it, to see someone limping toward you?"

Mandy tightened her cat tail and stroked back her long black whiskers. She felt calm and excited at the same time. "That's where you're wrong, James," she said. "Imagine hearing not just two thumps approaching you in the dark, but *three* — a foot and two crutches! We'll scare those vandals out of their socks!"

She bent down and gave Blackie an encouraging pat. "And you look very batlike, Blackie," she said happily. "You'll be terrifying."

The black Labrador did look faintly batlike in his red luminous collar. With his glossy black coat, the rest of him would blend in beautifully with the trees.

"Are you sure you aren't missing your Halloween party?" Araminta Greenwood asked.

"We'll be back in plenty of time for the party," Mandy assured her. "It doesn't start for an hour and a half. This is much more important."

"What if the vandals don't come back tonight?" said John.

Mandy smiled. "Of course they'll come back. It's Halloween! They won't be able to resist trying to spook Ms. Greenwood on the scariest night of the year. Now, what props have you brought?"

John dug around in his backpack. "A CD of sound effects," he announced. "I borrowed it from my dad. Sometimes there are theme nights at the restaurant, you know? It's got some fantastic stuff on it — howling wind, baying wolves, creaky doors." He fished a little deeper into his bag. "And here's the CD player," he went on. "We'll put the speakers up in the branch of a tree, and I'll use the remote control to switch it on. It'll be great."

James held out a large jar full of green slime. Mandy made a face. "Ugh. What's that?"

"Green gunk," James explained. "It's my own recipe. We'll daub it around the gate and the fence. Wait till they put their hands in it!" he added.

"Excellent," Mandy said with satisfaction. "I've brought some cobweb spray that we can string across the trees. And I have Pumpkin, too, of course." She patted her sweatshirt pouch. "Get that meow ready, Pumpkin," she instructed. "Tonight's your big night."

She waited for the kitten to meow in response, but there was no sound from her pouch. Mandy carefully drew the kitten out and held him up close to her face. Pumpkin's nose stayed where it was, tucked beneath his tail.

"Is he all right?" James asked, leaning forward.

Mandy tickled Pumpkin's chin. "Hey, little fellow!" she said encouragingly. "What's up?"

Pumpkin sat up slowly in Mandy's hand and blinked at her. Then he yowled softly and tragically. It was the saddest thing Mandy had ever heard, and she realized for the first time that he must be feeling lonely, with no other animals to play with and no home except for a cage in the clinic's residential unit and a cushion on the kitchen table.

"He needs his mother," Ms. Greenwood said. "Youngster like that. Can't be right for him, having no home."

"I know," Mandy replied unhappily. "It's not fair, always carrying him around like a shopping bag. I'm trying my best to find him a home, Ms. Greenwood, but I'm not doing very well."

"He'll be fine," Ms. Greenwood said abruptly. "Bright spark like that. He'll make his home where he pleases."

I just hope he's not too sad to yowl for us tonight, Mandy thought miserably, tucking the kitten back into her pouch.

"I have something I would like to add to these sound effects of yours, by the way," said Ms. Greenwood as she walked with them down to the gate. She gave a sharp whistle, and Cor fluttered out of nowhere to land on her arm. "I can't guarantee that Cor will join in, but I hope that he will," she said.

Mandy was thrilled. "May I pet him?"

"Of course," said Ms. Greenwood. "He'd like that."

The crow seemed to enjoy the feel of Mandy petting his dusty black feathers and made soft croaking noises in the back of his throat, almost like a cat purring.

"Time is moving on," Ms. Greenwood reminded them. "Let's get everything in place and hope that our visitors don't arrive too soon!"

Setting up the props took longer than Mandy thought. She was acutely aware of every rustle out in the woods, but this time it wasn't because she was scared of ghosts. If the boys came too early, the whole thing would be ruined.

But they were in luck. When everything was in place, Araminta Greenwood folded her arms and looked at them. "I am not good at saying thank you," she said abruptly. "And I should probably discourage what's about to happen here. But I can't help thinking that this will be a much better way of getting the message across to my visitors than a trip to the police station in a thrilling police car." She smiled. "So thank you," she said. "And good luck." Then she turned around and strode back to the house.

Mandy, James, and John crouched down behind the

trees and began to wait. The minutes ticked away, and Mandy felt her first twinge of doubt. What if John was right? What if the boys never came? What if Pumpkin didn't yowl? She petted the kitten and bit her thumbnail anxiously, staring hard into the night.

Click, click, click. It was the unmistakable sound of bicycle wheel spokes, turning very slowly over the ruts and bumps of the woods. Mandy tensed as she heard voices.

". . . might be expecting us after last night," Adam Poole was saying in a low voice. "So keep quiet, OK?"

Peering around the base of her tree, Mandy watched as Adam Poole, Ben Stevens, Liam Collins, and Matt Burness crept up to the gate.

Adam Poole propped the bike up against the fence and smiled at his gang. "Liam, you dig up a few more of the witch's herbs. Ben, the witch's woodpile needs a little rearranging. And you, country boy," he whispered, turning to Matt Burness, "let's see if you have the guts to use this." He thrust what looked like a can of spray paint at Matt. Then he puffed out his chest and looked important. "And this little gate will do for me. Not really built to keep out the ghosties and goblins. Time it came off its puny little hinges — *eurghgh!*"

He snatched his hand off the gate in disgust and stared at the sticky mess on his fingers. Mandy nearly burst out laughing. She turned and nodded at John, who aimed his remote control at the tree just beside Liam Collins.

"*Whshooshwhshoosh* . . . The sound of a spooky wind on a lonely moor began to fill the air.

Adam Poole snapped his head around, still holding his green-gunked hand up in the air.

"*Arooooo!*" bayed a very large, very hungry wolf.

"Wolves!" Ben Stevens said and gasped, spinning around.

"In Welford?" Adam Poole scoffed, looking extremely uncertain. "Nah. Just . . . just the wind or something."

The sound of an enormous door began creaking open, slowly, horrifyingly. . . .

"I don't like this!" Liam Collins whimpered, backing straight into a line of sticky cobweb spray. He gave a shriek and frantically tried to pull the cobwebs off his neck.

Mandy raised her arm. It was the signal! The boys yelled in terror as four *things* rushed out of the trees toward them: a giant cat, a luminous ghost, a swirling cape, and an odd red stripe that seemed to bound through midair.

Craaaa! Right on cue, Cor flapped clumsily over the boys' heads and screeched. Mandy pulled Pumpkin out of her sweatshirt and held him high in the air.

Now's your moment, Pumpkin! she thought, desperately willing him to meow. *Yowl now, and I promise I'll find you the best home in the world!*

And the kitten, thoroughly overexcited by the commotion, gave the most terrific yowl of his life.

Yaiiiieeeeeooooowwwaarrrr!

Adam Poole wheeled around and blundered off into the woods, screaming his head off. Ben Stevens and Liam Collins crashed into each other, skidded in a puddle of green gunk, and fell flat on their faces. Shrieking and yelling, they scrambled to their feet as fast as they could and fled toward the path. But Matt Burness appeared to be frozen to the spot, staring in horror at a quaking bush just beside the gate.

Tucking Pumpkin back into her sweatshirt pocket, Mandy skidded to a halt. A quaking bush? That wasn't one of their tricks. James and John raced up to Mandy, breathing hard. They all stared at the bush in alarm. What was in there?

Matt looked around at them, his eyes huge. He didn't seem surprised to see that the four phantoms had turned into Mandy, James, John, and Blackie. He didn't even seem able to speak. He just pointed.

The bush rustled and shook like a living thing. Mandy's heart was in her throat. So far, everything had been a great laugh. But it *was* Halloween. And this . . .

this was unexplained, impossible — and totally the scariest thing she'd ever seen in her life. She squeezed Pumpkin so hard that the kitten mewed and wriggled in protest.

"What's in there?" John whispered, clutching onto Mandy's arm.

"I don't k-k-know," Mandy stammered. She glanced at Ms. Greenwood's house. How long would it take them to run to safety there before the . . . the thing in the bush *attacked* them?

The leaves at the bottom of the bush parted, and a long, pointed snout appeared. There was another frantic rustle, and it was followed by a broad set of shoulders and a thickly furred black-and-white back. Brock the badger emerged from underneath the bush and shook his head. He stared up at his astounded audience.

Mandy found her voice. "It's Brock!" she croaked. She began to laugh with relief. "It's just Brock!"

Blackie stepped forward and sniffed cautiously at the badger. Brock growled a grumpy warning and began to shuffle away, under the gate and up the path toward the house.

"Was that a badger?" Matt Burness sounded amazed. Mandy nodded.

"Cool!" Matt whispered.

They all stared at one another, realizing at the same moment how odd the situation was. There was an embarrassed silence, and Mandy felt confused. *Matt Burness is the enemy*, she thought. *Isn't he?*

"Good trick," Matt said at last, gesturing at their costumes. "The, er, wind and creaky door and stuff. How did you do that?" He sounded genuinely curious.

"Sound effects CD," John replied warily.

"It was great," Matt said. "Adam nearly collapsed."

Suddenly, they were all laughing at the memory of Adam Poole rushing off in terror, and hostilities were somehow forgotten.

"I always knew you were all right," Mandy told Matt, with a glance at James. "Anyone with a dog like Biscuit is bound to be OK."

Matt smiled shyly.

"Listen," John said, "why don't you come up to the house? It's getting cold out here."

Matt took a fast step backward. "With the witch? No way!"

"Yes, way," James said firmly. "You owe her an explanation. And an apology."

"You have to face Ms. Greenwood sometime," Mandy pointed out.

"But she'll turn me into something!" Matt insisted, looking fearful.

"Don't be dense," James scoffed. "She's not a witch. She's just a wise woman who lives in the woods."

Mandy rolled her eyes. "It's about time you figured that out, James."

James shrugged. "I've known all along," he replied casually. "I was just teasing you."

The front door of the house flew open, and a wide stripe of golden light flooded the yard. Ms. Greenwood was silhouetted on the doorstep, her arms folded and her shadow long and witchy on the path to the door.

"You caught one of the visitors, I see," she said icily. "Now, what are we going to do with him?"

Mandy watched Matt's reaction. At first, the redheaded boy seemed too scared to say or do anything. Then, rather awkwardly, he bent down, picked up Ms. Greenwood's bike, and leaned it safely against the fence. It was clearly a gesture of peace.

Araminta Greenwood regarded Matt in silence for a minute or two. Matt squirmed beneath her gaze and shivered.

"Are you cold?" the woman asked.

Matt nodded, shading his eyes from the light.

"No more than you deserve," Ms. Greenwood said severely. "Now, do I get an apology, or do we stand here all night?"

Matt shuffled his feet. "Sorry," he whispered.

Mandy, James, and John ushered Matt up the path and into the house. Blinking in the light, he looked around the little room uncertainly.

"Sit down," said Ms. Greenwood. "You've had a scare. A well-deserved one in your case, young man, but a scare nonetheless." She picked up the large teapot on the stove and poured out four cups of fragrant, yellowish tea. "Chamomile," she said. "Calms the nerves. Drink up, all of you."

Soon they were all sipping the warming tea. Mandy petted Pumpkin, who was fast asleep on her lap, and hunted around for something to say. She looked at the silent, subdued-looking Matt, and said the first thing that came into her head.

"How's Biscuit?"

Matt's eyes lit up. "He's fantastic," he said right away.

"How long have you had him?" James asked.

Suddenly, Matt started talking. He explained how his dad had bought Biscuit for the whole family, to help them adjust to moving to the country. "We always wanted a dog in Walton, but Mom never let us have one." He told them about how worried he'd been about leaving all his friends and how he was sure he'd never find any new ones. "Adam Poole and that gang were better than no friends at all," he said, sounding apologetic.

Mandy leaned forward. "And do you still feel the same way about Adam Poole?" she prompted.

Matt looked down at his hands. "He's not a friend," he said. "I don't know why I didn't see it in the first place. I've made a real mess of things, haven't I?"

Ms. Greenwood nodded. "You certainly have," she said. "But the damage doesn't have to be permanent."

"I'll help you clean up the mess in the yard," Matt promised. "And I'll clean your bike, too. I'm sorry, Ms. Greenwood. I really am."

"Good," said the woman. "In the meantime, can you promise me that those ex-friends of yours won't be returning to Welford?"

"They only came because I invited them," said Matt. "They kept on saying how boring it was here. I'm sure they won't come anymore." He looked sad for a minute. "So I really am friendless now, I guess."

Mandy smiled at him. "I wouldn't say that," she said.

Suddenly, she felt Pumpkin's small claws digging into her legs. The kitten had woken up again. "We'd almost forgotten about you!" she said, scooping up the kitten and kissing him on the nose. "You were a star tonight, Pumpkin. I'm sure that yowl was the final straw."

Pumpkin stretched and yowled obligingly, and Matt's eyes widened. "I thought you said you used sound effects!" he exclaimed.

"Pumpkin was one of them." James said. He grinned, as the kitten started sharpening his claws on Mandy's knee.

"He's very cute." Matt reached out and tickled the kitten on the head.

"I don't suppose you want a cat?" Mandy asked hopefully.

Matt shook his head. "Sorry. My mom's allergic. Is he looking for a home?"

"Yes." Mandy sighed. "And tonight's my last chance."

Cor stuck his head around the side of the sofa and made them all jump. Pumpkin sat up and regarded the large black bird with interest. Raising a paw, he batted it in the crow's direction. Cor's head retreated into his shoulders, and he clicked his beak warningly. Taking no notice, Pumpkin jumped off Mandy's knee and bounced over to the crow, wagging his tail and preparing to pounce.

Craaa! Cor screeched and flapped his wings. The kitten leaped sideways in fright, stuck his claws into Ms. Greenwood's orange-and-black-striped tights, and shinnied up the surprised woman as if she were a drainpipe.

"Steady there, little cat!" Ms. Greenwood exclaimed, reaching awkwardly for the kitten as he tried to burrow into her black sweater. "There's nothing to be scared of.

Remember what I told you about not bothering badgers? Well, the same applies to crows."

All at once, Mandy noticed two things. First, there was a kind of *rightness* to seeing Pumpkin in Ms. Greenwood's arms, tonight of all nights — the good witch and her familiar, together at Halloween. And second, with his black fur and orange eyes, Pumpkin looked as if he was made to match Ms. Greenwood's tights.

"Ms. Greenwood?" she said hesitantly. "I know you said you don't like cats and everything, but Pumpkin's got Burmese in him so he's really sociable and friendly and more like a dog anyway, and . . ." She shook her head impatiently at the muddle she was making of this. "What I'm trying to say is, well, Pumpkin really likes you, and I think you'd be perfect together. Would you consider giving him a home, please? He just looks like he's *made* to be with you."

Ms. Greenwood took a long, hard look at the kitten in her arms. Pumpkin wriggled, put out his tiny pink tongue, and started vigorously washing the elderly woman's thumb. Ms. Greenwood laughed out loud for the first time since Mandy had met her. Then she nodded, very slowly. "I think that perhaps you were right about finding a cat to suit me, Mandy," she said. "This kitten's a handful, but between us, Brock, Cor, and I will keep him in his place. Yes, he can live with us. We'll be pleased to have him."

Mandy jumped up and hugged Pumpkin and his new mistress. "That's perfect!" she exclaimed, beside herself with delight. "Just perfect!"

"Hey, look at the time!" John exclaimed suddenly. "It's five to seven. The party's going to start without us!"

Mandy swung around, looking horrified. "Oh, no! What's Mom going to say?"

"I have an idea," said Ms. Greenwood, reaching for her new cell phone. "Why don't I call your parents and invite them here instead?"

"Here in the woods?" James asked, sounding excited. "Wow! How spooky would that be?"

"It would be a pity to waste good cobweb spray," John pointed out. "And the sound effects are still up in the tree."

The evening was just getting better and better, Mandy decided. "That's your best idea yet, Ms. Greenwood," she said happily.

*   *   *

Mandy's parents were there within twenty minutes, with the bags of chips and the soft drinks. Tom and Dorothy Hope came ten minutes later, bringing with them Walter Pickard and Ernie Bell. Mandy's grandfather had somehow attached a small rubber spider to his mustache — "Just following the instructions on the invitation, Mandy!" — and her gran was wearing a splendid black witch's hat.

"We were with your grandparents when Ms. Greenwood called. She was kind enough to invite us, too," Ernie Bell explained, looking impressed at the sight of Cor perching on the back of the sofa.

"We were sorry to miss your costumes at the trick-or-treating earlier," Walter explained, grinning at the sight of the pumpkins on Ms. Greenwood's windowsill. "And I did always love a good Halloween party."

James's parents couldn't come, but John's dad popped in to say hello, apologizing that he wasn't able to stay for long. "It's a busy night at the restaurant," he explained.

"Did you bring the rest of the candy corn, Dad?" John asked.

His dad put his hands up. "Sorry. We gave it all away to the trick-or-treaters. It was very popular — even without kittens in it!"

Mandy grabbed John's arm and pulled him away. "Never mind. We have lots for the games. Come on, let's set them up!"

Ms. Greenwood had invited Matt's parents as well, so the little house was full of people enjoying themselves by eight o'clock. Matt took over as DJ and was extremely good at it, mixing Mandy's dance CDs with John's spooky sound effects. The slimy things in jars made Mandy scream, and Walter got covered in sugar from the doughnuts hanging on strings. Mandy's dad, meanwhile, won the cookie race.

"It's my diet," he laughed, putting his arm round Mandy's mom. "Sheer hunger drove me on!" He winked at Mandy, and she wondered if he'd been secretly practicing.

Pumpkin had cheered up immensely since his argument with Cor and wanted to join in everything: chasing Mandy's cat tail, batting pieces of candy corn through the powdered sugar, and swinging from the hanging cookies like a small furry monkey. Mandy watched him fondly. *It's as if he knows that he's come home*, she thought. Ms. Greenwood had already given him a saucer of milk and promised Mandy that she would keep Pumpkin in her bedroom at night so that he was safely out of Brock's and Cor's way. Food, love, and a bed for the night. What more could a kitten want?

The last game was bobbing for apples. Mandy and Ms. Greenwood were just about to duck for the one remaining apple when suddenly —

SPLASH!

Pumpkin fell from an overhead cookie string, straight into the water.

"There's never going to be a dull moment with Pumpkin around, Ms. Greenwood," Mandy said, gasping and wiping her face.

The elderly woman's eyes gleamed. "Who likes dull moments?" she replied. "Come on, Mandy. Race you to the last apple!"

ANIMAL ARK®

Kitten in the Cold

Ben M. Baglio

Illustrations by Shelagh McNicholas

To the real Amber

Special thanks to Jenny Oldfield.
Thanks also to C. J. Hall, B.Vet.Med., M.R.C.V.S.,
for reviewing the veterinary information
contained in this book.

One

"Mandy, are you sure you know what you're doing?" Grandpa Hope asked as she lifted Smoky onto the kitchen table at Lilac Cottage.

Grandma tut-tutted. "For goodness sake, Tom, you can see that the cat is in good hands. Stop fretting and let Mandy get on with it." She bustled to fetch a small bottle of cleanser, a bowl of hot water, and some cotton balls.

"We'll need a towel," Mandy warned. "Smoky won't like having his ears cleaned. He'll try to shake his head. The cleanser gets everywhere."

Grandpa brought a striped red towel and spread it on the table. "That stuff's not too hot, is it?"

Mandy dipped the bottle into the hot water, while Smoky strolled up and down to investigate.

"Tom!" Grandma said. "Why don't you go into the living room and read a nice gardening magazine until we're finished in here? I don't know about Mandy, but you're making me nervous!"

Mandy grinned. "It's OK. It doesn't bother me." Her grandpa worried about two things in life, his garden and his cat. It was Grandpa who'd noticed something was wrong with Smoky's ear in the first place. He told Mandy that Smoky was always scratching it and shaking his head. Mandy had gone back to Animal Ark and asked her mom and dad what it could be.

"Ear mites," Adam Hope had suggested. "The bites could be infected." He'd stopped by the cottage to take a look and left Mandy there to treat poor Smoky's condition.

"Don't look!" Grandma told Grandpa, as Mandy settled Smoky and gently took hold of the scruff of his neck. "Do you need any help, Mandy?"

She shook her head. "Smoky's a good boy, aren't you? You're not going to struggle." Speaking soothingly, Mandy very carefully put a drop or two of lukewarm liquid into the cat's ear. "See, it's not too horrible, is it?"

Smoky opened his mouth wide and meowed.

"There." She massaged a spot just below his ear.

"What's that for?" Grandpa ventured forward for a closer look.

"To soften the earwax. I have to clear it out before I put some other drops in." She worked patiently, glad that Smoky didn't fidget. Taking a cotton ball, she wiped cleanser from the ear canal.

"Oops!" Grandpa stepped back, as suddenly Smoky shook his head. Drops splashed onto the towel.

"Almost done," Mandy promised. She finished off with a cotton swab, easing it down the ear to clean out the tiny, delicate folds of skin. Then Grandma handed her the bottle of medicine that Adam Hope had given them. Mandy held the dropper to the infected ear and let three or four drops fall. A quick final massage and the job was done.

"Will that do the trick?" Grandpa asked.

Mandy handed Smoky over to him. "Yes. The drops will kill the mites and cure the infection." She'd seen it done many times at the clinic, but this was the first time she'd been trusted to do it herself. She felt pleased that it had gone well.

"Excellent!" Grandpa beamed at her. "We'll make a vet of you yet."

"I hope so," Mandy sighed. She longed to follow in her mom and dad's footsteps and run the clinic with them.

"Long hours, lots of stress," Grandma reminded her. She cleared the table and put on a clean cloth. "It's not an easy job."

But Mandy couldn't think of anything she'd rather do. She'd always loved animals. "More than people," her dad would joke. She spent most of her spare time lending a hand at Animal Ark with sick cats, dogs, hedgehogs; any animal that needed help. With her shoulder-length blonde hair and slight figure, Mandy could often be spotted around Welford village looking for animals in trouble.

Grandpa stroked Smoky under the chin. "You have a way with them, that's for sure. Doesn't she, Smoky?"

The young gray cat purred his agreement.

"Hardly any time off." Grandma went on pointing out all the minus points about being a vet. "Look at your mom and dad. It's almost Christmas, and they're busier than ever."

Now that the kitchen table was back to normal, Mandy followed her grandma into the living room and helped her lift a big cardboard box full of Christmas decorations down from a closet. She peered inside at the silver baubles and colored lights. "It's because of the cold," she explained. "Animals seem to have more accidents and illnesses this time of year."

"Just like human beings, when you come to think

about it." Grandpa put Smoky down on his favorite red cushion on the sofa and came to help. "Coughs and colds, snuffles and sneezes." He took a tangle of Christmas lights from the box. "That's funny. I'm sure I put these away nice and tidy last year."

Mandy laughed at his puzzled frown. "Should I untangle them for you?" She loved Christmas; putting up the decorations at Animal Ark and Lilac Cottage, making and buying presents. Smoky jumped down from the sofa and came to play. He lifted his paw to bat a light that dangled from Grandpa's hand.

"Yes, please."

So Mandy sat cross-legged on the carpet with Smoky on her lap, patiently untying the knots in the wire until the lights were straightened out, ready for use.

> *"Away in a-a manger,*
> *No-o crib for a bed*
> *The-e little Lord Jesus*
> *La-ay down his sweet head!"*

A carol singer stood at the door.

"Dad!" Mandy recognized the voice. He sang in the church choir. "He must be practicing for a concert."

Smoky cocked an ear, meowed, then crept off under a chair. Grandma and Grandpa laughed.

*"We three Kings of Orient are,
One in a taxi, one in a car. . . ."*

Grandma dashed to the door to let him in before he had a chance to ruin the song any further. "Adam, come in out of the snow!"

Mandy looked up as he stopped to take off his boots at the door. There were snowflakes in his short brown hair and melting on his beard. He was zipped up inside his winter jacket, blowing warm air into his cold hands. "Did you like my singing?" he said with a grin.

"Fantastic, Dad!"

"What's Smoky doing under there?" He unzipped his jacket and took it off.

"Hiding from the carol singer."

"Hmm. He's got no ear for music, that cat." Mandy's dad settled in a chair by the fire. "Speaking of ears, how is it?"

"Cured, we hope." Mandy handed the lights to her grandpa. "Smoky seems to have stopped scratching already."

"Well done. It gave me time to stop by Bleakfell Hall. I had to check up on Pandora for Mrs. Ponsonby. She has a little chill, that's all. Poor Mrs. P. was worried stiff."

"*Poor Pandora,* you mean!" Grandma didn't always see eye to eye with fussy Mrs. Ponsonby. "That little Pekingese gets carried everywhere. She has no chance to run around and play like any normal dog." She brought in piping hot tea and chocolate cake from the kitchen. "By the way, Adam, did you mention Father Christmas to Mrs. Ponsonby?"

Mandy pricked up her ears.

He snapped his fingers. "No, sorry. I completely forgot."

"Brain like a sieve." Grandma tapped the top of his head. "We need to know if she has room for Rudolph at the Hall."

"What's this?" Mandy was full of curiosity.

Grandma's eyes twinkled. "Rudolph the red-nosed reindeer. You know the tune?"

"Da-dum, de da-da da-dum . . ." Mandy's dad came in with a deep bass version.

"Don't encourage him," Mandy sighed. "Yes, so what about Rudolph and Bleakfell Hall?"

"Father Christmas is going to bring his reindeer to Welford for Christmas Eve!" Grandma announced. "Of course, Rudolph will be a very tired reindeer, coming all the way from Reindeerland. So he'll need a place to stay . . ."

"Oh, Grandma!" Mandy sighed. She knew better than to believe all this stuff. "Everyone knows there's no such . . ."

"Hush. You wash your mouth out with soap and water, Mandy Hope! Father Christmas and his sleigh will be here in person, complete with reindeer. And if you don't believe me, ask your grandpa!"

Mandy looked from one smiling face to another. "Grandpa? . . . Dad?"

They nodded back.

"What's going on?" The grown-ups were up to something. Mandy reached down to pick up Smoky, who'd come creeping close to the warm log fire. She cuddled him to her.

"Father Christmas will make a special guest appearance in the village square this year," was all Grandpa would say. "Everyone's going to be there. Why don't you bring James along and find out?"

James Hunter, Mandy's best friend, lived on the edge of Welford. "Will there really be a reindeer?"

"Two!" Grandma said.

Mandy considered it. "Maybe we will come and have a look." Real reindeer with antlers, trotting through the snow! "Wait a minute, I didn't think there were any reindeer left in this country. Didn't they all die out ages ago?"

"Aha!" Grandpa winked. "But there are plenty in Reindeerland!"

"Anyway," Adam Hope said, "that's where you're wrong. We do have reindeer in Britain. In Scotland, as a matter of fact. They belong to well-managed, domesticated herds in the Cairngorm Mountains. There! *Rangifer tarandus*, to give them their Latin name. They're supervised by the Reindeer Council and looked after by a Mr. Donald McNab."

"Ask me anything you want to know about reindeer!" Grandpa boasted. "For instance, why do reindeer have cloven hooves?"

"I don't know; why *do* reindeer have cloven hooves?" Mandy joined in the fun. It really did seem as if Rudolph was coming for Christmas!

"To help them walk on frozen snow." Grandpa rushed on. "And did you know, a reindeer can pull a sleigh carrying three hundred pounds for a hundred miles a day?"

She shook her head. What was going on? How come they all knew so much about reindeer all of a sudden?

"Stop teasing," Grandma said at last, "and tell poor Mandy why we're all reindeer mad."

"It's all for a good cause," Grandpa explained. "This special guest appearance in the village is in aid of a little girl who lives at Beechtrees. That's the bungalow next to the main road. She and her family came to live in Welford earlier this year. Jeremy Hastings is the new groundsman at the tennis club. Their daughter, Alex, is only five, but they've recently found out that she's seriously ill."

Mandy tried to connect the reindeer's visit with Alex Hastings. She'd seen the girl from a distance — a tiny, red-haired child, with a bigger brother. Their hair was the first thing you noticed about them both. It was curly and shone reddish-gold in the sun. "What's wrong with her?"

"Something to do with her heart. She needs an operation, Mandy dear." Grandma spoke softly, seriously. "There's only one place in the world where she can get this kind of operation, and that's in America. But the Hastings can't afford to take her there. Your grandpa heard about it one day at the tennis club. A few people put their heads together and came up with various ways of raising money so the family could go to the States."

"Fund-raising," Mandy's dad chipped in. "Everyone has been having great ideas. Your grandpa came up with this special invitation to Father Christmas and his reindeer. We hope all of Welford will come along, sing a few carols, and put lots of money in a collection box."

"People have been very good so far," Grandpa said. "We've already raised enough money for the operation, but we need another eight hundred pounds for the air-fares to send Alex and her family for treatment. And we need it quickly. She must go early in the New Year for the operation, otherwise it'll be too late."

"You mean, if she doesn't get it, she'll die?" Mandy whispered.

"I'm afraid so, love."

For a while, everyone was silent. The logs crackled in the hearth, Smoky rubbed his soft face against Mandy's cheek.

"But if she goes to America and has the operation, the doctors think she will be completely cured," Grandma said. "So you see, Father Christmas's visit is going to be extra-important this year."

Slowly Mandy said, "Does Alex know about going to America?"

Grandma shook her head. "Her mom and dad think it's best to keep quiet until they're sure they can take her. She doesn't really know how ill she is. And she certainly doesn't have a clue about Father Christmas's visit!"

Adam Hope finished his cup of tea and brushed cake crumbs from his sweater. Smoky jumped from Mandy's arms and went to see whether the crumbs were worth eating. "I saw Alex's dad today, as a matter of fact."

"At Animal Ark?" Mandy found the little girl's story sad but fascinating.

"Yes. He brought a kitten in for her vaccinations. They just got her. Alex loves animals, apparently. Her dad says the walls of her bedroom are plastered with pictures of them!" He glanced at Mandy with a little smile.

"Just like someone else we know!" Grandpa teased. Mandy's own room was a portrait gallery of pets, wild animals, and endangered species.

"Beechtrees is just past Susan Collins's house, isn't it?" Mandy ignored them and got to thinking ahead instead.

"That's right. Why?" Her grandpa bent to plug in the Christmas lights. They lit up, a brilliant chain of blue, green, and pink. "Hey, presto!"

"Oh, nothing . . ." A five-year-old girl with a new kitten! "What's the kitten like?" she asked her dad, as casually as possible.

"She's a little brown-and-black tortoiseshell."

"Sweet!" Mandy stared wistfully at Smoky, now a fully grown cat. "How old?"

"Four or five months, just at the playful stage. You know, she chases everything, including her own tail."

"Aah!"

"And she has the most amazing eyes," her dad continued. "Big and shiny in her cute little dark face."

"What color?" She wanted to picture the kitten perfectly.

"Her eyes? They're a sort of bright gold color. Traffic-light orange. Yes, that's it!" Dr. Adam smiled as he stood up, ready to take Mandy home. He stroked Smoky. "Not as good-looking as you, of course," he said with a grin. "But the Hastings's kitten does have the most amazing amber eyes. And that's what they've called her. Alex chose the name herself; Amber."

They put on their jackets and boots, said good-bye to Mandy's grandparents and Smoky, and began to tramp through the snow up the lane to Animal Ark, Dr. Adam whistling as they walked.

"Dad?"

"What?" He stopped midtune.

"I wonder if I should go and visit Alex and Amber," Mandy said dreamily. There was a white wonderland of snow-laden trees, drifts almost three feet deep against the walls, and stars in a moonlit sky.

"I don't see why not."

"And, Dad . . ."

"Uh-oh!" He gathered snow from the wall top and patted it into shape. His eyes gleamed as he aimed the ball at Mandy. "Come on, this is a challenge!"

"No, Dad, I want to ask you something!" But she

couldn't resist scooping up snow and making her own snowball.

"So I gather. Am I going to say yes? I know you when you give me that look!" He was laughing now, as the first snowball flew toward him. He dodged just in time.

"Listen!" Mandy dived for more ammunition. "You know Grandma thought that the two reindeer might be able to stay at Bleakfell Hall?"

It was her dad's turn to fling a snowball. It thudded against Mandy's shoulder. "Direct hit! Yes, Mrs. Ponsonby has an empty stable at the back of the Hall."

"Well, we could look after them at Animal Ark instead, couldn't we? We've got room in the residential unit. I mean, reindeer aren't all that big!" She stood with her arm raised, fresh snow poised ready.

"Gi-normous!" Dr. Adam dodged and slipped. He landed flat on his back.

Mandy ran over and stood, hands on hips. "But Mrs. Ponsonby wouldn't have a clue how to look after them. We would! You and mom must know all about reindeer."

"Flattery will get you . . . everywhere!" He grinned back up at her.

"You mean yes? The reindeer can stay with us?" She hauled him to his feet.

"For a couple of nights. As long as your mom agrees."

"Yippee!" Mandy charged into a drift and kicked up loose snow. It sprayed up and sparkled. "Oh, Dad, thanks! That's so great." She ran ahead up the lane to Animal Ark. Real reindeer were coming to stay!

Two

"Two reindeer?" Emily Hope was talking on the phone in Reception. Jean Knox, Animal Ark's receptionist, stood listening, her glasses perched high on her forehead. Simon, their nurse, came through from the treatment room, ready for morning office hours. He raised his eyebrows at Mandy when he overheard the conversation.

It was early the next morning; only three days to go until Christmas Eve, and Mandy was keeping her fingers firmly crossed. Her mom had just called the owner of the reindeer herd in Scotland to make arrangements for the visit.

"Rudolph and Dasher?" Dr. Emily smiled. "And you'll bring their food with them?"

Mandy's eyes shone. "We're having two reindeer to stay this Christmas!" she whispered to Simon.

"You must be joking!" Glancing up from the appointment book, he realized that Mandy was serious. "When?"

"Tomorrow, Wednesday."

"How will they travel? By flying over the rooftops?" Simon winked at Jean, who seemed to think that the entire Hope family had finally gone crazy.

"I don't know yet. Hang on a minute." Mandy listened in again.

"We have an open-air compound at the back of Animal Ark, where we exercise the patients. It's small but secure. I think that should be all right. You say the reindeer need to stay out overnight. . . . Yes, OK, someone could meet you in Walton and show you the road over the moor to Welford. It's hard to find if you don't know your way around. . . . We've had snow, but the main roads are fairly clear. Yes, fine."

They waited as arrangements went ahead.

"Tomorrow afternoon? Yes, one of us will be there. We'll meet you outside the bus station in town . . . you should be able to park a trailer there. . . . Just look out for our Animal Ark Land Rover . . . yes, bye, Mr. McNab!" Emily Hope nodded as she put down the phone.

"Correct me if I'm wrong, but did I just hear you break your strictest Animal Ark rule?" Jean asked in disbelief. She'd known the Hopes a long time, and never in living memory had Mandy's mom and dad agreed to let an animal who didn't need treatment come to stay.

"You did." Dr. Emily put on her white coat.

"Here comes our first patient." Mandy hopped off her stool and went to the window. She wanted to change the subject. A car struggled down the lane through the snow.

"Well, I never!" Jean still couldn't believe it.

"They're coming down from a place near Aviemore," Dr. Emily said. "It's quite a journey. Donald McNab is driving down in a trailer . . . to help Father Christmas deliver presents in Welford!"

"Mom!" It looked as if Mandy would have to go along with the Father Christmas thing, though she considered herself much too old.

"What's wrong? You still hang up your stocking for him, don't you?"

"Yes, but . . . oh, OK, you win!" Mandy beamed.

"It's all in a good cause." Her mom explained to Jean the idea behind the reindeer's visit. "We're trying to raise money to send little Alex Hastings to America. You know about her operation, don't you?" Soon everyone in Welford would be in on it, thought Mandy.

"Good idea. I'll be there," Jean promised. "After all, it is Christmas."

"Seven-thirty in the square on Christmas Eve?" Simon asked. "Count me in, too." Mrs. Parker Smythe and her eight-year-old daughter, Imogen, had just come into the clinic. Simon showed them and their pet into a treatment room. "Did you hear about Father Christmas's special visit?" he asked them, as the door swung closed.

"The more the merrier," Emily Hope smiled. She turned to Mandy. "Happy now?"

"I can't wait!"

"Well, why not go and visit Alex, like you planned? I'm sure she could do with some company."

"Now?" Mandy would normally help out in the clinic during vacation.

"Why not? We won't be busy here, not in this weather. And you could tell her there's a special treat in store this Christmas."

"But not exactly what the treat is?" Mandy scrambled out of her white coat and grabbed her jacket.

Dr. Emily put her head to one side, ready to start work. "No," she said. "Let's keep Father Christmas a nice surprise!"

*   *   *

"Alex likes animals," Mandy promised James. She'd stopped by the Hunters' house, and James had decided to bring his dog, Blackie, along to Beechtrees.

The black Labrador padded through the snow ahead of them, leaving a narrow trail of footprints. When he came to the wide gates of Susan Collins's enormous house, he stopped.

"No, Blackie, that's not where we're going today." James ordered him on. James was dressed for the snow in a padded jacket and a baseball cap. The wind had reddened his cheeks, and his glasses reflected the bright light as he and Mandy loped along after Blackie.

Beechtrees was tucked away under the shadow of some tall trees a few hundred yards down the main road from Susan's house. Today there were few cars on the road; only a yellow snowplow trundling toward them, with Jeremy Hastings sitting at the controls. The plow had been clearing a track from the tennis club toward the main road after the snowfall of the previous night.

"Hello there." Mr. Hastings drew near, then leaned sideways. He was puzzled by the sight of Blackie, James, and Mandy knee-deep in the fresh snow.

"Hello." Mandy knew him as friendly in a quiet sort of

way, never excited or annoyed. She and James had seen him at work around the tennis courts that autumn.

Blackie spoiled the introductions by barking at the snowplow.

"Sorry." James blushed and told him to sit. "He's never seen one close up before."

"That's OK." Jeremy Hastings decided to take a break. He climbed down from the cab. "I know you two, don't I?"

"Yes. I'm James Hunter, and this is Blackie."

"And I'm Mandy Hope." Somehow, because Mr. Hastings was shy, Mandy was self-conscious, too. She felt her face grow hot behind her woollen scarf and hat.

"The vets' daughter?"

She nodded.

"I took Alex's kitten up to Animal Ark for her yesterday. Nice place." He didn't waste words. "Alex doesn't get out much at the moment."

"No. That's why we brought Blackie to see her," James said.

Mandy's blonde hair fell around her face as she took off her hat. "We heard she likes animals."

"She's crazy about them!" For the first time, Jeremy Hastings smiled. "Completely nuts. She'll love you, Blackie. Why don't you all come in?"

Mandy felt that the ice was broken. She grinned at

James and followed the groundskeeper between two tall beech trees, up a path toward the bungalow.

"Alex!" Mr. Hastings opened the door and knocked snow off his boots. "You've got visitors!"

They waited for an answer, but none came.

"She's a little shy with strangers," her father told them. "Hang on a sec." He kicked off his boots and went inside.

"Sit, Blackie." James made him wait on the porch. He and Mandy stared curiously into the hallway.

"What do you want?" a voice challenged from behind them.

They spun around. Blackie jumped up. There in the front garden, peering from behind a bush, was a small boy with bright ginger hair. His eyes were greeny-gray, his face covered in freckles. He wore a navy-blue fleece jacket zipped to his chin and an expression that said, "Get lost!"

"We came to play with Alex," Mandy answered carefully. The boy looked about seven years old.

"Oh, her." He turned away in disgust. "She doesn't want to play." He trudged back onto the lawn and kicked at the deep snow. "I'm her brother, and she won't even play with me."

Mandy couldn't tell who the boy was most angry with, but his tone of voice and his deep frown made her guess that it was everyone and everything. He was what

Grandma would call "moody." That meant he sulked a lot.

"I'll play with you," James volunteered. It was chilly standing on the porch waiting for Alex to appear. "We could build a snowman."

"Where?"

"There on the lawn."

"How tall?"

"As tall as you like."

"Up to the roof of the bungalow?" The boy looked up at the single-story house.

"Well, maybe not that tall." James went ahead anyway. He jumped from the step into the garden and began to scoop snow into a rough pile. "Let's see how fat we can make him."

Mandy pulled her hat from her pocket. "He can wear this when you finish him."

Slowly the boy came and took it. "Can he wear your scarf, too?"

"OK." She unwound it and handed it over.

Satisfied, he ran back to James. Soon they were both hard at work on the snowman's body.

"There, what did I tell you?" Mr. Hastings returned at last, holding his daughter's hand. "Here's a dog that came all this way in the snow to see you. He's called Blackie."

Blackie stood up and wagged his tail at the sound of his name.

Mandy knelt and put an arm around his neck. "He won't bite," she said softly. "He's a nice doggie."

Alex Hastings let go of her father's hand and took a halting step forward. She was small for a five-year-old — pale and thin, wearing a dark blue corduroy dress. Her curly hair was even brighter than Mandy's mom's — the reddest hair that she had ever seen.

Alex's big green eyes grew wide as she reached out a tiny hand to stroke Blackie. "He's all wet!" She took it quickly away.

"That's melted snow. Blackie likes the snow. He tries to eat it!"

Alex stroked him again. "His ears are nice and soft."

"He's one big softie really." Mandy smiled as the little girl grew bolder. "Would your new kitten like to meet him?"

Alex looked up at her dad. "Won't the dog chase Amber?"

"I don't think so. Blackie's probably used to cats. Why don't you get Amber from your bedroom and see?"

As Alex went slowly through one of the doors leading off from the square hallway, Mr. Hastings smiled at Mandy. "Bring Blackie inside and let me close the door.

Alex's mom is fixing hot chocolate for everyone. We could all use some on a day like today."

Mandy smiled back, stepped in, and looked around at the cream-colored walls, the big mirror, and framed family photographs.

"Dad, Amber won't come!" Alex called in a high, panicky voice. "She's hiding under the bed."

There was a faint meow. Blackie pricked up his ears and whined.

"No, she's not! She's running away!"

They heard rapid little feet pattering and jumping

from surface to surface, then a small black-and-brown shape hurtled through the door. The kitten somersaulted into the hall.

"Oh, Amber!" Alex cried from her bedroom.

"It's OK, here she is!" Mr. Hastings cornered the kitten and picked her up.

Mandy held onto Blackie as Alex came slowly over and took Amber from her father. All Mandy could see was a bundle of wriggling fur, a long, fluffy tail, and a little pair of pointed ears. "She's gorgeous!" she exclaimed.

"Amber, be good," Alex scolded. "Say hello to Blackie."

But the kitten caught sight of the big black dog and stared. Her golden eyes flashed, and she opened her mouth wide and hissed.

"No, you have to be nice to him," Alex insisted. She brought her up closer. "Nice doggie. See, Amber; nice, nice doggie!"

Good-natured Blackie sniffed at the kitten. Amber's ears and whiskers twitched. She put out a paw to pat the dog's black nose.

"See, you like him!" Soon it was safe to let go of the kitten. Alex put her on the carpet and watched the two animals stalk in circles around each other. Blackie towered over the kitten, but he was very gentle. Amber, on the other hand, thought that playing meant jumping up at Blackie and catching hold of his neck. She clung on for dear life.

Alex gasped, then laughed. "They're playing a game!"

Mandy told her all about Blackie and James. "James is my best friend. He helps us with the animals at Animal Ark." She explained that her mom and dad looked after sick animals.

Alex didn't take her eyes off Amber and Blackie. "Are they all sick?" she asked slowly.

"Who, the patients who come to my house?" Mandy nodded. "But most of them get better. It's like a hospital for animals."

The little girl turned to her with a serious face. "I've been to the hospital."

"I know," Mandy said gently.

"I might have to go again, so they can make me better. Then I can play outside with William."

"That's her brother," Mr. Hastings explained.

"I know. We met him in the garden. James is out there building a snowman with him." Mandy took Alex to the glass door to look outside. The snowman was already as high as William's shoulder.

"Who's building a snowman?" Alex's mother popped her head around the kitchen door.

"William and James." Alex peered out wistfully at the

snow scene. Then she turned her attention back to the two animals. "Amber's got a friend," she told her mom.

Mrs. Hastings stepped into view. She was small and neat, in dark pants and a soft, fawn-colored sweater. Her short hair was a darker red than her children's, with rich coppery tints.

She smiled at Mandy. "So have you," she said to her daughter. "A new friend. What a lovely surprise!"

Mandy was soon made welcome in the Hastings's house. Alex took her and Blackie into her bedroom. From there they could see James and William out in the garden. The snowman was growing; he had a head and a face made from twigs and stones.

"What's Father Christmas bringing you?" Alex sat on her bed with Amber on her lap. Surrounded by pillows and cushions, she looked like a little red-haired doll.

"I'm not sure." Mandy smiled.

"Do you believe in him?" Alex asked solemnly. She didn't give Mandy a chance to reply. "I do! I wrote to him with a list of things."

"What did you ask for?"

"Well, it's not things exactly. Anyway, I can't tell. It's a secret. Otherwise it won't come true, like a wish."

Beneath the cheerful chatter, Mandy suspected that Alex was sad. From the way she sat stroking her kitten, she could even imagine what Alex's wish might have been. "Dear Father Christmas, Please give me an operation to make me better, so I can go out and play."

"Do you like reindeer?" Alex chatted on. "I do! My favorite is Rudolph. Who's your favorite?"

Mandy glanced up at the giant color pictures of kittens and puppies, ponies, and hamsters. She could hardly see a square inch of bare wall space. "Rudolph." She bit her lip. Sometimes it was difficult not to spill the beans. Little did Alex know it, but she was about to get a visit from her favorite reindeer!

"Poor Rudolph, he couldn't join in any reindeer games, could he?" Alex sighed.

"Because his nose was too red. They didn't like him," Mandy reminded her.

"I would have let him join in anyway."

"Me, too." Mandy sat on the floor with Blackie, happy to talk to Alex as if Rudolph was a real, live reindeer. Alex seemed to know the story inside out.

"Why did it matter what color his nose was?" Alex was determined to stick up for Santa's problem solver. "When I'm better, anyone who wants to can play with me! I'll go back to school, and *everyone* can be my friend!"

Mandy agreed. Suddenly, there was a loud thud

against the window. They turned quickly, in time to see a flattened snowball sliding down the glass.

"William!" Alex gasped. The windowpane had rattled. Startled, Amber had jumped from her lap and gone into hiding. Blackie gave a sharp bark.

"Alex, come and look!" The boy's voice from the garden was high and bossy. Another snowball landed against the glass.

Slowly Alex uncrossed her legs. Mandy helped her from the bed. She could only move at a snail's pace, Mandy realized, and was quickly out of breath.

"Come here. Look at this!"

From the window, the girls could see two snowmen. One wore Mandy's red-and-white-striped hat and scarf. The other had James's cap perched on his head.

"What's going on in here?" Mrs. Hastings came rushing into the room with a worried frown. She glanced at the melting snowballs sliding slowly down the windowpane. "What was that noise?"

"William's snowballs. Look what they built in the garden!" Alex's face was bright with admiration.

But Mrs. Hastings was annoyed as she came to the window.

From outside, William saw his mother and yelled. "Mom, look!" He sounded faint through the glass, but they could tell he was proud of the snowmen. "Can Alex come out and see?"

Mrs. Hastings tapped hard on the window. "No, she can't!" she mouthed. "And you come inside at once!"

Mandy saw the smile vanish from William's face. James stood by, unsure.

"Alex, it's time for your medicine," her mother said sharply. Frowning, she left the room to get it.

"William's going to get it now," Alex whispered. "He's not supposed to do things that make me jump." She sighed and retreated to her bed. "Now he'll think it's my fault that he's in trouble again."

"Oh, I'm sure he won't," Mandy began. But she heard doors bang and Mrs. Hastings's voice speaking to her son.

". . . No consideration . . . making loud noises . . . you are seven years old; old enough to know better, William!"

Alex hung her head and put her hands over her ears.

"We'd better go," Mandy said quickly. James still stood out there in the cold.

Alex nodded. "I have to have a nap after my medicine anyway." She blushed and smiled. "Thanks for bringing Blackie to see me."

"Thanks for showing me Amber." The kitten peeped out from under the bed, her eyes shining big and golden. "Enjoy the snowmen!" Alex would be able to see them from her bed. Mandy smiled again and left.

Outside, she found James waiting for her, and, at the gate, the worried figure of Jeremy Hastings.

"Alex has to be kept nice and quiet," he said to explain Mrs. Hastings's anger about the snowballs. "No exertion. It's doctors' orders. Of course, if she gets her operation, it'll be a different story. She'll be running around just like she was before."

"Grandpa says the fund-raising is going really well," Mandy said.

He nodded and smiled grimly. "A lot depends on this Father Christmas thing."

"Don't worry. It'll be amazing; a sleigh, real reindeer — Alex will love it!"

"You didn't mention it to her?"

"No." It had been hard, but Mandy had kept the secret.

"Good. It's bound to cheer her up, isn't it?" Mr. Hastings gazed up at the trees, as if he would find an answer there to his family's problems. "Alex has always loved Father Christmas and his reindeer."

Mandy and James said good-bye. They left Mr. Hastings standing by his snowplow, gazing up at the gray sky.

Three

"I'm sorry I'm late." Donald McNab strolled up to the Animal Ark Land Rover.

It was just before dinner the next day, and Mandy and James had driven into Walton with Dr. Adam to meet their special guests. After an hour of sitting freezing in the car, with James snuffling and sneezing into his hankie, Mandy's dad had hurried off to buy warm drinks. It had been a long, cold wait.

"Aye, I lost my way," the Scotsman explained in a heavy accent. He sounded very calm. "Took a couple of wrong turnings in York. Terrible place to drive through.

I went around the old city walls three times before I found the right exit. My head was spinning by the time I got out."

"That's OK." Mandy and James looked eagerly for the reindeer in Mr. McNab's trailer, which he'd parked a few yards up the road. They weren't interested in why he was late.

"I thought maybe I'd missed you." He shook hands as first James, then Mandy jumped down onto the pavement. His gray eyes shone with good humor, his handshake was firm. "It was good of you to wait."

"Dad won't be long," Mandy said. "Mr. McNab, can we go and take a look?" All day she'd been looking forward to this.

"At Rudolph and Dasher? Aye, go right ahead. And call me Don!" He fished deep in the pocket of his weatherproof jacket. "Here, you can give them a wee treat for being cooped up in that trailer for so long."

They took a handful each of what looked suspiciously like scraps of chewed leather. James sniffed them and wrinkled his nose.

"Dried mushrooms," Don laughed. "They love 'em!"

Mandy couldn't wait a moment longer. She ran ahead. From inside the gray trailer came a loud shuffling and knocking of hooves. She saw that the back doors were half open, like stable doors, and as she drew near, two heads loomed out; two long noses, two pairs of dark brown eyes, and two sets of enormous antlers.

Mandy held her breath. The animals were only the height of a small Welsh pony, but their antlers were huge, branching off like mighty boughs on a tree. They curved over the reindeer's heads as they nodded and poked them out of the trailer.

"Go ahead!" Don encouraged. "They won't harm you!"

Gingerly, Mandy reached up with the mushrooms. The nearest reindeer bent to nibble at them with his velvety mouth.

"That's Dasher."

James followed suit, letting the other reindeer take food from his palm.

"And that's Rudolph. Say hello, boys!"

The reindeer snorted and grunted. The trailer shook as they shifted their weight.

By now a small crowd had gathered. Walton had never seen a reindeer in the flesh. Word went around for people to come and look at their magnificent antlers. Mothers came with children, shopkeepers stood out on the pavement. One bus driver even stopped his bus to let his passengers see, while Don McNab fielded eager questions.

"They've come to help Father Christmas," he explained to the smallest children. "They have to pull his sleigh through the snow."

"When?"

"Where?"

"Will we see them?" More questions, more round eyes and open mouths.

"Aye, you will if you come to Welford on Christmas Eve," Don told them. "That's when the old gentleman will bring your presents!" He winked at James and Mandy.

Through all the fuss, Rudolph and Dasher chewed contentedly, until Adam Hope came back with the drinks and the children had to say good-bye.

"Do you think you'll be able to follow us OK?" Mandy's dad asked Don after the two men had met.

But Mandy came up with a better idea. She arranged to drive with Don in the reindeer van. "Just in case they can't keep up," she explained.

"Och aye, I don't want to get lost again!" Don helped her into the passenger seat. All the way home, out of town and across the moor, Mandy was able to fire questions at him.

"What do reindeer eat?" she asked, hoping she'd be able to help feed them later.

"Grass, moss, ferns, bark, oh aye, and mushrooms, of course," Don answered, as he drove carefully down the hill toward Welford. The whole valley lay under a blanket of snow, and the village lights twinkled in the dusk. He stifled a yawn. "I'm away to my bed early tonight."

Mandy smiled happily. "We'll take care of the reindeer for you," she promised.

"Aye, I know you will. Anyhow, I've a busy day tomorrow."

It would be Thursday tomorrow, the day before Christmas Eve. "Where do you have to go?" Mandy asked.

"I've to drive the reindeer to a children's hospital in Leeds tomorrow morning. The old gentleman will be handing out presents there."

Mandy shot a puzzled look at the cheerful little Scotsman. He had short gray hair, a square face, a nice, outdoorsy feel. "This old gentleman . . ." she began.

"Father Christmas, aye?"

"I mean, aren't you . . . Isn't it really . . . ?" She stammered to a halt. Here was another grown-up who liked to tease.

"Me?" He roared with laughter and thumped the steering wheel. "Oh, no, dearie! Don't ever let him catch you saying such a thing, or there'll be no presents for you this year!"

He went on chuckling as they followed Dr. Adam and James through the village, past the pub and the post office, along the lane to Animal Ark.

Four

"Hold him steady," Don told Mandy as she led Rudolph down the ramp from the trailer into the yard.

The reindeer tossed his head and pawed the ground stiffly until he grew used to his new surroundings.

"Here come the guests of honor." Emily Hope stood on the doorstep after evening office hours.

"They're . . . awesome!" Simon gave a low whistle. "Look at those antlers!"

Rudolph grunted suspiciously, then allowed Mandy to lead him on. She took him around the back to the residential area and gave him a reward. "Good boy." She stroked his thick white winter mane.

"Steady as you go." Don steered James and Dasher down the ramp. He took a look at the high wire fence surrounding the exercise compound. "Aye, this'll do nicely."

Mandy breathed a sigh of relief. The reindeer's long journey had ended safely. "Will they need food?" she asked Don, anxious again as Rudolph and Dasher began to paw at the snow. "They must be hungry."

"No need. They can dig, see."

The reindeer lowered their heads and began to scrape with their antlers, using them as giant snow shovels. Soon they were down to green grass and grazing happily.

Mandy, James, Adam and Emily Hope, Simon, and Jean all gathered around to watch. "They don't seem to mind an audience," Dr. Adam said quietly.

"Och, they're used to it. They're at the center of the action wherever they go." Don went to fetch his own bag from the battered white van. He looked up at the soft snowflakes floating out of the dark sky. "Good reindeer weather. It reminds them of home."

"Come inside and get warm." Unless there was an emergency call during the evening, Emily Hope had finished work for the day. She took Don's bag and carried it into the house. Simon and Jean went inside to clean up the clinic.

"Aye, in a wee while." Don grinned at Mandy and James. "I just want to show these two the sleigh belonging to the old gentleman himself!" He stayed out in the yard as the other grown-ups went indoors.

James and Mandy shrugged and followed.

"But it's the trailer!" James was disappointed. Father Christmas's sleigh was just like any other trailer that you would see on a farm or at a horse show.

"Not just any ordinary trailer, young Jim!" Don McNab leaped into action. He unscrewed nuts and bolts, removed the detachable roof, folded down fiberglass flaps, and soon transformed the trailer into what looked for all the world like an old-fashioned sleigh.

"Wow!" James was impressed. The painted side panels hid the wheels and looked like imitation sleigh runners.

"Abracadabra! We hitch the reindeer onto the front, and jingle bells, off we go!"

"That's really neat," Mandy said.

"Aye, it is."

"Who thought of it?" James tipped his glasses more firmly on to his nose and went to inspect it more closely.

"I did." Don was proud of his handiwork. "I use it to tour the country at Christmastime. In two shakes I can turn the trailer into the old gentleman's sleigh. He arrives in style to visit the kiddies in the hospital or turn on the Christmas lights, whatever they want."

"I like it!" James examined the hinges and molded fiberglass and the metal shafts that harnessed the reindeer.

"Then why not come with us tomorrow?" Don promptly invited them both along. "We're off to visit the little kids in the hospital in Leeds. You two can keep me on the right road." He reminded them how hopeless he was at finding his way.

"Great; we could help look after Rudolph and Dasher!" Mandy jumped at the chance. She ran inside to ask her mom and dad.

"Yes, fine," Emily Hope said. She stood by the stove in the warm kitchen. "Would you tell Don that supper's ready?"

They sat down to steaming bowls of thick soup and piles of fresh bread. Don McNab ate with a ravenous appetite, entertaining them with stories of the reindeer herd at home. Mandy lapped it all up; the rolling sound of the Scotsman's voice, the picture he painted of snowy mountains and magnificent animals.

Before she went to bed, Mandy went outside to check one last time on Rudolph and Dasher. They were still happily shoveling snow with their antlers to reach the grass. Tomorrow, Mandy and James would go with them to visit the children in the hospital. The day after would be Grandpa's fund-raising event for Alex. Mandy sighed and let the light snowflakes settle on her nose. This was going to be the most exciting Christmas ever!

"Two days to go before I open my stocking!" Simon rubbed his hands as he came in the next morning. He was wearing layers of sweaters under his jacket, and a woolly hat was pulled down over his forehead. Outside, it was sunny but freezing cold.

Mandy had been up bright and early, along with her parents, while their Scottish guest slept in. She'd already answered the phone to half a dozen worried pet owners. The appointment book was full.

"Just think, back home for Christmas Day; sleeping in, presents, turkey, and Christmas pudding!" Simon put on his white coat.

"Can we fit Mr. Pickard in?" Mandy ran her finger down the list of appointments. Walter was on the phone to say that his old cat, Tom, was under the weather.

Simon nodded. "We'll squeeze him in, but don't tell Jean."

So Mandy made the appointment. "He'd like to come in right away. He sounds worried."

And that was the start of a pre-Christmas rush at Animal Ark. At half-past eight, Jean arrived and took over for Mandy at the desk. Mandy put on her white coat, ready to help her mom and dad. There were three dogs, two cats, a hamster, and a hedgehog to feed and clean.

And of course, there were Rudolph and Dasher to see to. As she went out with a special mix of oats and molasses recommended by Don, the reindeer raised their heads in greeting. Dasher trotted right over to his dish of cereal and began to eat, but Rudolph took one sniff at his and turned up his nose. *That's strange*, Mandy thought. She patted his shaggy neck, frowned, and went back inside.

Then there was a waiting room full of patients, with old Walter Pickard and Tom at the front of the line. Mandy was on hand as they came into Dr. Adam's treatment room.

"Let's take a look at this old fellow." Mandy's dad waited for Walter to lift Tom out of his basket.

Tom appeared, sad and bedraggled. Normally a sturdy, heavyweight cat, black and white, barrel-shaped, with a black patch of fur over one eye, today he looked thin and ill. He snuffled, his head hung low, his eyes dull.

Adam Hope examined his eyes and throat. "Has he been eating properly?"

Walter shook his head. "He's stopped eating his grub. It's not like Tom."

"Has he been sneezing? Coughing?" Dr. Adam beckoned Mandy to take a look. "See these little ulcers on his tongue?"

She nodded. "Is it cat flu?"

"It looks like it." He took Tom's temperature and confirmed that it was high.

Walter sighed. The old man treated Tom as a companion. Like him, the cat was a tough customer, but getting on in years. And this year, Walter had forgotten to have him vaccinated. "Can you do anything for him?"

Dr. Adam stroked Tom. "He'll need antibiotics to treat any secondary infection and plenty of fluids, but you should be able to take him home and nurse him there. You'll have to keep him warm. Clean up his eyes and nostrils if they get blocked. Poor old guy, he's having trouble breathing."

"He's feeling sorry for himself all right."

Dr. Adam decided to dose Tom with antibiotics there and then. Mandy helped to hold the cat, as her father showed Walter the best way to get the syrup down his throat. "Remember, this is a viral infection," he explained. "You'll have to wash Tom's bedding and feeding bowls, then disinfect them. Don't let him near other cats, OK?"

Walter promised to take good care of him. "Thank

you, Dr. Hope," he said meekly, as he put Tom back in his basket.

"Give us a call to let us know how he's getting along with the medicine. And don't worry, we'll soon have him back on his feet, terrorizing the neighborhood again!"

The old man smiled weakly. "I hope you're right." He shuffled out of the room with his pet.

Dr. Adam glanced at Mandy. "And don't you worry! Tom will be fine."

"It's not that." Mandy frowned. "It's Rudolph." She remembered that he too had sounded chesty when she took out the dish of food. And he had the look that Tom had come in with — dull-eyed and moping. She told her dad how the reindeer had turned down the oats.

"Hmm. Do you want me to take a look?"

Though the waiting room was full to overflowing, Mandy nodded.

"Come on then, quick!"

They went out together into the snowy compound, where the difference between the two reindeer was now quite clear. Dasher, whom Mandy recognized by his shorter antlers and dark coat, came trotting nimbly, hooves clicking. But Rudolph kept his distance and gazed listlessly. When Mandy and Adam Hope ap-

proached him, he simply lowered his head and sat down in the snow.

"Not so good." Adam Hope frowned. "It looks like you were right, Mandy. We may have a sick reindeer on our hands."

They examined Rudolph and brought Don out to look. Dr. Adam diagnosed a viral infection that needed the kind of treatment he'd prescribed for Tom. "Plenty of food, plenty of water. Keep him separate from Dasher."

Don nodded. He had talked Rudolph back onto his feet and stood patting his neck.

"He should be over it in a day or two. Perhaps even in time for Christmas. It's a kind of twenty-four hour reindeer flu."

But this left Don with a problem. "I can't let the kiddies down this morning," he told them.

"Can Dasher pull the sleigh by himself?" Mandy asked.

"He can manage it if Father Christmas walks alongside instead of sitting on top. You think I should go ahead and leave Rudolph behind to recover?"

"I'll stay here to look after him!" Mandy promised.

So when James arrived, with a cold but ready for the trip into Leeds, he and Don led Dasher into the trailer and prepared to set off alone.

"You're sure you don't mind, Mandy?" James asked.

"No. We're really busy at the clinic in any case. I'll be more use staying here."

"Aye, you look after Rudolph." Don sat at the wheel, ready to move off.

". . . the red-nosed reindeer!" James grinned.

"Ha-ha!" She grinned back. "Don't get lost!" she called, as the van and trailer eased out of the yard.

"Very funny!" James leaned out and waved a map. "Don't worry, we'll be back by dinner!"

"Mandy!" Jean called her inside. "Would you mind manning the telephone for the next hour? The clinic is running late, and I did promise that I'd dash into the village to meet Lydia Fawcett for coffee. I tried to ring High Cross to cancel it, but she'd already left."

Mandy agreed willingly. She took over in Reception, seeing the last patients into the treatment rooms and answering the busy phone. Every now and then she would glance out at Rudolph. He seemed the same — no better, no worse.

"Welford 703267, Animal Ark!" She picked up the phone. It was nearly lunchtime. Her dad had gone out on an emergency call to Sam Western's dairy herd at Upper Welford Hall. Her mom was busy treating patients in the unit.

"Hello?" A woman's voice hesitated. "This may not be the right thing to do, but I wondered if you could give me some advice?"

"Mrs. Hastings?" Mandy recognized the voice. "Is it something to do with Amber?" Her first thought was that the kitten might have developed a case of cat flu, like Walter's Tom.

"Oh, hello, Mandy. Actually it is. It's OK, she's not ill. It's nothing like that."

Mandy was relieved but puzzled.

"It's a silly thing in a way . . ."

"Shall I fetch Mom?"

"No, I really don't want to bother her. Perhaps you could help. You see, Amber's been really naughty this morning. She was in a mischievous mood, playing hide-and-seek. Anyway, Alex lost her. We looked, but we couldn't find her anywhere inside the house. But when my husband came home for lunch a few minutes ago, he saw where Amber was." Mrs. Hastings paused for breath.

"Where?" Mandy pictured the garden path, the porch, the single-story building.

"On the roof! I went out to look, and there she was, the naughty little thing, perched halfway up, refusing to come down!"

"Do you think she's stuck?"

"We don't know. Jeremy says that if she managed to get up, surely she can manage to get down. He thinks we should wait and see."

Mandy knew that cats, even kittens of Amber's age, had excellent balance. On the other hand, it must be very cold up there on the roof. "Have you tried to tempt her down?"

"Yes. I've just put out a saucer of milk on the front step. We've been calling her, but she takes no notice. What do you think we should do?"

"Keep trying," Mandy decided. "Try some food as well

as the milk. And tell Alex that cats usually come down when they're ready."

"All right." Mrs. Hastings sounded reassured. "It's just that at the moment we don't like anything to upset Alex. But anyway, you're probably right. We'll try the food, Mandy. Thank you very much."

"That's OK. Will you call us when Amber comes down?" Mandy would be uneasy until the problem was solved. She put down the phone and checked with Simon that she'd done the right thing.

"Fine," he confirmed. He brought a list of things for Mandy to do. "Can you help me put a fresh dressing on the cocker spaniel's leg? Then we have to fit a cone collar to the border collie."

"To stop him from biting his stitches?" The farm dog had a jagged wound on his back. The collar made a cone shape around the dog's head so that he couldn't turn and tug at the affected area.

Simon nodded. They went ahead with the routine tasks. Then, in the middle of the afternoon, Emily Hope popped her head around the door to check in with them. She looked busy but perfectly in control. The phone rang again. "Get that, Mandy, would you?"

Mandy dashed into Reception. Perhaps it was Lisa Hastings with good news about Amber. "Welford 703267."

"Hi, Mandy, it's me!" James sounded far-off. "Listen, you'll never guess what happened."

"Hi, James. You got lost?"

"No. We found the hospital OK. Father Christmas did his bit even though I didn't actually see it. The nurses said my cold made me infectious. Anyway, all the kids got their presents. Dasher went into the ward with him. They loved it."

"So?" She leaned sideways to look out of the window for a quick check on Rudolph.

"We're snowed in."

"What?" Her jaw dropped.

"We're stuck here in Leeds. It's snowing like crazy, the roads are blocked, and we can't move!"

"Oh, no!" If they didn't get back before tomorrow, this would turn into a major crisis. "For how long?"

"No one knows. They're out with the snowplow and salt trucks, but you should see it, Mandy! People are saying that it might go on all day and all night!"

"Where are you exactly?"

"We're still at the hospital. Don was able to put Dasher out on the lawn, so he's happy. But he figures we might not get back to Welford tonight."

"What about tomorrow?" Christmas Eve; Father Christmas's special appearance. The collection for Alex. Her operation! Mandy's heart sank.

"We don't know. We hope we can make it. Don says to keep our fingers crossed. He said to ask how Rudolph is."

"He's OK. He still looks down in the dumps, though. Listen, James . . ."

"Quick, Mandy. My money's running out."

The phone line crackled. "What are we going to do if you don't make it?"

Bip-bip-bip! The line buzzed and went dead. Mandy put down the phone with an empty click. She almost panicked. What a day! One crisis after another. And now, with just twenty-four hours to go to the big event, they had no sleigh, just one sick reindeer, and no Father Christmas!

Five

"Mandy, what on earth's the matter?" Her grandpa strode into the clinic in his walking boots, thick socks, and a down jacket. He was on his way to the village and had stopped by to see if they needed anything from the general store.

"Oh, Grandpa; Father Christmas — Don McNab — is snowed in. He might not be able to get back for tomorrow night!"

"Well, I never!" Even Tom Hope was thrown for a loop. "But we've already told everyone to come. They're even coming in from Walton to see him. They're expecting us to put on a good show." He sat for a moment on a chair in the waiting room. He took off his thick gloves and ran a hand through his gray hair. "And we're relying on that collection money to raise the final eight hundred pounds."

"I know." Mandy began to think. She stopped panicking, determined not to look on the bad side. "If worse comes to worst, at least we'll still have Rudolph."

"But no sleigh and no Father Christmas," Grandpa groaned.

"No, and I suppose we don't even know if Rudolph will be better in time." Mandy's nerve faltered as she glanced outside. It was the darkest time of the year. The light was already fading from an overcast sky. But at least it wasn't snowing here in Welford, and Rudolph was starting to scrape away at the snow to find the greenest grass shoots. "But let's say he does make it," she went on. "Dad said it might be a twenty-four hour thing."

"Yes?" Grandpa looked weary. "All that planning, and it could come to nothing," he mumbled.

"Listen!" Mandy went and crouched beside him, willing him not to give in. "Rudolph looks OK; at least we'll have one reindeer!"

"And one is better than none?"

"Yes, and maybe the sleigh isn't that important. Or maybe someone like Mr. Western or Mr. Collins could lend us a trailer. We could decorate it with Christmas lights to make it look like a sleigh!"

"A do-it-yourself effort?" Grandpa perked up.

"Yes!" There was no stopping Mandy now. "Ernie Bell's good at making things. Maybe we could get him to help. And it would be easy to get a substitute Father Christmas. All we need is a big red suit with a hood and some white fur trimming. A big white beard, a sackful of presents . . ." Her imagination ran on.

"And someone to wear it," Grandpa reminded her.

"Yes." She stopped and looked him in the eye. "Grand . . ."

"Oh, well, I don't know about that." He coughed and stood up. "I don't know that I'd be any good at dressing up. But you're right about the rest, Mandy. What we have to do now is mention it to a few people. I'm sure someone will volunteer right away!"

". . . I'll think about it." Julian Hardy, the landlord at the Fox and Goose, listened to Grandpa and Mandy's request. "It's kind of short notice, but I'll consider it."

They'd left Animal Ark and walked into the village to look for a substitute Father Christmas. The landlord was an obvious choice. The plan was for the procession to start outside the pub with traditional carols and the collection, before it moved up the road to Beechtrees.

"Come on, Dad!" John Hardy encouraged him to be a good sport. "They need someone to say yes right now."

"Ho-ho-ho!" The landlord practiced his laugh. "No, it's not me," he said with a frown. "Besides, we'll be busy in the pub."

"Oh, Dad!"

"Let me think about it." This was his final word for now, so Mandy and Tom Hope continued across the square to Walter Pickard's corner house.

". . . Me, dress up as Father Christmas?" Walter snorted. He'd invited them into his kitchen, but now he evidently wished he hadn't. "I never heard anything so silly!"

"Wait a minute. Think about it." Grandpa Hope stood there, perfectly reasonable. "You're the right age for the job, Walter."

"And so are you," he retorted.

"Yes, but I'm more on the management side of things. I'm a behind-the-scenes kind of guy."

Walter's eyebrows shot up. "Oh, really?"

"Yes. Whereas you're more the hands-on sort. I can just see you in a Father Christmas outfit, Walter. Besides, you wouldn't want to let everyone down, would you?"

Walter hemmed and hawed. He coughed and shuffled. He said his rheumatism was bad, Tom was sick and needed full-time care.

"Then you won't be in the Fox and Goose for a pint tonight?" Grandpa said with a sly wink at Mandy.

"Oh, I don't know about that," came the instant response. He glowered at his visitors, unable to turn them down flat. "I'll think about it," he said as he showed them to the door. "I'll mention it to Ernie. He's more your man!"

". . . Father Christmas?" Adam Hope considered it. "I'm a little on the young side, aren't I?"

They'd bumped into him outside the post office on his way back from Sam Western's place. Customers came and went, rushing in to mail late Christmas cards and out again to do last-minute errands. Dr. Adam had stopped the Land Rover to offer Mandy and her grandfather a lift.

"I don't mind calling Sam Western to ask if we can borrow his trailer," he told them when he heard about the crisis. "But I'm not so sure about playing the old man."

"You'd be good at it," Mandy pleaded. "Wouldn't he, Grandpa?"

"Perfect. Just the right, friendly sort of fellow." But it looked as if Grandpa Hope was beginning to think he would have to do the job himself after all. "Look, if no one else wants to, I suppose I could go home and get an outfit together before tomorrow night. . . ."

"I might be out on call. Anything could happen between now and then." Mandy's dad certainly wouldn't commit himself. "Nice try, Mandy. I'll think about it."

"What's the problem?" A familiar voice interrupted. Mrs. Ponsonby appeared at the post office door, ready to step into any breach. "Do I take it that the real Father Christmas has disappeared?" She chortled at Mandy as she descended onto the pavement.

Mandy swallowed hard. Given half a chance, Mrs. Ponsonby would step in and start bossing them around. "He's stuck in Leeds," she admitted. "It's still snowing there. The roads are blocked."

"Oh, dearie me!" And take charge Mrs. Ponsonby did, standing there on the pavement with her two dogs, Toby and Pandora, both dressed in their little tartan jackets. "We must do something!" She braced herself. The feathers in her red hat blew in the chilly breeze. Her round figure stood firm. "We must find another!"

"Which is exactly what we're trying to do." Mandy's grandpa tried to get a word in.

Mrs. Ponsonby swatted him away with her hand. "Hush, Tom, I'm thinking. . . . Yes, of course! Now look, you just leave it all to me!"

*   *   *

When Mandy and her grandfather had done everything they could in the village, they went back to Animal Ark. It was late, so Grandpa continued down the lane to Lilac Cottage to hatch his own plans, while Mandy went into the house, tired and hungry.

"Which do you want first, the good news or the bad news?" her mom asked.

"The good news." Mandy sighed and kicked off her boots. "Please, tell me that it's stopped snowing in Leeds and the roads are clear. Don is on his way back."

"If only." Emily Hope gave her a quick hug. "But Rudolph is definitely on the mend. His temperature's down and he's eating normally."

"Thank heavens for that." Now the Christmas procession wouldn't be a complete flop. Rudolph could be the star of the show.

"Rudolph saves the day, just like in the song." Adam Hope was on the phone. "I'm calling Susan Collins's dad to arrange for him to bring his trailer over first thing in the morning."

"So what's the bad news?" Mandy asked warily. Her mom was dressed to go out into the snow in her hat and jacket.

"I just heard from Lisa Hastings at Beechtrees. Amber's still up on the roof."

"Oh, no! Didn't the food tempt her down?"

"Apparently not. And the temperature's dropped below freezing again. I said I'd go over to see if there was anything I could do."

"I'll come!" Though she was exhausted, Mandy immediately offered to help.

"Good. Come on, then. The sooner the better."

So Mandy turned around, stuck her feet back into her boots, and went with her mom.

"Tiring day?" Dr. Emily drove confidently down the narrow lane. The snow sparkled yellow under the headlights. When her four-wheel drive caught a low branch or a bush, a shower of soft snow fell to the ground.

Mandy nodded. "Poor Amber. She's been up there for hours."

"I know. And it's turned very cold again. I'm worried about hypothermia." She glanced at Mandy. "When body temperature falls below a certain level in an animal, or a person for that matter, it makes the victim sleepy. If it's bad, they become unconscious."

"And Amber's only a kitten."

"That makes it worse, I'm afraid. Kittens are more susceptible. They don't have as much body fat to protect them against the cold."

Mandy bit her lip and tried not to think that far ahead.

Beechtrees came into sight as they drove past the Collinses' house. The main road was busy with traffic driving home from work or from last-minute Christmas shopping in Walton. Soon the car pulled up outside the bungalow.

"There she is; she's still up there!" Mandy scrambled out of the car as she spotted a tiny dark shape on the long slope of the white roof. Mr. Hastings stood in the front yard. A ladder leaned against the side of the house.

"Let's hope it's not too late." Emily Hope carried her heavy vet's bag to the porch. She had a quick word at the door with Mrs. Hastings.

"We're sorry to drag you out," Alex's mother began, "but we've tried everything, short of actually climbing onto the roof. It's very slippery. And besides, Jeremy's afraid that it would scare the kitten even higher and make her lose her balance."

"We don't mind." Dr. Emily gave a reassuring smile. "Where's Alex?"

"She's in her room. She's worried sick about poor Amber. No one knows how the kitten got onto the roof, but Alex is convinced it's her fault for not taking better care of her. She's crying her eyes out."

"Tell her to try not to worry." Emily Hope stepped back from the porch and together with Mandy went to join Mr. Hastings at the foot of the ladder.

"It's no good." He shook his head. "Every time I climb up there, she just creeps farther away. I don't want to scare her into making a false move."

Mandy craned her neck to see the tiny kitten. She could just make out a sorry bundle of fur shivering on the roof. She heard a feeble meow. Amber was too frightened to move a muscle.

"How cold will she be up there?" Mr. Hastings asked, anxious but helpless.

"Very cold. She'll get frostbite if she has to stay any longer." Dr. Emily made a quick decision. "Mandy and I will take a shot at getting Amber down, but meanwhile I think you should call the SPCA. They have the right equipment to get up there. Explain the situation to them, and see if they can come out right away!"

He nodded and ran inside. As he opened the door, Mandy caught a glimpse of William hovering in the hall-way. It seemed he was curious to know what was going on but was also trying to keep out of the way. The door closed again and shut him inside.

"Let me go up the ladder, Mom," Mandy said quickly. "Amber knows me. She's more likely to come when I get up there and call her."

Emily Hope checked the ladder. "OK, but don't try anything risky when you get up there. I don't want you climbing onto the roof under any circumstances. Got that?" She knew Mandy would be willing to risk it unless she ordered her not to.

Mandy had to agree. She would have to rely on coaxing Amber down.

"Good luck," her mom said, holding the ladder firm as Mandy set her foot on the first metal rung.

She counted the steps; six, seven, eight. At nine, her head reached roof level. She peered up the snowy slope to the ridge. Amber sat and shivered against the chimney. Her eyes gleamed orange in the dark. "Here, Amber!" Mandy edged up another rung. The kitten backed away.

"That's far enough, Mandy!" her mom warned from below. "If she won't come when you call, we'll leave it to the SPCA!"

Mandy leaned against the gutter and reached out with both hands. Her legs had begun to tremble. The icy wind whipped up loose snow and blew it in her face. "Amber, don't be scared. Come this way!"

In her confusion, Amber thought that Mandy's outstretched arms meant danger. She edged back again, almost lost her footing on the snow-covered ridge, and half slipped from sight. Mandy gasped. With a struggle, the kitten found her balance and cowered against the chimney.

"Any good?" Dr. Emily called.

"No!" Mandy looked desperately along the treacherous surface. The roof was smooth and white except for two raised squares where windows had been built in for extra light. These, too, were snow-covered, but they gave Mandy an idea. "I'm coming down!" Forcing her trembling legs into action, she climbed down the ladder.

"What next?" Emily Hope looked at her watch. "Where's the SPCA?"

"I'm going to try from inside!" Mandy ran to explain to Mr. and Mrs. Hastings. "Can you open the roof windows from inside the house?"

Jeremy Hastings nodded. "They work on hinges and lift up. Come and see!"

He led her to Alex's bedroom.

"Mandy, please get Amber down!" The little girl sat huddled on her bed, crying at the thought of Amber freezing to death.

She put on a brave show of confidence. "Don't worry, we'll get her back for you." She was shocked by Alex's pale, tear-stained face, her tiny, distressed voice.

"Don't let her die, please!"

"Now Alex, we're all doing our best, love." Jeremy Hastings looked around the room for something to stand on.

She sobbed quietly and hid her face as her dad put a

chair in the middle of the room and began to push at the snow-covered window in the sloping ceiling.

Mandy waited impatiently, hoping that the noise wouldn't frighten the kitten outside.

"No good, it's frozen solid." Mr. Hastings gave up and jumped to the floor.

"What about the other one?" Mandy had seen the shape of a second window.

"In William's room!" He left Alex crying and ran next door, bursting in without knocking.

Mandy followed. What was William making of all this? She saw him on his bed, pale and silent, pretending to read a book, but obviously scared. She stood under the skylight while Mr. Hastings ran for a chair to stand on. Looking down, she saw that the fawn carpet had a darker stain, a patch of wet about ten inches across.

William followed her gaze. He slammed his book shut and glowered.

Had water leaked in through the window frame? Mandy looked up. Or had snow drifted in through the open window? This window was lower, just out of reach. She shot another glance at Alex's brother, who went whiter still. His lip began to quiver as he heard his dad coming back.

"William?" It struck Mandy all at once; that was how

Amber had gotten stuck on the roof. The boy had opened the window and put her there on purpose! Then he'd slammed it shut and locked her out!

"Don't tell!" he whispered, guilty, terrified.

Mr. Hastings dashed in and put the chair over the wet patch without noticing it. He climbed up on it. This time, the window opened easily. He eased it up and propped it into position. "Come on, Mandy, take a look. See if you can coax Amber down from here."

Recovering from her shock, she stood on the chair and peered out. She was closer to Amber but still not

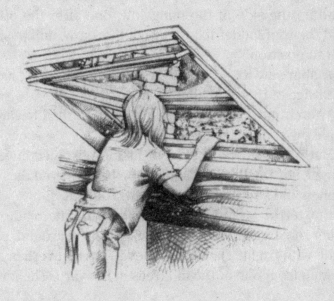

able to reach. The kitten saw her, but this time she didn't react. She blinked and shivered but didn't try to escape.

Mandy knew the signs. This was worse than before; Amber was so cold that she was growing sleepy. But it was the kind of sleep before she fell unconscious and froze to death. "Amber, here!" Mandy cried. She tried desperately to slither onto the roof.

"Careful!" Mr. Hastings yelled.

Out on the road, an SPCA van pulled up at last. From her vantage point, she could see two men rush into the Hastings's yard with special roof ladders. They scrambled up the side of the bungalow, one after the other, laid the roof ladder flat on top of the snow, and pushed it into position.

Amber saw it and gave a cry. She darted away, along the ridge of the roof, almost slipped and fell.

"Watch out!" Mandy warned. The first man began to scale the roof. "She might fall!"

But it was now or never. If the kitten stayed out any longer, she might die. Mandy hoped and prayed that the men would succeed where she had failed.

But terror jerked Amber into action. She made another run, farther out of reach. She looked around, eyes wide with fright. There, just above, was an overhanging branch from one of the tall trees in the yard. The kitten saw it and crouched. The man hesitated. Then he lunged to grab her.

Amber jumped. She sprang up onto the nearest branch. It dipped and swayed. The kitten hung on.

"I've lost her!" the man shouted. Outside, someone else yelled, and the traffic on the road rumbled by. The dark shadow of the tree had swallowed Amber.

"Quick!" Mandy slid back into the bedroom, bringing a shower of loose snow with her. She ran out through the hall onto the porch. Her mom stood with her bag, ready to treat the kitten. "She's up in the tree. We can't see her!"

"Bring a flashlight!" Emily Hope told Jeremy Hastings. They ran to the base of the tree.

"Shine it up into the branches!" The SPCA man held his own flashlight. The yellow beams shone through the dark.

"She's up there somewhere!" Mandy whispered. "She has to be!"

But though the SPCA men brought their ladder and climbed up once more, they couldn't find Amber.

"She can't just disappear!" Frantic, Mandy ran into the road to see if she could see Amber from out there. The moon shone through the bare branches; there was no sign.

"Watch the cars!" Mr. Hastings warned.

Mandy kept close to the side, searching the road just in case the kitten had lost her balance and fallen. Again, nothing!

Amber's mighty leap from rooftop to tree had ended in mystery. They searched and searched, but the kitten seemed to have vanished into thin air!

Six

"What shall I tell Alex?" Mr. Hastings asked as he clicked off his flashlight.

They felt empty and cold. The men from the SPCA had stacked their ladders on top of the van and driven away from Beechtrees.

"I think we should tell her the truth." Mandy's mom offered to help him explain.

They trudged into the house. Mrs. Hastings brought Alex from her room and they broke the news that Amber was lost. There were tearful questions: "How can she be? Isn't she stuck on the roof? Where is she now?"

The grown-ups were gentle, but they had to admit that they had failed.

"At least until it gets light," her mom told her. "Then we can begin to look again. We'll be able to see more in the daylight."

"But it's so cold!" Alex shivered with fear. "Why can't we try to find her *now*?"

"We *have* looked for a long time," Mr. Hastings began. But he saw the look in Alex's green eyes. "OK, I'll try again."

Mandy said she would go with him, while Mrs. Hastings and her mom did their best to calm Alex.

"William, come and give us a hand," Jeremy Hastings called from the front porch.

The boy's bedroom door opened slowly. When he saw Mandy, he closed it quickly again.

"What's gotten into him?" His father was impatient. "As if we didn't have enough to worry about, without William going into a sulk."

Mandy waited while he went to fetch his son. William appeared reluctantly, grumbling about having to go out in the cold. He avoided Mandy's gaze.

"It isn't even my kitten," he complained, as his dad made him put on his jacket and boots.

"But Alex is upset. Don't you want to help us find Amber for her sake?"

William screwed his mouth up tight. He said nothing.

"Come on, try and put someone else first for a change." Mr. Hastings handed them each a flashlight and they went outside. They searched behind bushes along a low wall, across the lawn where the two snowmen still stood, gleaming white in the moonlight.

"Let's look for paw prints," Mandy suggested. She aimed her flashlight at the ground. "If Amber did fall out of the tree and manage to run off, we should soon be able to pick up her trail."

For a while, their search had a new purpose. Surely Mandy was right; the kitten would have left some evidence in the snow. But the minutes ticked by. They looked on the lawn, then under the beech tree for the telltale prints. Mr. Hastings even went up his ladder to investigate the roof for fresh signs. He had no luck up there, either.

"I'm freezing!" William moaned. He sniffled and whined. "My toes hurt! I can't feel my fingers!"

"Well, just think how cold Amber must be!" Mr. Hastings refused to let him retreat into the house. "Now go with Mandy and look on the road. Watch out for cars!"

"It's all clear," Mandy called. She stood at the gate, shining her flashlight along the wall top where the tree branches hung over the road. "Can you see any prints?" she asked William.

He scowled. "No. And it's not my fault if the stupid cat is missing! Why can't Alex take better care of her?"

Mandy bit her tongue. She hated it when people called animals stupid. All of a sudden she had to say something. "Listen, William!" She pulled him to one side and whispered urgently.

"Let go! What?"

"Are you sure it's not your fault that Amber is missing? What about that patch of melted snow on your carpet?"

"Don't blame me. I was only trying to rescue the stupid thing before Mom went and called you!" He looked at her at last, eyes flashing angrily. "Anyway, I know you won't believe me. No one ever does. They never blame Alex. It's always me!" He pulled his sleeve free and ran into the yard. Mandy quickly followed.

She saw William jump the low wall onto the lawn. He headed straight for the snowmen that he and James had built, threw himself at the nearest one, and began shoving and kicking it until it toppled and shattered. It lay in frozen lumps. Soon he had destroyed the second one, too.

"There!" He turned to her, as his father came running down the path. "That's what I think of stupid snowmen. And I hope you never find Amber! I hope she freezes to death!"

*   *   *

"He didn't really mean it," Dr. Emily explained as she drove Mandy home.

"He sounded as if he did." Mandy had been shocked by the outburst. In the end, Mrs. Hastings had come out and taken William inside.

"He is only seven, remember. And his family has a lot of problems at the moment."

"Yes, and William's making them worse." Mandy couldn't forgive his cruel taunt about Amber. She sat looking out at the snow-covered hillside, staring disaster in the face. For one thing, there were the snags over Father Christmas. Grandma and Grandpa's fund-raising treat could well fall completely flat. For another, Alex was so upset about Amber that she might be too ill to enjoy the procession even if it did take place. And then, of course, there was the kitten out all night in the cold.

"I'm sure he doesn't mean to make things worse," her mom insisted. "I don't think he can help it, poor boy." She swung down their lane, talking things through. "It must be hard for him, having a little sister who gets all the attention. Alex is ill, so naturally her mom and dad worry about her. They don't have much time to spare for William at the moment. I expect he feels left out."

"Jealous?" Mandy considered it for the first time.

"But that doesn't mean he had to go and spoil the snow-men. That makes no sense."

"Sometimes things don't make sense." They turned into their own drive and pulled up in the yard.

"Mom . . . ?" Frowning, Mandy unclicked her seat belt. "I know what you mean. William's getting his own back."

"Yes. But he's having to take it out on things that never did anything to him in the first place. Like the snowmen."

"And Amber?" Mandy wondered out loud. William had denied it, but the suspicion lingered that he was the one who had put the kitten on the roof.

"Possibly." Dr. Emily listened quietly to the full story as Mandy saw it. She sighed. "Oh, dear, I hope not. The poor boy must be feeling wretched."

"Poor *Alex*, poor *Amber*!" If it was true, William had taken out his problem on the thing his sister loved best. And now an innocent animal was suffering because of it.

"Cheer up!" Adam Hope greeted them with a smile. "Don't tell me you didn't see them out in the yard?"

Mandy shook her head wearily. "No. Who?"

"Not who; what. The van and trailer. Don's back!"

"Och aye, I'm back, all right." The wiry Scotsman

came downstairs in T-shirt, jeans, and bare feet. "I've had a long, hot bath and now I'm ready to put my feet up in front of the TV."

"Is Dasher with you?" It took a while to sink in. The last Mandy had heard was that the trailer was stuck in a snowdrift outside a Leeds hospital.

"Aye, and young James. All home safe and sound." Don's face was shiny red after his bath. "Now where did I put those sneakers?" He scratched his head and began to search the kitchen.

"But how did you get here?" For a moment Mandy had a vision of the reindeer rising magically above the rooftops, pulling the sleigh.

"The snowplows dug us out. They did a great job. By late afternoon they had the traffic moving again. We couldn't get a message through to you, so we headed for home. It's a good wee story, though." He chuckled over it. "Now where *did* I put those shoes?"

"At least I won't have to get dressed up in that red suit." Dr. Adam sounded relieved. He made Mandy sit down to her supper. "You had us worried for a while, Don. Mandy's grandpa has been all over the village trying to round up a substitute."

"And no one wanted to do it," Mandy added. She ate her supper, glad that at least one of the major crises was over. "Everyone said, 'Let me think about it,' which means, 'No,' doesn't it? But anyway, Rudolph's better and you're back."

"No problem!" Don was cheery as ever. "Maybe I left them in my bag," he muttered to himself. He shuffled off in bare feet, upstairs to the spare room. They heard a few thumps and clomps as he came back down — shoes on but unlaced, and wearing a puzzled frown. "That's not like me. I'm usually a very organized sort of person!"

Mandy rolled her eyes at her mom and dad. Don was

many good things, but organized wasn't one of them. "What have you lost?"

"Och, I wouldn't say 'lost' exactly. More mislaid. Aye, but I could have sworn I put them in my bag."

"Your shoes? They're on your feet, Don." Mandy broke it to him gently.

"Och, no, not my shoes. No, I'm talking about Father Christmas's clothes; the old gentleman's best red suit and black boots. I told him I'd spruce them up for Christmas Eve, so he left them with me. I've looked, and I can't find them anywhere!"

"He left them at the hospital," Adam Hope confirmed as he came in to say good night to Mandy. "They just called and left a message. Father Christmas's suit is neatly folded on a bed in an empty side ward!"

Mandy made a noise halfway between a groan and a giggle.

"Yes, and you thought *I* was absent-minded!" He sat down for a moment on the edge of her bed. "Your mom says you've had a hard day?"

She nodded. "We looked everywhere for Amber, Dad, but we just couldn't find her. What do you think could have happened to her?" She knew that she was so worried she wouldn't sleep.

Her dad shrugged. "I don't know for sure, but let's try

and work it out. Because one thing's for sure; a cat really can't just vanish. So, first off, you say she definitely jumped off the roof?"

"Yes, into the tree by the wall. We saw her land, but it was so dark among the branches that we lost sight of her."

"And she's absolutely, definitely not still up there?"

"No. So where can she be?"

"Well . . ." He spoke gently. "We have to face the fact that Amber might have fallen."

Mandy scrunched up her face and closed her eyes. She didn't want to hear this.

"No, listen, love. Say she did fall; after all, it was dark and she was very frightened. But you know cats have this amazing ability to land on their feet. We call it a head-on-body righting reflex."

She opened her eyes to look at him. "Meaning what?"

"It works like this. A cat falls from a height. First it twists so that the top of its head faces upward. Then the neck and body line up in the reflex action so that the cat falls feet first. It only takes milliseconds, and lo and behold, she lands safely. One of her nine lives is saved!"

Mandy took a deep breath. "Do you think that's what happened to Amber?"

"It's possible. She falls and lands the right way up, no

damage done. Then as quick as she can she darts for cover, waits for all the fuss to die down."

"Yes. Maybe she didn't like the flashlights and all the noise." Mandy pictured the kitten tucked safely out of harm's way, sheltered from the wind and waiting for the all clear. Tomorrow morning the Hastings would open their front door and discover her, sitting on the mat and meowing for her breakfast. "I just hope she found a nice warm place to hide."

"Me, too." Her dad stood up and turned off the light. "After a day like today, we deserve some luck. So try not to worry too much, OK?"

The door closed and left the room in darkness. Mandy tried to sleep. But one thing bothered her. If her dad was right, and Amber had landed safely, why hadn't they found any paw prints in the snow? Mandy wrestled with the problem until well after midnight. No paw prints, no evidence, nothing. Poor little Amber; it seemed that she had simply been spirited away.

Seven

Grandma turned up at Animal Ark before breakfast, armed with scissors, sewing pins, and an armful of old red curtain material. "We'll just have to make do and mend!" she cried, seizing hold of Don. She measured him for a replacement Father Christmas suit. "I expect Santa Claus is about the same size as you," she said with a wink.

"Aye, though he's a wee bit fatter around the waist." Don patted his stomach.

As usual, Mandy played along. She helped Grandma get him ready for the grand procession that evening.

They laid the fabric flat on the kitchen table, cut and shaped it, then Grandma began to sew to the whirr of the machine, making tucks, seams, and fastenings. By nine o'clock, Don was trying on the finished article.

"Beard?" Grandma stood back to judge the effect.

"Cotton balls!" Mandy ran into the clinic. She dived through the busy waiting room, grabbed a pack from a cabinet, and raced back to the house. By hook or by crook they would be ready for the big event.

"Boots?" Grandma was almost finished. The beard was a miracle of cardboard, glue, and cotton balls, with elastic loops to hook over the ears.

"Dad's rain boots!" Mandy jumped up to get them. Then, when they were satisfied and Don had gone outside to groom Rudolph and Dasher so that they would look their best for that evening, she called James to see if he would come along to Beechtrees with her.

"What time is it? Have you called them yet?" James inquired sleepily.

"No, not yet." Mandy had been putting it off. "And they haven't called us, either." Her hopes that Amber would turn up on the doorstep of the bungalow were fading. She knew that the Hastings would have telephoned with any good news about the kitten. "I wondered if you would come and help us look." She would be glad if he said yes. James was wonderful in a crisis. He kept a clear head and always came up with bright ideas.

"Sure. What time?"

"In half an hour."

"See you there." He was alert now and didn't waste time talking.

In fact, he was at the bungalow before her. When Mandy arrived, he was already looking for the lost kitten with Mrs. Hastings. Mr. Hastings had gone to work at the tennis club, and William and Alex were inside.

"How is she?" Mandy asked.

"Not quite so upset as yesterday. But she's very sad," Mrs. Hastings told them. "I can't think of anything to cheer her up. She's completely lost interest in Christmas."

Mandy knew how Alex must feel. Even making Father Christmas's outfit with Grandma hadn't stopped her from worrying about Amber. "Should I go in and see her?"

"Would you mind, Mandy? You're the only person Alex is interested in talking to right now. I'm afraid she sees you as some kind of heroine, like Superwoman!" Mrs. Hastings gave a sad smile and led Mandy and James through the hallway.

James stayed in the kitchen while Mandy tiptoed into Alex's quiet room. The curtains were drawn, and a dim lamp shone. All around the walls, pictures of animals seemed to stare down at the sick little girl who lay motionless in bed.

"Hi, Alex." Mandy sat close by. There was a full glass of water on the bedside table, next to an unopened book.

Alex turned her head. When she spoke, her voice was a whisper. "Hello, Mandy. Guess what, I don't think Father Christmas read my letter."

"Why not?" Mandy saw now what Mr. and Mrs. Hastings meant when they insisted that Alex must keep calm. Being upset drained her of her strength. She looked as white as a ghost.

"I wrote and asked him for a collar for Amber; one with a little bell."

"Well, you never know." She tried to sound cheerful. "He might bring you one. He hasn't delivered his presents yet, remember!"

Alex's eyes filled with tears. "No, but if he got my note, he'd know I have a kitten. Then he wouldn't let Amber get lost, would he?"

"I don't think even Father Christmas can do anything about a missing kitten," Mandy explained gently.

"But he knows everything! He knows what we'd all like for Christmas. He can even fly through the air with his reindeer. He must know about Amber!"

Mandy nodded. "Well, maybe he does."

Alex had a sudden idea. She wiped her eyes and looked at Mandy. "Yes, and maybe he's looking after her for me! That could be where Amber is right now — with Father Christmas!"

"I hope so," Mandy whispered. Before Mrs. Hastings came in to give Alex her medicine, Mandy crept out of the room to join James in the kitchen.

After a few minutes Mrs. Hastings followed. "She's sleeping," she reported. "It's an extra strain on her heart when she's upset. She isn't strong enough to take it." It was Alex's mother's turn to brush away a tear.

"Come on, let's start," James suggested, ready to take up the search. They went out onto the porch.

"I dread what sort of time we'll have if we don't find this kitten." Mrs. Hastings scanned the trampled lawn. "We've been over and over the ground, but there's still no sign."

James agreed. "I thought we might find prints in the snow, but it's all trodden down, so even if there was a track last night, it's disappeared by now."

"I did look," Mandy told him. "And I couldn't see one. William and I even searched out on the road." She glanced at the house to see the small, pale face and ginger hair of Alex's brother staring solemnly at them through the window.

James studied the beech tree where Amber had last

been seen. Then he went out to look at the road, which was quiet at this time of day. He stood under the overhanging branches and looked up, pushing his hair from his forehead. "Who saw her up there?"

"Let's think; me, Mom, Mr. Hastings, and the two men from the SPCA."

"And the people driving by," James suggested. "If Amber managed to scramble down the tree on this side, then ran off, maybe someone in a car saw her?"

Mandy nodded. "All we need is one clue to find out which way she went. But how do we find out if anybody saw her?"

"We could ask in the village. There would be plenty of people around on Christmas Eve, doing their last-minute shopping. It's worth a try!"

Mrs. Hastings agreed. "You two go and ask. I'll stay here and make some fliers to put up on trees and gateposts to say we've lost a kitten. I'll get Alex and William to help me." She seemed glad to have something to do.

So Mandy and James went into Welford. They called at the McFarlanes' and the Fox and Goose. They saw James's dad talking in the square to Mrs. Collins. They saw Ernie Bell and Walter Pickard.

"Tom's right as rain!" Walter called. "Back to normal, as bossy as ever!"

They passed the message; the Hastings's kitten, Amber, was lost in the snow. Had anyone seen a stray tortoiseshell with bright golden eyes? Each time the answer came back: "No, sorry. But we will keep a lookout!" Even the people who remembered driving past the bungalow at about the right time hadn't seen a thing.

They asked the Parker Smythes and Sam Western, as well as the farmer from Graystones, David Gill. All promised to do their best, but they shook their heads as if to say, "What chance does a little kitten have out in the freezing cold at this time of year?"

By lunchtime Mandy and James had done all they could. They headed back past the square, where Julian Hardy from the pub was stringing up big Christmas lights. "Ready for Father Christmas," he said. "I hear everything's going ahead?"

Mandy nodded. Her legs were weary from tramping through the snow. And so far, all for nothing. They were no nearer to finding Amber. She forgot to mention to Mr. Hardy that Don McNab and Dasher were back in Welford, ready for tonight's procession.

"We're busy baking mince pies. And John's made Christmas candles for the kids. The vicar's bringing a tape of Christmas carols, and I'll rig up loudspeakers so we can all sing along."

Everyone was pulling out all the stops in support of

Alex's lifesaving trip to America. Mandy and James watched for a while, then went on, deep in thought. "You know something?" Mandy said, "Unless we find Amber, I don't think Alex will go!"

"For her operation?" James began to see how important the missing kitten was. "You mean, she's just too upset?"

Mandy sighed and nodded. "And too ill to travel. Come on, we'd better go and see what's happening."

"If only *I'd* seen something." James strode along beside her. "Don and I drove along this road yesterday afternoon, on our way back from Leeds."

"Along with a hundred other cars." She was beginning to feel that it was like looking for a needle in a haystack.

"Well, it looks like William is finally trying to help." James spotted him in the garden. William climbed the wall and stood, watching them approach. As they drew near, he dropped to the ground and ran to meet them.

"Alex is even more sick! They went and got the doctor." His eyes were wide and scared. "Did you find the kitten?"

Looking up the drive, they saw a red car and the front door of the bungalow standing open. A tall woman came out carrying a dark bag. She stopped to talk earnestly to Mrs. Hastings. The moment William spotted them, he ducked behind the wall. "That's her," he told them. "That's the doctor!"

They waited until the woman had gotten into her car, backed out of the drive, and driven off. By this time, William was shaking from head to foot.

"I never meant for her to get sick!" He trembled and fought back the tears, refusing to go any nearer to his house. The front door was closed, the bungalow strangely quiet.

"Just like you never meant Amber to get lost in the snow?" Mandy asked quietly.

James stepped back in surprise. William hung his head. "I only wanted her to be on the roof for a little while. I didn't know she wouldn't come down again." He mumbled and choked over how his plan had gone wrong.

"You mean, *you* put Amber up there?" James was stunned.

Mandy nodded. "I thought so. Listen." She knew the whole story would soon come tumbling out.

"Yes, but I thought I could get her down again. They'd all be looking for her, and I'd be the one who saved her, see?"

"But it didn't work out," said Mandy. Instead of rescuing the kitten and being the hero, William had to watch Amber climb out of reach on the roof, then get too scared to move, slowly growing colder and colder as night fell. "Why didn't you tell someone?"

"I was scared," he confessed. "I thought Amber was going to die because of me." Tears welled up and rolled down his cheeks.

"Look, don't worry about that now." James knew there was no point crying over it. "At least we know how it happened."

Mandy wondered how James could be so kind. She found it hard to forgive William. But the little boy looked

miserable as he realized just what he'd done, and Mandy remembered what her mom had said; William was feeling left out. He was a lonely child who knew he'd done something wrong. "We won't tell anyone," she whispered. "Don't cry any more. Just help us find Amber!"

William sniffed and dried his eyes on his cuff. "I don't want to go in," he pleaded.

"OK." James was practical. "Let's stay outside and look."

"Again!" Mandy stood at the gates, hands on her hips. It almost drove her crazy to think how often they'd gone over this ground since Amber had disappeared.

But William shook his head. "No!" he insisted. He pulled back as James tried to persuade him to come into the yard.

"Why not? The least you can do is help us look!" For the first time, James sounded angry.

"I can't. Anyway, there isn't any point!"

Mandy turned. "Don't, James. What's wrong, William?" She suspected there was more to come.

"Amber's not here."

"How do you know? Did you see what happened?"

Slowly he nodded. "I was looking out of the window. She was in the tree. Everyone was using ladders and flashlights, but I knew there wasn't any point."

"Why not? What did you see?" She wanted to shake the truth out of him, but she forced herself to be patient.

William stood at the roadside, pointing up at the tree. "She was in that branch, there. I saw her. I shouted, but you didn't hear because there was too much noise." There was a long pause. "Amber fell."

"Where? Into the road?" James was the one to prompt him, as Mandy held her breath.

"No. She fell onto a sort of truck. I saw her slip from the branch. The next second the truck went past the gate and I saw Amber on top of it, hanging on."

"Alive?" Mandy gasped.

He nodded. "The truck kept going. I couldn't stop it."

James's mind flew ahead. Mandy was dazed but overjoyed that Amber had survived the fall. "What kind of truck?" he asked.

"A gray one. It was a kind of trailer."

James stared. "What was pulling the trailer?"

Mandy grabbed James's arm, waiting in suspense for the reply.

"A big van, a dirty white one. It was covered in snow. I've never seen it before."

They gasped. "Don!" they said together.

"The reindeer's trailer!" Now, at this moment, Mandy

could have hugged William. Here was the clue they needed. "Amber fell on top of it!"

"It looks like it," James breathed. "The kitten must have driven home with Don and me!"

"To Animal Ark!" Mandy cried. "Oh, James, Alex was right; Father Christmas has been looking after Amber all along!"

Eight

"William saw what happened to Amber!" Mandy told Mrs. Hastings, so excited that she could hardly get the words out. "At last we've picked up a lead we can follow!"

Mrs. Hastings went right away to tell Alex the latest news while William slipped quietly back into the house. "I won't get her hopes up too high just yet," Alex's mom said. "But at least this should help to cheer her up!"

"We hope!" James whispered to Mandy as they set off down the road, as fast as they could, toward Animal Ark. Back at Animal Ark, Mandy and James found the

395

reindeer's trailer standing in the yard. Its doors hung open and the ramp was down. They nearly fell over themselves getting inside it. Their feet thumped up the ramp, and they almost tumbled over.

But, once inside, they soon realized that the dark trailer was empty. Mandy had longed for it to be simple. She had hoped Amber had clung onto the top of the trailer and during the journey home had clambered inside to safety — to spend the night in the warm straw. But no, the trailer was bare. No kitten, not even any straw.

"Don must have cleaned it out," James said, his voice flat.

"Let's make sure." Mandy took one last look around, then went out and hoisted herself up onto a ledge to look on top. There was no kitten there, but something caught her eyes. "James, come and look at this!"

James joined her. Together they peered onto the snowy roof of the trailer.

"See there." She pointed.

Frozen into the deep snow was a trail of paw prints that led from a scuffed patch. "You think that's where Amber fell?"

"Yes, then she crept to that far edge, there."

"Well, at least we know William's telling the truth,"

James agreed. "But that's not to say that Amber stayed there all the way back here." He jumped down and tried to think what to do next.

"Let's ask Don if he knows anything." Mandy caught sight of him in the compound with the two reindeer. "Don!"

He waved as she ran over.

"Don, did you just muck out the trailer?"

"I did." He hummed cheerfully. Rudolph was enjoying a grooming session, getting ready for the big night. Dasher nibbled at a dish of sugar beets.

"Did you see anything there?" Again she was in such a rush that the words tumbled out. "Like a kitten, for instance?"

"Whoa, slow down!" His eyes crinkled with amusement. Mandy hopped from foot to foot, and now James came running. Rudolph grunted and nudged at Don's hand. "Aye, steady on, Rudi. I haven't forgotten you!"

"A brown-and-black tortoiseshell kitten with amber eyes!" Mandy gave a full description to a mystified Don.

"Aye, as it happens, I did."

"Oh!" Mandy clasped her hands together. "Oh, Don, where is she? What did you do with her?"

"Well, I didn't do anything with her." He scratched his

head. "I went into the box and there she was, curled up in the straw, cozy as you like. Cheeky wee thing."

"You didn't chase her away?" James asked anxiously.

"Och, what do you take me for? It was a pity to disturb her; she'd found a grand spot for a wee nap. No, I went off to fetch her a saucer of milk, but wouldn't you just know it? The minute I turned my back, off she ran." He shrugged and started again on Rudolph's thick coat. "She's a wicked wee cat, right enough."

Mandy stared. "She ran off?" she faltered.

"Aye, but don't worry. Kittens don't stray far from home. You'll soon have her back safe and sound."

"No," James cut in. "Amber doesn't belong to Mandy. She doesn't live here at Animal Ark."

"But I thought you said you were looking for her?" Don stood up straight and wrinkled his forehead.

"For someone else," James explained. "Did you see which way she ran?" Of course, Don couldn't realize how important this was. They'd been so near to finding Amber, yet now they'd lost her again.

He sighed. "I didn't. She nipped away when my back was turned. I just got on and mucked out as usual. I never gave the wee cat a second thought."

Mandy hid her disappointment. "Never mind. Thanks, Don."

"Och, I've a feeling I've let you down," he apologized.

"No." She managed to smile. "At least we know Amber was here."

"How long ago?" James fitted together all the information he could gather.

"Half an hour. Maybe a wee bit longer."

Mandy nodded at James. "Then she can't have gone far!" she said, jutting out her chin and looking across the yard. The hunt for Amber was on.

In the small village of Welford, news of the missing kitten traveled fast.

"Little Alex Hastings is ill with worry, poor child!" Mrs. Ponsonby spread the word. She'd heard it from Emily Hope when she went into the clinic with snuffly Pandora. She told Mrs. McFarlane that the kitten was still alive. "Isn't that wonderful? And wouldn't it be the best Christmas present in the world if we all helped to find her?" Warmhearted in spite of her bossy manner, Mrs. Ponsonby gathered a search party.

"I suppose I've nothing better to do." Ernie Bell hid his willingness to help beneath a grumpy surface. He picked up a shovel from his garden shed and set off for Animal Ark, ready to dig through snowdrifts and do his very best.

Walter Pickard, not to be outdone, went with him. "We can't have the little lass making herself sick over it, can we?"

And John Hardy, the serious, studious son of the landlord, went along with Susan Collins. Even Brandon Gill, the shy boy from Graystones Farm, heard about Amber and tramped across the snowy fields to Mandy's house. Soon a dozen people, young and old, were helping James and Mandy in the search for Amber.

"We must spread out in different directions!" Mrs. Ponsonby was wearing a bright pink anorak with a white fake-fur trim. She had a master plan. "Mandy and James have checked the house thoroughly, so we can be sure that the kitten has gone farther afield. We will split into twos and search the lane with a fine-tooth comb. Now, Mandy, please give a detailed description." She clapped her hands quickly. "Attention everyone, please!"

Mandy blushed as she gave the information. "Amber is a black-and-brown tortoiseshell with golden-orange eyes. Her tail is mostly black. There's a flash of white on one back leg. She's five months old." Even as she spoke, she realized that the short daylight hours would soon draw to a close. They must get the search underway as soon as possible.

They left it to Mrs. Ponsonby to divide people into

pairs. "Walter, you come along with me!" she instructed, after she'd sent all the others off.

Mandy raised her eyebrows. James breathed a sigh of relief. Walter got no chance to object.

"Go on, Mandy. You and James head for Lilac Cottage. See if your grandparents have seen or heard anything useful!" Mrs. Ponsonby implied that the two of them were slacking.

They shot off, leaving Walter to be bossed around by her, passing Brandon and Susan who had been sent to look in the field opposite Animal Ark.

"Here!" Susan said, suddenly excited. She pointed to a track that led right across the field. "A set of footprints!"

James and Mandy jumped the ditch to peer over the wall.

Brandon stopped to examine them. "A fox," he said quietly, shaking his head.

"Oh, Brandon, are you sure?" Susan was dismayed. She clung onto her discovery. "But they look like cat prints to me!"

"Fox," he said stubbornly. "They're too heavy for a kitten."

Susan sighed and gave in. Mandy and James jumped back into the lane and went on. The snow still lay deep and pretty as a Christmas card along all the wall tops and gates, weighing down the dark tree branches. By the time they reached the cottage, they'd passed Ernie, John Hardy, and Mr. Hastings, who'd rushed over from work the moment he heard the news.

"Thanks, you two!" He raised his head and called after him. "You don't know how much we appreciate this!"

"Thank us later," Mandy told him.

"When we find Amber!" James added.

At Lilac Cottage, Grandpa stood holding the gate open for them. "Come on. Your grandmother and I have been having a good look around, but no luck so far, I'm afraid."

It was the same old story; everyone doing their best but getting nowhere.

"That kitten certainly has a knack for vanishing!" Grandma was in the front garden, looking under benches and behind bare trellises where, in the summer, roses grew.

"Poor thing. It must be a big, cold world out there for her." Grandpa pictured her lost and frightened. It made James and Mandy concentrate even harder.

"Here, Mandy!" James called at last. His warm breath turned to clouds of steam as he trod carefully in Mr. Hope's vegetable garden at the back of the cottage. "Come and look!"

Mandy walked delicately between the mysterious white humps and clumps. Under the snow lay Grandpa's precious rhubarb and fruit bushes. Her footsteps were the first to spoil the smooth surface of the carefully tended ground.

James crouched by a round water barrel at the bottom of the garden. The barrel was covered over with a thick layer of ice, but it was the base that he was interested in. There, around the back of the barrel, leading along the garden boundary toward the house, was a beautiful, clear set of paw prints!

"What do you think?" he breathed. "Not a fox's this time?"

"Definitely not! Not so close to the house." She followed the track to see where it led. "Anyway, they're too small for a fox."

Excited now, they followed the trail onto the patio. They lost it, then found it again. The prints led along the patio, straight up to the sliding glass doors.

Mandy turned to James. "What now?"

He shook his head. "It looks like she went inside."

"But who would let her in? Grandma and Grandpa would have mentioned it." Doubts came to the surface; doubts that she didn't want to admit.

James pressed his face to the glass and peered inside. "Uh, Mandy . . ." he said dully.

She forced herself to look. *Please let it be Amber!* she prayed. But there, sitting peacefully in his favorite armchair, carefully grooming behind his ears, was the sleek gray shape of Smoky, Grandma and Grandpa's own precious cat.

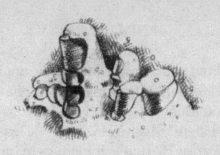

Nine

Smoky saw two surprised faces peering in at him. He opened his mouth in a great big yawn. Then he stood and arched his back, rousing himself from sleep.

For the first time ever, Mandy wasn't glad to see him. In fact, her heart gave a thud of disappointment. As Smoky leaped from his chair and came padding across the carpet toward them, tail up, ready to say hello, she turned away.

"No, wait a minute . . ." James chewed his lip. "Maybe Smoky can help us!"

Mandy didn't see how. She stood on the patio, trying to get over this latest disappointment. Grandpa's garden, all covered with snow, with its bare apple trees and empty greenhouse, looked as bleak as she felt. Would they ever find Amber?

"Mandy, listen!" James insisted. "This garden is Smoky's territory. He thinks it belongs to him."

She agreed. "That's right. He keeps watch over it."

"Just like Eric at home. He has a track that he follows, like the one by the fence. He kind of travels a network of paths on his home turf." He knew that male cats were especially anxious to keep invaders out.

Mandy began to see what he was getting at. "So, if there's another cat around, Smoky would soon chase him off."

"Or *her*!" James suggested. He stared through the glass door at Smoky, who meowed silently to be let out.

"You mean, if Amber is anywhere around here, Smoky would soon find out?"

James nodded. His eyes were wide with excitement behind his round glasses. "What do you think?"

"It's worth a try!" Immediately Mandy seized the handle and slid the door open for Smoky to step out. "Come on, Smoky. There's a good cat." She stopped to stroke him and let him rub against her leg. He trod delicately into the snow, lifted one front paw, and shook it.

James eased the door closed behind him. "Just in case he prefers to run back inside into the warmth!" he whispered.

Smoky raised his head and looked around at the strange white world. His ears twitched and he followed the flight of a sparrow from Grandpa's fence to the apple tree. He flicked his tail and meowed.

Mandy and James held their breath. They watched Smoky stalk toward the tree. He crouched by the gnarled trunk, staring up at the sparrow. The bird hopped and twittered in the branches above. As Smoky sprang for the trunk and his claws dug into the bark, the sparrow fluttered and flew off. Smoky dropped silently to the ground, disappointed.

When cats chased birds, they were like tigers, Mandy thought. Or like jaguars stalking through the jungle. Smoky settled low on the ground, haunches raised, tail flicking to and fro.

"What's he seen now?" James breathed. They didn't dare move as Smoky marked out his territory and went prowling through the garden between the rows of snow-covered vegetables.

"Shh!" Mandy crept quietly after the cat. Smoky had picked up a scent. He padded around the water barrel, set off on his track by the fence, sniffed again, then turned back in his tracks. He trotted quickly toward the greenhouse, stopped by a half-buried stack of over-turned flowerpots, and hissed.

They heard a tiny noise, a faint, frightened meow. The fur rose along Smoky's back as he arched and let out a loud yowl. Mandy and James ran for the greenhouse as fast as their legs would carry them.

Yet, when they got there, expecting to find Amber cowering in a corner, there was only Smoky. He hissed and growled, the fur on his back standing on end as he arched and spat.

"Let's look inside the greenhouse!" Mandy dived for the door. She wrenched it open and peered inside. Empty shelves, empty flowerpots and trays. No kitten.

"Out here!" James listened again and traced the fee-ble meow to the row of overturned pots. Some had top-pled sideways and lay higgledy-piggledy around the back of the greenhouse. They were heavy clay pots, big enough for a kitten to get trapped inside. . . .

Mandy rushed to help. The faint pleas grew louder. Smoky backed off. He sensed danger and crept to the edge of the vegetable patch, where he crouched, growl-ing steadily.

"She must be stuck under one of these pots!" James tried to reach down the narrow gap between the green-house and a tall fence. He overbalanced and fell against the glass panes. The whole greenhouse shook, but nothing broke. Instead, there was the sliding, rushing sound of heavy snow gliding down a smooth slope.

Mandy glanced up at the greenhouse roof. An avalanche of snow hung over the edge, a huge weight of snow just above James's head. "Watch out!" She darted to pull him clear.

Just in time! The snow inched down the roof, hung for a second, then plunged to the ground in a shuddering thud. The kitten's cries were drowned as a mountain of snow buried her alive.

Grandma and Grandpa Hope came rushing from the front of the house. "What was that?" Grandpa had heard the noise. He stared in dismay at the solid mass of snow.

"Oh, quick!" Mandy cried. "Amber is under there! We heard her, then the snow fell on top of her. We need something to dig her out!"

In a flash Grandpa headed for his garden shed. Grandma rushed into the house to fetch the fireplace shovel. Meanwhile, Mandy and James kneeled to scrape at the pile of snow. There was no sign of Smoky; he had fled across the garden in the rumble of falling snow.

Mandy dug with her bare hands. "What if she's been crushed?" The snow was heavy, packed into the gap between the fence and the greenhouse. It was about three feet deep.

"Don't think about it!" James scrabbled through the heap.

Soon Grandpa came back with his spade. "Try this!" He handed it to Mandy over James's head. She began to dig.

"Careful!" Grandma warned. She gave the smaller shovel to James. He worked at the bottom of the pile, going in sideways.

At last Mandy's spade hit something solid. She scraped at the snow to reveal a cracked flowerpot, tumbled side-

ways under the avalanche. Digging carefully around it, she pulled it free.

"What's under there?" Grandpa craned to see.

"More pots." Mandy put the spade down and began to scoop with her hands again, while James dug his tunnel through the base of the pile.

"We've got to get air in there!" he gasped, his face red with the effort. "Amber has to breathe!"

"Perhaps she's trapped under a pot, in a pocket of air," Grandma whispered.

"I hope you're right," Grandpa murmured.

Mandy pulled a second pot from the heap. It was broken in two. She thought she heard a faint cry from deep in the snow. Her heart leaped. "Did you hear that?" In a frenzy she scraped at the snow, digging deeper and deeper.

"Yes!" James stopped tunneling to listen. "I heard it!"

"Oh, be careful, Mandy!" Grandma repeated. Any second the pile of snow could collapse and crush the kitten to death.

Mandy lifted out another shard of broken pot. The snow shifted and slid. She stopped, gathered her nerve, and began again. This time she brought out a whole flowerpot, then another.

The cries grew louder, more insistent: *Meow . . . meow . . . meow!*

Mandy scraped at the snow. She uncovered a pot. It was turned upside down, like part of a giant sandcastle made of snow. She did more careful scraping. The pot tilted then jolted back into position. The kitten wailed, then went quiet again.

"Ready?" Mandy breathed. She seized the pot with both hands, fingers frozen, arms trembling. She lifted it inch by inch so that the surrounding snow stayed in place. And there, under the flowerpot, hunched in a bedraggled ball, her orange eyes staring up at them, was Amber!

The news spread down the lane like wildfire; Mandy and James had found the kitten. Ernie, Brandon, Susan, and Mr. Hastings came running to Lilac Cottage. Mrs. Ponsonby went to the village to proclaim the good tidings. Walter stopped by Animal Ark to tell the Hopes. Soon everyone knew.

By this time Mandy had carried Amber into the house. She asked her grandmother for a towel and began to rub the kitten dry. Amber shivered and huddled inside the towel, mewing quietly.

"What about a hot water bottle?" Grandpa asked. They were still worried about hypothermia.

"No, she shouldn't have direct heat," Mandy said. "We mustn't warm her up too quickly. We just have to get her dry." She said she didn't think there were any broken bones, but that Amber might have frostbite. She couldn't tell yet.

"Can she have warm milk?" Grandma asked. They stood peering over James's head at Mandy kneeling on the kitchen floor with the kitten on her lap.

Mandy nodded. Soon Amber's fur was dry and fluffy. Grandma brought a saucer of milk and Mandy set her gently on her feet. The kitten wobbled, then stooped to lap with her pink tongue. Mandy rested on her heels and looked up at the worried faces. Her wet blonde hair was streaked across her cheeks and neck. Her skin still tingled with cold. "I think she's going to be all right!" she whispered.

A crowd had gathered outside the gate as Mandy wrapped Amber in a thick red blanket and took her out to Grandpa's camper. They planned to drive to Beechtrees to deliver the kitten safely back home.

"Well done!"

"Isn't that great!"

"Oh, she's gorgeous!" There was a general murmur of approval at the sight of the rescued kitten.

Mandy let the helpers have a peep. There Amber sat, warmly wrapped up, purring like a little engine. She peered out from the red blanket at the row of strange faces, gave a puzzled meow, and snuggled deeper into Mandy's arms.

Grandpa thanked everyone as he opened the gate. "All's well that ends well!" He smiled and went to wait in the van.

Grandma beckoned from the doorstep. "Come on, Mandy. Don't keep that poor little girl waiting a moment longer!" She went to wave them off through the gate.

Mandy sat in the front with Amber, James in the back. Mr. Hastings climbed in too, then slid the door of the camper shut.

They were on their way at last to give Amber back to Alex.

"Just in time," Jeremy Hastings murmured. He stared out the window across the valley at the twinkling lights of Welford village.

Just in time for Christmas, just in time for the grand procession; above all, just in time for Alex.

Mandy took Amber into Alex's bedroom. The kitten was still wrapped in the red woolen blanket. "Look who I've brought," she whispered.

Alex was still in bed, staring at the ceiling. Her hair shone coppery-red against the white pillows. She turned her head, hardly daring to believe her eyes.

Mandy tiptoed forward. "It's Amber!"

"Really and truly?" Alex propped herself on her elbows. Then she sat up. "Let me see!"

She unwrapped the blanket. Amber's round face peered out, eyes alert as she recognized the room. She sprang from Mandy's arms onto the bed and went padding softly toward Alex.

The little girl held her arms wide open. She was speechless with delight. Amber stole straight into her arms. Alex wrapped them around the kitten, put her cheek against Amber's soft head, and looked up at Mandy. "Did Father Christmas tell you where to look?"

Mandy smiled. Alex's dream had come true. No more worries, no more tears. Now she could concentrate on getting better. "In a way, yes, I suppose he did," she said.

Ten

Don McNab was polite about Grandma's specially made Father Christmas outfit. "It's very good of you to go to all this trouble," he said as she brought it into the yard at Animal Ark. He was busy transforming the trailer into the reindeer sleigh. "But the old gentleman won't be needing it after all!"

Mandy and James were helping Don. It was seven o'clock; they had just half an hour to get the sleigh ready and to harness Rudolph and Dasher, before they were due in the village square. The evening was crisp and clear, a perfect Christmas Eve.

"Are you sure?" Grandma was puzzled. As far as she

knew, Don had left the proper outfit stranded in a hospital ward.

"Quite sure, thank you. I got a message to Father Christmas and he had a spare one especially sent down from Reindeerland!"

"Ah, well." She raised her eyebrows, then tucked the homemade suit back into her shopping bag. "Perhaps it will be useful another year." Intrigued by the sleigh, she walked around it. She admired the fiberglass side panels as James bolted them into place and inspected the bulky pile of presents in the back. "Lovely!" she told Mandy. "I may be an old lady, but I confess I'm very excited!"

Mandy nodded. "I know. I can hardly wait."

"They're ready for you in the square," Grandma told Don. "The holiday lights look beautiful. They've hung huge, old-fashioned lanterns outside the pub. And the music is already playing."

"Is there anyone there yet?" Mandy asked. All they needed now for the procession to be a success was a huge crowd of people singing carols, all gathered to see Father Christmas and his sleigh.

"Quite a few. Your grandpa and I are on our way back there now. Would you like a lift?"

But Mandy and James weren't quite ready. "No, thanks. We'll come down with Mom. Dad had to go out on a call, so we'll meet him there." She wanted to help Don hitch Rudolph and Dasher to the sleigh before they set off for the village.

So Grandma said she would see them later. "Don't be too long," she warned, "or you'll miss all the fun!"

But Mandy and James couldn't think of anything better than helping with the reindeer. They went to lead them out of the compound, smartly groomed, hooves clicking, white manes fluffed out. Their velvety antlers cast wonderful shadows across the yard.

"That's right, steady on!" Don encouraged as they entered them in between the shafts of the sleigh. "Come on now, Dasher, back a wee bit farther! That's it, Rudolph, you show him how it's done!" Slowly they eased the reindeer into position.

Dasher grunted and pawed the ground. The sleigh shifted behind him. Rudolph stood, the picture of patience, as if he sensed that their big moment had come.

"Grand!" Don was satisfied at last.

They stood back for the full effect. It was as good as they could possibly imagine; a gleaming sleigh with polished white sides, decorated in red and gold. There was a pile of presents stacked high on top and two beautiful reindeer to pull it along the snowy lane. James glanced at Mandy, stuck both hands deep in his pockets, and raised his shoulders in a contented sigh.

"All right, you two!" Emily Hope called from the drive. "We haven't got much time. I'll race you there!"

Mandy grinned. Her mom was dressed in a brown velvet hat with a fake-fur brim, a long, dark, Russian-style coat, and long boots. She looked too dressed up to race, Mandy thought. "Can't we wait for Don?" she pleaded.

"No!" came the instant reply. Don was still busy checking the harness. "Father Christmas doesn't like having folk around when he gets here. He's a wee bit on the shy side, like young James there!" He winked, and James blushed. "You go on ahead," he told them. "Go and enjoy yourselves!"

So they had to say good-bye for now to Rudolph and Dasher.

"Twenty minutes to go," Mandy's mom said as they set off on foot.

"I hope Dad gets back in time," Mandy said. As luck would have it, the phone had rung and he'd had to go out. "A vet's life," he'd sighed. "Always on call, always having to go and tend the sick and wounded!"

"Aah!" they'd cried. Mandy and James had felt truly sorry for him.

"Pay no attention," Emily Hope had told them. "He's only fishing for sympathy!"

So now they walked quickly along the lane in a threesome — Mandy, James, and Dr. Emily. As they drew near the main street, they saw a row of parked cars and heard carols playing over the loudspeakers. Then they saw the square. It basked in a glow of lights — yellow, red, and green. A giant Christmas tree stood proudly in the middle, all lit up. A huge crowd was gathered around it.

Mandy felt a thrill of excitement. There were children running around or perched on grown-ups' shoulders. There was Walter leaning on his garden gate, watching events, the Parker Smythes standing with Sam Western. Simon was talking to Jean, and shy Brandon Gill and his father stood munching on mince pies.

Then Julian Hardy came out of the pub to conduct the singing. He handed out carol sheets. Everyone stood ready.

"There are hundreds of people here!" James tried to count but gave up.

Mandy smiled at her mom, then slid in among the crowd. She took a song sheet, on the lookout for her father, but instead she spied Grandma and Grandpa. They gave her a wave. She waved back, continuing to thread her way toward the front.

"While shepherds watched their flocks by night,
All seated on the ground,
The angel of the Lord came down,
And glory shone around!"

Faces in the crowded square were lit by lantern light. They opened their mouths and sang. The music floated into the night sky, a chorus of happy voices.

> *"Away in a-a man-ger,*
> *No-o crib for a bed . . ."*

Mandy sang her heart out. But where was her dad? Surely he should have finished his call by now. She edged sideways out of the crowd, to look down the road for the Animal Ark Land Rover.

But there, by the side of the Fox and Goose, she was waylaid by the strange sight of two Father Christmases arguing.

"Aye, well, when I heard they were short of someone to do the job, I thought I'd better step in." A grumpy voice growled from behind a fake white beard. The figure was hidden behind a red hood and cloak, but Ernie's trousers and sturdy boots were unmistakable.

"Yes, and that was very kind of you!"

Mandy opened her eyes wide. Here, too, was a voice she recognized.

"It was really very thoughtful, Mr. Bell. But now I think you should leave it all to me!"

This figure was short and round, with a big chest beneath the red, fur-trimmed coat. The hood was pulled way up, and the voice was muffled behind an outsized white beard. But it was true; Mrs. Ponsonby was taking charge as usual. "I know how to deal with small children, you see. You might frighten the poor little things. Now step aside and let me pass. We mustn't disappoint our public, must we?"

Ernie muttered and grumbled. He wasn't going to give in without a fight. "Look here, I had to borrow this lot from the wardrobe department at the Welford Players. They didn't let me have it for nothing, neither!"

Mrs. Ponsonby eyed the moth-eaten costume as if to say that Ernie had been robbed. She smoothed her own posh costume and stroked her beard. Mandy choked back a laugh.

"Break it up there!" Julian Hardy stepped in with a smile between the two would-be Father Christmases. The carols soared on. No one except Mandy had seen or heard the squabble. "Didn't you hear? The real Father Christmas got back safely after all!"

"Surely not?"

"Well, I never!" Mrs. Ponsonby and Ernie were stunned into silence. They unhooked their beards and threw back their hoods in the shadow of the pub wall. Suddenly the music changed. Bells jingled through the loudspeakers. All the children squeezed to the very front and peered up the street.

A roar of voices struck up with the first lines of Rudolph's song as Father Christmas's sleigh came into sight.

It was magical. Rudolph and Dasher pranced toward the square. The sleigh was all lit up with tiny white lights, and silver bells jangled; it shone and sparkled as the reindeer drew near.

"Father Christmas!" the small ones gasped.

"Is he real?"

"Oh, look, it's Rudolph!"

They all looked on in wonder.

Father Christmas sat up high, holding the reins — a round man with a red face and a big white beard. He was definitely the most believable Father Christmas Mandy had ever seen.

Mandy felt James creep up alongside her. "Doesn't Don look great?" she said.

"Shh!" He glanced around to make sure that no one heard. "Don't spoil it!"

They grinned at each other. Don McNab certainly looked realistic as he stopped the sleigh in the square and stepped down. His loud voice boomed out a great "Ho-ho-ho!"

"What do you think of him?" a voice asked quietly over their shoulders. "The gentleman got here on time, just like I promised." The voice had a definite Scottish accent.

"Don!" Mandy and James jumped sky-high.

"But you're . . ."

"You should be up . . ."

They stopped dead. Don grinned back. He stood there large as life in his thick sweater and jacket. "Och, no," he protested. "You didn't still think *I* was the old man! Do you not believe in the real Father Christmas, after all I've told you?"

They gulped.

"They do now." Emily Hope smiled as she passed by with a collection box. She shook it in time to the tune. People reached deep in their pockets and gave generously. They said it was the best Christmas sleigh they'd ever seen.

When Mandy and James turned again to quiz Don, the Scotsman had melted away into the crowd.

Then there were gifts for the small children. They went up shyly one by one to whisper their Christmas wish. Father Christmas delved into the pile of wrapped presents and found the right one. The child went off hugging the parcel while moms and dads added money to the collection boxes. The line seemed to go on forever, as kids with shining eyes got to stroke Father Christmas's reindeer.

At last all the carols had been sung, the presents given out. Collectors returned to the pub with their tins, where Grandma and Grandpa Hope counted up the total. More mince pies were eaten, and then the crowd lined up along the street, ready for Father Christmas's sleigh to move on toward Beechtrees.

"He's due to make a special stop," Mandy's mom explained. She stood between Mandy and James, waiting to hear Grandpa's announcement of the grand total.

Grandpa climbed onto the sleigh, sheet of paper in hand. He asked for quiet. The music faded, the excited voices died. Clearing his throat, he read from the paper. "We have collected a grand total of eight hundred and seventy-nine pounds and thirty pence!" he announced proudly. "Which, I'm delighted to say, means Alex and her family will be off to the States as soon as possible in the New Year! Well done, everyone, and thank you very much!"

Grandpa got down from the sleigh to a round of applause. Then the crowd formed a long procession behind the sleigh.

"Come on." Emily Hope put her arms around Mandy and James's shoulders. "We can't miss the best part!" She led them into the procession. They walked slowly to the jingle of bells and the click of the reindeer's hooves.

Before they knew it, they were outside the bungalow, underneath the tall trees. Father Christmas drew the reindeer to a halt. "Ho-ho-ho!" he greeted the people at the house.

William appeared at the front window. He pulled back the curtain, gasped, then shot off. Soon the door opened and he stood on the porch, eyes bright, as Father Christmas beckoned him.

"Go on, William!" Mrs. Hastings appeared behind her son and whispered softly. She put a hand on his shoulder and nudged him down the step. He ran down the path, shook hands with the figure in red, and took a huge present from him. His mom stood by, smiling.

"Say thank you," she prompted.

William could hardly see over his mysterious box. "Thank you!" he whispered.

"And thank you, from Alex's dad and me, too," Mrs. Hastings told Mandy. "Your grandpa tells me we can all go to America for Alex's operation." Quickly she brushed a tear away as Jeremy Hastings hurried inside to fetch their daughter. She took Mandy in her arms and gave her a great big hug.

And now it was Alex's turn. She came to the step with her dad, all wrapped up in her coat, scarf, and hat, carrying Amber. The kitten blinked at the lights on the sleigh.

"Here, give her to me," Mr. Hastings urged Alex.

As if in a daze, she handed Amber over and came slowly down the path. Father Christmas welcomed her with open arms. She smiled up at him, a dazzling, disbelieving smile. Then he lifted her clean off her feet and into the sleigh.

"Choose a present!" he boomed.

Alex pointed shyly to a small, round parcel. All the people who had helped to make this the best Christmas ever looked on, as she tore off the wrapping. Inside was a tiny blue leather collar with a silver bell. She held it up to show Mandy. "Look! He must have got the letter. He brought this for Amber!"

Her dad came forward with a smile and handed her the kitten. Carefully, Alex fitted the collar around Amber's neck.

"Would you like a ride?" Father Christmas let her and the kitten snuggle up close.

Wide-eyed, she stared up at him and nodded. "Can William come, too?"

"Plenty of room!" Father Christmas replied.

No sooner said than done, Jeremy Hastings hoisted his son up on the sleigh.

Then Father Christmas took up the reins. "Gee up,

Rudolph! Gee up, Dasher!" The reindeer jerked once, then they were smoothly in step, clicking down the road.

Mandy and James ran to keep up. Behind them, the crowd struck up another verse from "Rudolph."

Father Christmas joined in the song as he drove his sleigh along the snowy road. His deep voice boom-boomed through the clear night air.

Mandy and James stopped dead.

"You don't think . . . ?" James stared and stammered.

Mandy swallowed hard. "No!" Father Christmas was fat and jolly, his beard was white. Her dad's was brown. "Then again, where *is* Dad right this minute?"

They watched as the sleigh turned and came back toward them.

"Magnificent, eh?"

Mandy whirled round at the sound of the familiar deep voice. "Dad!" He stood behind them, wrapped in his scarf and hat.

"What's wrong? I said I'd be back in time for the celebrations, didn't I?"

"B-but!" She gazed again at the splendid red figure on the sleigh.

Adam Hope smiled broadly and clapped his gloved hands. "Merry Christmas!" he shouted above the jingling bells.

The sleigh drew up beside them, the reindeer grunted and shook their harnesses. Alex held tight to her kitten. She and William beamed at them. Then Mr. Hastings came and lifted the children down to the ground.

Finally, the old gentleman looked Mandy and James straight in the eye. He gave one of his booming ho-ho-ho laughs. "Merry Christmas!" he said. They waved up at him, as he took the reins and drove off. "Merry Christmas, everyone!"